Smith's

MONTHLY

Every Month Original Novels, Stories, and Articles

USA Today Bestselling Writer **Dean Wesley Smith**

TABLE OF CONTENTS

I0554011

Smith's Monthly Issue #12

The Writings and Opinions of

Dean Wesley Smith

Introduction
One Year Old
and Learning to Walk

A CAKE, ONE CANDLE, change diaper… the kid turns one.

This issue marks the first full year of *Smith's Monthly*.

Twelve issues, one per month. I didn't miss a month.

Twelve completely original novels, one per issue.

Two ongoing serial novels.

One nonfiction golf/humor book.

Twenty-five poems.

And with the five stories in this issue, a total of 52 short stories.

Who knew all that was even possible?

One year down, firing onward. Who knows, soon this magazine will be walking.

Most of my friends didn't think this magazine was possible. Can't honestly say as I blame them.

In all of publishing history, I had never heard of this being done before either.

Now granted, I got the idea from a ton of magazines through history with an author's name on it, but usually the author only wrote a short novel for an issue or a short story or often didn't even have anything in an issue.

But never had an author filled an entire issue of a magazine month after month.

And certainly not for an entire year.

So next month starts the second year and I'm not stopping. I'm having way too much fun, to be honest. I am going for at least another dozen novels, more than fifty short stories, and who knows what else.

Stay tuned. This party is just getting interesting.

I want to say thanks right now for those who supported this project by subscribing or buying an issue in a bookstore or online. And also thanks to others who

---

Thanks for the Support

Dean Wesley Smith

supported it with great comments on my ongoing blog series.

Thank you, one and all. Without you all, I'd have tossed in the towel on this idea after a few months.

But most of all I want to thank my wonderful wife, Kristine Kathryn Rusch. She never once doubted I could do this, and still doesn't doubt in the slightest that I can keep right on going, past this first birthday bash, even though she has lived with this now for a full year.

She knows I'm crazy and still lives with me, encourages me, and is my biggest fan. How I got that lucky, I'll never know.

So I'm blowing out the single candle now.

On to year two of *Smith's Monthly*. I might be walking by the end of year two, but no bets on being potty trained.

Dean Wesley Smith
August 14, 2014,
Lincoln City, Oregon

#1... October 2013

#2... November 2013

#3... December 2013

#4... January 2014

#5... February 2014

#6... March 2014

#7... April 2014

#8... May 2014

#9... June 2014

#10... July 2014

#11... August 2014

#12...September 2014

Coming Next Issue in Smith's Monthly
A Return to the Ghost of a Chance Universe
in a brand new novel
HEAVEN PAINTED AS A CHRISTMAST GIFT

Dean Wesley Smith

USA Today Bestselling Writer

A POKER BOY STORY

THE War of Poker

Poker Boy somehow finds himself facing an imitation of his girlfriend, Patty Ledgerwood.

Within a fraction of a second he somehow saves himself and maybe the world from another war.

Or maybe he helps set up a new war in the future.

THE WAR OF POKER
A Poker Boy Story

I WAS STARTING to figure out that if I wanted a new case or some problem to come up threatening the world and everything I knew, all I had to do was stand in the main lobby of the Las Vegas MGM Grand. Someone, some problem, somehow would find me.

At the moment I really didn't want a new case, but I had learned as a superhero that people needing help or problems needing solving didn't happen when I wanted them to. Annoying, but true.

But even though it might lead to the end of everything I knew, I often spent time in the MGM Grand lobby wearing my black leather coat and black Fedora-like hat that was my superhero uniform, leaning against the same marble pillar, waiting for my girl-friend and sidekick, Patty Ledgerwood, aka Front Desk Girl, to get off work.

That I stood there was common knowledge and also might have something to do with people and problems being able to find me. Superheroes are not normally regular in their schedules.

But standing and waiting and sometimes getting cases was worth it as long as the world didn't end. I liked watching the crowds and watching Patty work. Her long brown hair, deep brown eyes, and wide smile always made me feel wonderful. To say I was in love would be an understatement.

The only place I spent more time was in poker rooms. But except for the poker room at Spirit Winds casino in the mountains of Oregon near my doublewide trailer, I seldom played poker in the same casino. My job as Poker Boy, a superhero in the gambling universe, was to help those who needed help and take the money at poker tables from those who needed it taken because of their poor play.

Sometimes the two parts of my job crossed and combined, but usually the money part just paid the expenses for the superhero part.

Technically, since I was a superhero in the poker-playing niche of the universe, I should only be solving problems associated around poker and poker rooms. But over the last few years I had managed to gather a team of superheroes around me from different aspects of the world. As a team, we had become known for solving some of the stranger problems to come along, including saving the entire world from tiny bugs one day, stopping an alien invasion on another adventure, and saving Lady Luck herself yet another day.

When the team got to work, things were never dull.

Patty, who was part of that team, was still fifteen minutes away from getting off work when I sensed a problem coming toward me. I call that sense my "tingly-warning bell" superpower. Sometimes, but not always, I know when danger is approaching. It's not the kind of power

I can trust like Spider-Man trusts his "Spidey-Sense." I often wished my power was that dependable. But when I feel that shiver and the tingle go down my spine like a drip of ice water, I have learned to pay attention. Danger is close by.

Right at that moment a river of ice was flowing all over my spine and I shivered like someone had turned up the MGM Grand air-conditioning to the Arctic setting.

I swung around to see the most beautiful woman I had ever seen walking toward me with a smile. She had long brown hair that seemed to just glow in the bright lights of the lobby, wide brown eyes, and a perfect smile. She wore the uniform of the MGM front desk crew and wore it better than anyone had a right to wear a simple white blouse and brown slacks.

In fact, the woman walking toward me looked exactly like my girlfriend, Patty.

I glanced around at the front desk wondering how I had managed to miss Patty leaving work.

I hadn't.

Patty was still standing behind the desk working with a customer. Her hair was still tucked up tight on her head. She never let it down until she got off work.

I spun back to the woman walking at me.

It was Patty all right, walking toward me smiling, giving me that "look" with her big brown eyes that could melt every ounce of resistance I had toward anything.

All I could do was stare.

How could there be two Patty Ledgerwoods?

The ice shivers running around on my back finally snapped me out of my shock and I stepped out of time, freezing everyone around me.

The loud sounds of the nearby casino and people talking and background music all vanished instantly.

I loved the ability to do that. I actually couldn't stop time, but I could pull myself out of the flow of time and into an instant so that it appeared to me that time had stopped around me.

I liked to think of it as me being in a bubble outside of time, but that wasn't right exactly either.

Around me kids were frozen in mid-scream, husbands were stopped in mid-look at another woman, bellhops were stopped with a bag halfway onto a cart.

And there were no sounds.

None.

The superpower came in very, very handy and I had learned that when in doubt about anything, I should just get out of the flow of time and give myself some time to think.

I turned toward the front desk again. My girlfriend, Patty, was frozen in mid-sentence behind the front desk of the MGM Grand hotel talking to a woman with a bored-looking husband in bright red shorts. I knew that was Patty. Everything about me could sense that was the woman I loved behind the counter.

From the other direction, the woman who looked just like Patty was frozen in mid-stride about ten steps from where I stood. Her smile looked artificial when frozen like that.

The loud sounds of the nearby casino and people talking and background music all vanished instantly.

And every sense I had told me she was nothing but danger.

Extreme danger.

I went over and walked around her, studying every detail about her.

She was an exact duplicate of Patty, right down to the tiny mole on her neck.

Same height, same shape, everything.

Creepy didn't begin to describe what I was feeling and I quickly went back to my original position. My damn warning power kept making me shiver like I was fighting upwind through a cold snowstorm in nothing but a swimming suit.

I needed help and I needed it now.

As a superhero, I had learned a long time ago that there were many, many things in the world I did not understand. And with that learning I had lost all fear of just calling for help when there was something I flat didn't understand.

Right now I had no idea what was happening, but I knew it couldn't be good. One Patty Ledgerwood was more than enough for me.

I glanced at the ceiling and shouted "Stan! Need help!"

I have no idea why I look up when I am calling out for Stan, the God of Poker and my immediate boss, but I always do, and he has never failed to show up at once.

And this time was no exception.

He appeared next to me, also out of time. I had no idea how he could do that, jump right into my frozen moment in time and join me, but he had done it in the past so now was not the time to be asking him how. It seemed for the gods, time was a lot easier to deal with than for us mortals and superheroes.

Stan had on a plain pair of brown slacks and a tan, open-collared dress shirt. His brown hair was perfectly combed as always and you could walk by him a hundred times and never notice him. He was a perfect master of disguise and blending in.

He glanced at the woman who looked like Patty walking toward me, then frowned, something I hated when my boss and the God of Poker did it around me.

"That's not Patty," I said. I pointed back at the main desk of the hotel. "That's Patty."

"I know that," he said, only glancing back at the real Patty. He eased toward the imitation Patty slowly and carefully, like trying to sneak up on a sleeping bear.

He was clearly seeing something I was not seeing.

After two steps, he stopped. "We need help. How long can you hold this field?"

"Another half hour," I said, checking in with how I was feeling holding the bubble with me and Stan out of the time stream. I had gotten pretty good at this super power.

Suddenly I could feel that it was slipping.

"Less," I said, now straining to hold the field. "It's slipping."

Stan nodded and focused for a moment.

The field holding us out of time solidified again.

"What caused that?" I asked, trying to catch my breath. It actually felt like I had just run a hundred-meter sprint.

"She did," he said, pointing at the imitation Patty.

Suddenly I could feel the time bubble starting to slip again.

Stan suddenly looked a little panicked and some beads of sweat broke out on his forehead as he too struggled to hold the field.

"She knows what we are doing," Stan said.

I didn't want to know how he knew or how she could know unless she was some god. I didn't want to think about the fact that I had frozen in time a god and she would be angry at me.

Stan moaned and sweat started to run down his neck. I felt like the time bubble I was working to hold now weighed as much as a large truck. No chance I could hold it much longer and as a poker player, there was nothing on the planet more frightening to me than to see the God of Poker sweat and strain.

Stan glanced up at the ceiling. "Burt! Laverne! Help!"

Every ounce of energy I had was going to hold Stan and me out of time at that moment, or I would have just sat down stunned. Stan had just called for Burt, the God of Casino Operations and Lady Luck herself, the most powerful god I had ever met.

Who or what was this Patty imitator and why had she scared me and Stan so much?

Burt and Laverne appeared next to the now sweat-covered Stan. Burt wore a gray, three-piece silk business suit and his short stature made him look more like a mob boss than a major god. Laverne was dressed in a black pants suit with matching jacket and had her hair pulled back tight.

"What is the…"

Then she saw the Patty imitator and Lady Luck herself actually flushed.

Suddenly the pressure was off holding the time bubble as both Burt and Lady Luck took over, giving Stan and me a rest.

My rubbery knees wanted me to slump to the floor and give them a rest, but instead I managed to keep on my feet trying to catch my breath.

"Who is that?" I managed to ask.

"Morrígan," Lady Luck said, walking over around the imitation Patty. "The Phantom Queen as she is often called. And why she is coming to you, Poker Boy, is a mystery."

Now I was officially and formally scared. When Laverne, Lady Luck herself, didn't know something, I knew I was in deep trouble. So I didn't ask the next question on my mind…Who was Morrígan?

"I thought Morrígan was only a myth," Stan said, looking very worried. "Right along with her sisters."

I still had no idea who Morrígan was.

"Nope, all three are real," Burt said, looking very worried. "Just not around much these days."

I am sure I looked worried as well, but that was because I had no idea what was going on and because they were all worried and they were far more powerful than I was.

"After Atlantis," Laverne said, "Morrígan pretty much stayed in the Alps and out of any of the world's problems."

"I heard she was around for the two big wars," Stan said. "After all, she is known as the Goddess of War."

Oh, wow, it was *that* Morrígan who stood there frozen looking like my girlfriend. When a very, very old god started pretending to be your girlfriend, things could not be going well.

Laverne shook her head. "Both wars Morrígan stayed in Switzerland, neutral."

"What is she doing in Las Vegas?" Burt asked.

And instant later Morrígan, still looking like Patty, moved and smiled at Laverne as she stepped into our frozen time bubble. "You could just ask me," she said.

"That's why I brought you out of time," Laverne said, her voice cold and as hard as I had ever heard Lady Luck sound.

"Nice seeing you again as well," Morrígan said to Laverne.

She might look like Patty, but the voice was nothing like Patty's at all. Patty had a softness to her voice. This imposter sounded harsh, with a coldness in every sentence.

Laverne just stared at Morrígan and the stare was returned in kind. There was clearly no love lost between the two women.

After a moment the woman's appearance shifted. The Patty-look sort of melted and formed into a woman who had long, black hair, a very, very thin face with a long, thin nose, and eyes that were coal black. She had on a white pants suit and was as thin as any supermodel I had ever seen. She towered over all of us because not only was she tall, but she somehow managed to stand on six-inch heels.

Laverne said nothing.

Finally Morrígan smiled at Laverne. "Fine, if you want to be that way, I came to ask a favor of Poker Boy."

Morrígan smiled at me, then went back to staring at Laverne.

I figured if my heart was ever going to explode out of my chest at any point in my life, now was the time. I was stunned I hadn't just fainted dead away under that look. The woman was totally terrifying. I hadn't been this scared in any recent memory. And that was with three of the most powerful gods in existence standing beside me.

"You could have just come to me," Laverne said.

"And you would have agreed?" Morrígan asked, smiling.

"Of course not," Laverne said.

Looks like I was off the hook at least for the moment.

"That's why I had to take a chance on approaching Poker Boy directly," Morrígan said. "But he is as good as his reputation and saw me coming, clearly."

I think I had just been complimented by an enemy of Lady Luck. Not something I would ever want as a poker player.

"So what was the favor?" Laverne asked, her voice perfectly level and very, very cold.

"I wanted him to teach me how to play poker," Morrígan said.

"I assumed as much," Lady Luck said. "Why?"

The idea of teaching that woman anything, let alone poker had my knees weak again. I would rather have five guns pointed at my head than do that.

My warning chill was doing tap dances up and down my spine.

Morrígan laughed, but there was no real humor in the laugh and it brought no smiles to anyone around me. It just made the cold shivers on my spine increase. I was shivering so hard from my danger warning sense, it was lucky my foot wasn't pounding on the ground like an excited dog.

I was going to need to figure out a way to turn that warning signal off when I needed to.

"You might know I have been hanging around with Ares lately," Morrígan said.

I wanted to shout *The God of War!* But somehow I managed to stay silent.

"I heard you have been living together since the Cuban Missile Crisis," Laverne said.

"Yeah, he got depressed," Morrígan said, "He was so looking forward to that war. He thought it would have been epic. I've been trying to nurse him back to health."

"I'll bet," Laverne said.

"So we've been playing some poker and I'm tired of losing," she said.

"He cheats," Laverne said flatly. "Get a new deck of cards that he has not touched and see how you do."

Morrígan stood there staring at Laverne for a very, very long moment. Laverne just stared back. For a moment I thought they had stepped outside of the time bubble and were frozen in the instant of time like everyone else in the lobby of the MGM Grand.

Then Morrígan smiled a very mean and angry smile and slowly shook her head. "That bastard."

And then she vanished.

It was as if the sun had come out after weeks of rain and I had won the lottery all in one instant. The cold chills that had been running up and down my back suddenly vanished as well.

"I hate her," Lady Luck said.

"But you might want to let her win some now," Burt said, chuckling.

"Yeah, we'll see," Laverne said.

With that they both vanished.

Stan just stood there shaking his head. Then he laughed and turned to me. "Nice job."

"What did I do?" I said, still feeling stunned.

"You saw her coming," he said. "That's amazing. It's not many people who can see through a Banshee's disguise, let along Morrígan's, the war goddess. And you got out of time without her

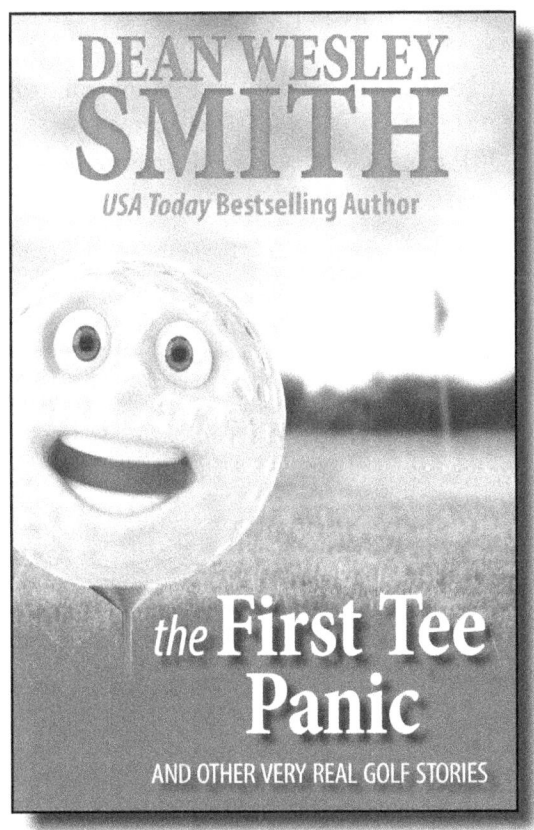

noticing at first. Impressive against a god that powerful."

"And she's living with Ares? Right?" I asked. "The same Ares of war fame?"

"Yup," Stan said, "as long as they keep themselves entertained with each other and out of the spotlight, the planet is a lot safer."

"Until they get mad at each over a poker game," I said, suddenly feeling less hopeful for the survival of the human race.

"Yeah, until that," Stan said, thinking it was funny now.

"And she and Laverne have issues, clearly?" I asked, trying to get my mind wrapped around what had just happened.

"From way, way back," Stan said, laughing. "A long story I'll tell you about sometime, at least the parts I've heard. It predates me by a few hundred thousand years."

He patted me on the back. "Again, great job. Who knows what kind of problem or major war you just avoided."

"Thanks, I think," I said.

He laughed and vanished.

The pounding sounds of the real world came crashing back in around me as he let go of the bubble outside of time. The fine patrons of the MGM Grand Casino and Hotel were back in motion, laughing, talking, and being very human.

And right now that felt wonderful.

I moved over and leaned against the stone pillar, trying to slow down my racing heart. Patty looked up at me and smiled before going back to helping her customer.

Somehow my poker face allowed her to not notice that I had just escaped an encounter with a very dangerous woman. And who knew what else would have happened if Morrígan had gotten to me.

But how in the world was I going to tell Patty what had just happened in an instant in time right in front of her?

She was never going to believe me.

I turned my gaze to the high ceiling of the lobby. "Stan, can you meet me and Patty at the Diner in thirty minutes? Milkshakes are on me. I need help explaining what just happened. I'm still not sure myself."

I could hear a low, rumbling chuckle echo over the noise of the lobby, then his voice, "Sure thing, kid."

Patty looked up and frowned. She clearly had heard Stan's voice as well.

"Long story," I mouthed at her and she frowned, but went back to work with the customer.

A long story that had only taken an instant to happen.

And a story I had a hunch wasn't over just yet. Morrígan playing poker against Ares just couldn't turn out well. If not this century, then maybe next. That was the nature of the war of a poker game.

Especially now that Morrígan wanted to win.

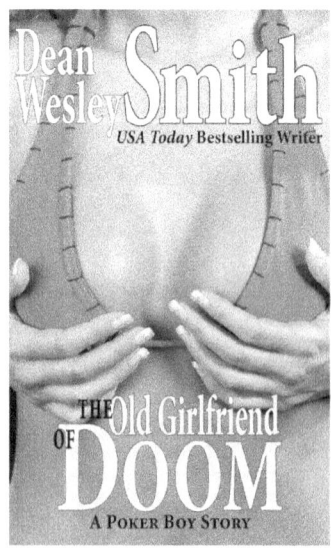

Now Available
from all your favorite booksellers in trade paper and electronic editions.

FANTASY

USA TODAY BESTSELLING AUTHOR

DEAN WESLEY SMITH

THE SLOTS OF SATURN

A POKER BOY NOVEL

DEAN WESLEY SMITH

BUTCHERED WHALE

ON A RED BEDSPREAD

Sometimes a detective can see with more than just his eyes. And sometimes a detective must take steps to stop murders, steps that seem harsh in the cold light of day.

A woman, killed in her own bedroom, brutally skinned like an animal, seems to be just another victim in a ritualized killing. But to one special detective, she plays a much larger roll than victim.

She might very well be a savior.

BUTCHERED WHALE ON A RED BEDSPREAD

YOU COULD SAY it wasn't a pretty sight. I never would, but you could say that, and I'm sure it would be the truth. I never say anything about how something looks, because I am blind. But I "see" just fine in other ways.

I can tell you a mile away that there is a dead raccoon rotting in the heat on the side of a road. I can tell you what the last shudder of a common fly with its wings ripped off sounds like. I can even tell you what it feels likc to shake a lying man's hand.

But telling you exactly what a dead whale on a red bedspread in a small bedroom *looks* like just isn't possible for me to do.

But I do have enough to visualize it.

I know the bedroom was that of a woman who wore perfume and used Ivory soap to wash her clothes. I know the bedroom has one bed, a dresser to the right of the door, and a window on the street side.

I know the woman is dead on the bed-spread.

My partner, J.P. Rancher shuddered beside me, meaning the sight in front of us was just plain ugly. J.P. very seldom shuddered at the sight of a dead whale. But for some reason this one made him shudder.

I knew J.P. almost as well as he knew himself. For instance, this morning, before coming to pick me up, he'd had sex with his girlfriend. He hadn't told me, but he slurred his words slightly, laughed at everything, and just reeked of passion. I may be blind, but I know a happily-screwed man when I smell one.

"That bad, huh?" I asked in response to J.P's reaction.

"Yeah," J.P. said, softly. The last word was more like a sigh than a word.

"Man or woman?" I asked, trying to get him and me back on track. I knew it was a woman, but I had to get him focused as well. We had a job to do.

"Woman," JP said.

"How big?"

"Small, maybe five-one. One hundred and ten pounds. No fat. Nude. She had been a looker..."

"...before this," I said, finishing his sentence. "Standard death?"

"Yeah," J.P. said, "harpoon through the chest, then the hunter skinned and gutted her."

There was bile mixed with blood and fecal matter in the smell. "The hunter must have nicked an intestine. Sloppy work."

"Yeah, real sloppy," J.P said.

"Lamp?"

"Gone," J.P. said. "Looks like it used to be on the bed stand."

"I'll bet the house was tossed as well," I said. "This hunter was a rookie."

"Got it in one," J.P. said. "I'll get all the standard crime boys into action. With someone this new we might get lucky."

I nodded as J.P left my side. My hearing was so good I could have listened to his conversation in the next room, but I knew almost word-for-word what he was going to say. So instead I stood there in the middle of the room and studied everything.

The smell was that of blood and shit and fear.

The room was stuffy, the air still, so clearly the windows were closed tight, with no drafts.

I took a deep breath of the thick air and made myself relax into the place. I used my senses to search out the light smell of breakfast made and cleaned up after hours before.

I imagined the woman, opening the front door and being surprised by a hunter, who shoved her to her bed and shot her with a harpoon. I imagined the skinning, the ceremony of taking the lamp, the final slashing of the skull to destroy the clone link before the hunter left.

But J.P had not mentioned the skull slash. Was this hunter that sloppy?

Of course, I knew there was another thing missing. In all the whale deaths I had investigated, there had always been a clear odor, at least to me, of fish. This room had no such smell.

J.P claimed he could never smell it, but he was a sighted person and he hadn't learned how to use his nose and other senses like I had.

Without even looking, I knew this wasn't a whale that had been killed. The person on that bed, harpooned and skinned, had been human.

I did not smile.

I stood and waited for my partner to come back into the room. I knew better than to move around a crime scene, no matter how good I was at getting around without sight. I needed J.P. to get here and help me outside, and he was still giving orders in the next room to the techs.

Having a human killed in a ritual whale ceremony confused issues greatly. Detectives had to figure out why this poor woman had been targeted as a whale? Had it just been a mistake? Or was this a copy-cat killer by someone who wanted her dead?

Besides the clone chip in the skull behind the left ear, there was no real difference between whales and humans. And the clone chip had been made to look like skull bone on any scan.

So it was impossible to know the difference at a glance. And I believed there really was no difference. Intelligent beings were intelligent beings, but my viewpoint was still in the minority around the world.

Whale intelligence had been first put into cloned human bodies thirty years before in an underground lab in Greenland. The theory was that the twenty scientists in the lab were looking for a way to help save the whales from extinction. I personally think they were just making excuses to justify their working on clones.

The scientists were shocked to learn that whale intelligence could be transferred, unlike human brains, and that the whales were as intelligent as humans. With a human cloned body and training, whales quickly learned a human language and how to function completely in the general population.

Having a human killed in a ritual whale ceremony confused issues greatly.

And they liked it, at least most whales did. They wanted to stay out of the water, they wanted to keep their fingers, their ability to move around freely on land.

Without telling anyone what they were doing, the scientists in the underground lab worked for years to grow and transfer as many whale intelligences into human cloned bodies as they could. These whales were then sent out all over the world to live normal human lives, with the only drawback being they had to have a certain light every night for a number of hours to stay healthy.

I had been dealing with whale killings for years and I still didn't completely understand the light. But with the hunters, the lights were the real trophies. The skin was the only proof offered to other hunters in the ritual celebration at their lodges. But each lamp was placed in a spot of honor, with the hunters name on it.

It had become illegal to kill whales in human cloned bodies shortly after the news of their existence became public. But arresting humans for killing what many considered to be nothing more than animals was not a popular job. J.P. and I had been doing it for years, and we had gotten used to the names and the anger and the lack of respect that came at us. We were catching killers and that was all that mattered to us.

Over time I started to understand what made humans in general so angry at the whales. It wasn't that they were clones. It was because they were alien in nature and had a chance of living forever.

The early scientists discovered a way to move whale intelligence not only from a whale's body to a human clone, but from one human clone to another. For some reason scientists have yet to figure out how to move human brains from one to another, let alone do it for a second time, so we humans are still stuck with a short hundred years of life, while whales can possibly go on living forever.

A lot of people don't much like that.

By five years ago the anger against whales in general had become so great that there were only a few thousand natural whales left in the oceans. But who knew how many there were living and having children in secret tanks and labs to be put into cloned human bodies.

And like the old days in the south, organizations had been formed to keep the whales in their place, to get rid of the whales if possible. They were called hunting lodges, and they developed their own rituals that they followed with every killing.

I very much wanted to skin every member of those lodges, just as they skinned the whales.

J.P.'s footsteps told me he was headed back toward me.

"We have a problem," I said, lifting an arm in the general direction of the body. "She wasn't a whale."

"What?" J.P. asked.

"Unless whales have managed to get rid of the underlying fish odor, that woman was completely human. Is her skull caved in?"

"Yeah," J.P. said. "Let me check it."

I could sense that J.P had waved for a tech to come into the room to help him, and after a moment a man with a slight after shave habit who had had bacon for breakfast entered the small bedroom.

I knew the guy stared at me for a moment, then turned his breakfast breath away to work with J.P over the body.

"Shit!" J.P said after eight seconds.

"No clone chip, right?" I asked.

"No clone chip. She was human."

"Third one this month," I said. "Detectives with the human division seem to have a problem on their hands."

The tech snorted and said nothing. I liked to use the words "human division" when talking about human crimes, even though J.P. and I were the only members of the "whale division" of the force.

No one much cared that a whale got killed. No real cops moved to close down the hunting lodges. Some cops were even members. But after more and more humans died they were going to care. Of that I had no doubt.

And then, maybe, the whale hunting would be stopped by the decent people of the world. I could only hope, because it was a large sacrifice some people were making to have this change happen.

I didn't know the woman spread out harpooned and skinned in front of me, but she had given her life for the cause of humane treatment for whales. Other humans would do the same until the hunting lodges were a thing of the past, and the law dealt with whale hunters like they did any other sick killer.

"Looks like we're done with this case, partner," I said. We never took cases in which humans were killed. The whale deaths kept us busy enough.

"Sure does," J.P. said. "Let's get out of this mess and let the next detectives in line take the ball."

J.P. touched my elbow and with only slight pressure made sure I made it out of the room and the house without stepping on any evidence. With luck the

Now Available
from all your favorite booksellers
in trade paper and electronic editions.

detectives would catch this killer and string him up.

I got to J.P.'s car and slid in as he talked to the cop we were leaving in charge until the new set of detectives got there.

I was glad that we had not been in that home long enough for me to get to know much about the victim. She had been killed by the stupidity and fear and hatred that had grown in our culture against the whales. I had had very little to do with it.

Granted, I had given her address twelve days ago, a perfectly random address, to someone on the internet who I knew would pass it on as a possible whale home, and then have it passed on again, and then again, through underground meetings in five countries, until it found a hunting lodge in this city and a sick killer who would do the job.

My involvement could never be traced, that much I made sure of. I hadn't done the killing, I had just given out an address.

A random address. There might have been a whale living there. There might have been a human. I didn't know, but I hoped for a human, and again this time I had been right.

Tonight I would start another address for this city floating out there on the underground streams of information about whales. Every night, in a different way, I started addresses in major cities around the country.

The increase in killings of humans thought to be whales was starting to make the national news.

People were starting to get unhappy.

Whale killings were starting to drop off.

So far the deaths were paying off. I would continue until finally enough humans had died to make the hatred and killing stop.

If nothing else, each human death helped remove a killer of whales from the street if the detectives did their jobs. And as far as I was concerned, that seemed only fair.

I wondered what the great hunter who had skinned that woman in there was going to think when he discovered she had been one hundred percent human?

"What are you smiling about?" J.P. asked as he slid in behind the steering wheel and started the car.

"The piece of cheesecake I'm going to buy you at Audry's."

"Oh, man," J.P. said, roughly pushing the car forward and into the light traffic I could hear on the road. "I was hoping you were going to say that. Just keep on smiling until I get us there."

I thought about the hope for the future whales had. I thought about their hope of living as equals with humans, and it did keep me smiling.

Right up to the moment that I picked the next random address.

The Third Seeders Universe Novel
now available from all your favorite booksellers in trade paper and electronic.

USA *Today* Bestselling Writer

DEAN WESLEY SMITH

THE LIFE AND TIMES OF BUFFALO JIMMY

Chapters 34-36

What Came Before…

Nineteen-year-old Boston native Jimmy Gray had been traveling with his parents and older brother, Luke, headed west to find a new home and new riches. Before even reaching Independence, they were attacked and robbed by Jake Benson and his gang. Jimmy's parents were killed, his brother wounded.

In one of the wildest towns in all of American history, Jimmy Gray, a sheltered, educated son of a banker from Boston suddenly finds himself very, very much alone. But then through some luck, he finds other young men about his age and down on their luck who might be able to help him.

Together, the five of them head west after Benson. They end up hunting buffalo as he always dreamed of doing, but then they are hit with a massive flash flood and Jimmy is left alone, his friends more than likely dead. Luckily, they all meet up again and are all safe. So they continue west, knowing that Benson is just ahead of them.

Suddenly they come upon Benson and his men killing a farm family. They manage to get one of the men separated from the others, but in a fall he accidently dies. So they scatter to meet up later at a camp. They managed that but found a survivor of the killings. So one of them had to go back with the kid while the others followed Benson.

They caught him once again terrorizing a small wagon train and managed to scare him and his men off. But then they had to cross the forty-mile desert. And right from the start, things started off deadly. Then, in the middle of the worst part of the desert, they find a wagon train, horses stolen, water gone, only women and children left to die by Benson.

But what can they do? If they try to take them along, everyone will die. They decide they can't leave them and take them, barely making it to the river. Barely. Then, after getting help, they go back into the desert to get the women's wagons and supplies, again risking their lives. They make it and head to Virginia City looking for Benson.

THE LIFE AND TIMES OF BUFFALO JIMMY

Part Thirty-four
The Search Goes On

JIMMY HAD BEEN stunned at the excitement, the energy, and the feel of Virginia City when they rode in that first day. It was very much like Independence, only with far more drunks and fighting. The mines and mine tailings seemed to be everywhere, bright brown scars on the rough land. The mineshafts riddled the ground right under Main Street.

Over half of the buildings along the main streets were two story wood structures, and more were going up all around. Clearly, since there were no trees nearby, they were hauling in the lumber from some distance.

Long had been right to stay out of town. Jimmy soon discovered that a few years earlier, there had been a massive misunderstanding that had led to the building of Fort Churchill by the Army and then the Pyramid Lakes Indian battle. Feelings around town were still running hot on what had happened, so it was better that Long had just stayed on the sidelines.

There was no sign at all of Benson or his one remaining man.

They met back up with Long and Truitt, then made camp on a river a few miles upstream from Fort Churchill. The location gave them fresh water and was up against a rock wall that could be defended if for some reason they were attacked. Jimmy had a hunch that they would be using the camp for some time to come. It was going to take time to search for Benson.

Then, early the next day, with Long and Josh staying in the camp, the rest again went in search of Benson.

C. J. had suggested that they would cover more ground if they split up, so Jimmy and Truitt went into Virginia City. Zach and C.J headed in the other direction for Carson City.

Unlike the search in Independence, this time more than Jimmy knew Benson on sight. They also knew who Benson's riding companion was, and what the men's two horses and saddles looked like.

That first day of the search was long and hot, and left Jimmy feeling frustrated. Suppose Benson had gone ahead and stayed on the trail and went on over the mountains to Sacramento. Now, after all the time on the river, he might already have the gold deed registered in his name. That night, Jimmy talked to the rest about his worry and suggested that maybe they should split up, with some of them riding for Sacramento.

None of them had agreed with Jimmy's fears. They were all convinced that Benson was still in the area. As C.J. had said, "It's certain he's here somewhere."

Josh said, "It wouldn't be in his character to move on. He's going to drink and spend the money he stole from the women's company before he leaves here, just as he has done every time before."

Jimmy still wasn't sure, but he felt better that at least they all agreed that staying and searching was the right thing to do.

So the next day, Jimmy and Zach and C.J. and Truitt stayed together instead of going two different directions. C.J figured it was better that they cover one town per day completely and Jimmy had agreed. They planned to split up in each town.

As it turned out, it didn't take long to prove C.J. and Josh correct. Benson had stayed.

It was in Virginia City, as they rode into town just after dawn, that Jimmy spotted Jake Benson, the man Jimmy hated more than any man alive. Benson's horse was roped in front of a saloon and the murderer was just walking down the sidewalk as if he had no care in the world.

"That's Benson," Jimmy said to his friends, pointing at Benson's back.

"So that's what the poisoned snake looks like," Truitt said.

"Deadly and mean," Zach said.

Zach and Truitt had never seen Benson before, since they had been taking the only survivor of Benson's Goose Creek killings back to Fort Hall when Jimmy and the others saved the wagon train.

"That's him," Jimmy said, not even trying to hide the disgust in his voice.

They quickly dismounted and tied up their horses in front of a general store.

"Now what?" Zach asked.

"We follow him," Jimmy said. "From now on, he never leaves our sight. Any time of the day or night. We just have to wait for the right moment."

The others nodded and they all moved after Benson down the main street.

Jimmy could barely contain his anger. Right in front of him was the man who had killed his mother and father. And many others along the trail from Independence.

Jimmy had to stop Benson, but he had no idea how.

And it was clear that the others wanted to stop Benson almost as much as Jimmy did, after burying that family on Goose Creek, and those men and women in the desert.

Benson had left a trail of bodies in his wake and it seemed that Jimmy and his friends had been doing nothing but cleaning up after him and digging graves. If Jimmy had anything to say about it, that was going to stop right here in Virginia City.

Benson just kept walking, his boots rumbling on the wooden sidewalk like it didn't matter. He was almost swaggering.

It was clear to Jimmy that Benson believed no one was after him for all that he had done. That was good. Even after

being chased off from that wagon train back on Goose Creek, Benson didn't feel threatened, which meant they still had surprise on their side.

"Split up," Jimmy said. "Truitt, you and Zach pace him down the other side of the street."

Truitt and Zach crossed over between two wagons while Jimmy and C.J stayed behind Benson.

Jimmy had no idea what they would do now that they had found him, but one thing was for certain, they weren't going to lose sight of him again. They would be on him like a tick on a yard dog until Benson did something that would allow them to act.

Benson walked most of the length of the booming mining town, going by saloon door after saloon door. The wooden sidewalk ended and he kept on going downhill, out of the main part of town, passing some smaller buildings and a few large tents that housed different businesses.

Then finally, near the lower south edge of town, Benson turned into a small wooden-planked building that had a painted barber pole hanging on the front wall. The building was no bigger than a shack and had been built up against a rock bluff. It had a tin roof. Jimmy couldn't imagine how hot that must make it inside the little shack in the middle of the day. Even with the front door standing open, Jimmy doubted Benson would be in there long.

"Stay here," Jimmy told C.J. "I'll be back.

Then, as if on a mission, he walked past the front of the shack and got a quick

> **"That's him," Jimmy said, not even trying to hide the disgust in his voice.**

look inside, keeping his hat low on his head.

He then circled around, went back up the other side of the street, and met the others off to one side of the street in the shade, where Benson couldn't see them.

"It's only Benson in there with a barber," Jimmy said. "Any ideas?"

Zach shook his head, as did Truitt.

But C. J. smiled. "I just might have something we could do. But if it fails, we might get shot."

"After watching that scum of the earth walk up the street like he had done nothing," Jimmy said, "I'm willing to take some risks. That man in that building killed my parents."

Zach nodded. "And a lot of other innocent people. After seeing how he left those women out in the desert to die, I agree. We have to stop this animal."

"All right," C.J. said, nodding. "But my plan is going to take some rope and a blanket."

Jimmy glanced around. There was a general store about a half block back up the street. He had maybe just enough money left for what C.J. needed. "You three stay here," he said. "How much rope?"

"Thin and strong and about thirty feet."

Jimmy nodded and turned toward the store without even asking C. J. what his plan was.

"Get a shovel, too," C.J. called after him. "With a long handle."

Part Thirty-five
The Plan

JIMMY TRUSTED C.J., but he sure hoped this plan would work as he headed for the general store at a fast walk. They had rope on their horses, and blankets and shovels back in their camp, but that would take far too long to get. He was going to have to spend the very last of his father's money for this. He sure hoped it worked.

It took him less than five minutes and he was back with what C.J said he needed.

C.J. took the shovel, gave the blanket to Truitt. Then he quickly explained his idea on how they could capture Benson and maybe get him to the Virginia City Sheriff. After they captured Benson, the boys would have to ride to catch the women in the wagon train. The women could then testify to the Sheriff about what Benson had done to their men. Jimmy was sure the women hadn't made it too far up into the Sierras yet.

"This is crazy," Zach said, smiling at Jimmy. "He has a gun and clearly doesn't mind killing people."

"I know," Jimmy said. "But we got to try."

"I'm not saying we don't," Zach said. "I'm just saying that this is crazy."

"No argument from me," Jimmy said, smiling back at his friend.

"You know," Truitt said as they headed across the street, "that if this works, we're going to have to come up with a name for it."

"Let's see if it works, first," C.J. said, clearly worried, even though it was his idea.

Near the barbershop, with the rope trailing behind him in the dirt, Jimmy walked past, again keeping his face from being seen clearly.

Inside the barbershop, he could see Benson still sitting in the chair and the barber working at Benson's beard and hair. Both were looking away from the door.

As Jimmy got to the other side of the barbershop and out of sight of Benson and the barber, he stopped and eased the rope right up near the front step up into the small shack.

On the other end of the rope, Zach pulled tight. To Jimmy, the rope seemed clearly obvious tucked against the bottom of the step, but C.J. had assured them that if they got Benson to come out fast and hard, he wouldn't notice it.

Truitt unfolded the dark wool blanket that Jimmy had bought and moved over against the barbershop front wall, his back to the wooden planks, the blanket held in both hands.

Then, when he was ready, it was C.J's turn.

C.J stepped up so he could be seen through the front door of the small shack.

"You Jake Benson, mister?" C.J. asked, leaning on the shovel like he always stood that way.

Jimmy was impressed that C.J. sounded so calm, like none of this mattered.

"Yeah, what's it to ya, kid?" Benson said from inside.

Jimmy felt a chill go up his spine. He hadn't heard that voice since before his parents were killed. He hadn't liked it then, he didn't like it now.

"I was told to come down here and tell you that he's taking your horse and gear in payment for what you owe him."

"Who!" Benson shouted.

The shout echoed off the tin roof.

Jimmy could hear from the scraping sounds that Benson had stood up. Both Jimmy and Zach made sure they were braced and ready with the rope.

"He didn't give me his name," C. J. said. "Black beard, brown hat, black mare with a silver braid on the saddle."

C.J. had just described Benson's remaining riding companion.

With that, C.J. stepped back a few steps into the middle of the street, allowing room for Benson to come straight out of the building.

"I'll kill that snake," Benson shouted as he stormed out of the barbershop, putting his hat on as he came.

Jimmy and Zach instantly yanked the rope up as Benson stepped for the street. The rope caught him in the shin and Benson went forward hard, face down into the dust.

Truitt moved faster than Jimmy thought possible, sprawling on Benson from behind with the blanket, covering the killer's head and arms.

Zach and Jimmy moved in and quickly wrapped more of the rope around Benson's legs.

But Benson was clearly fast and angry. He was bucking Truitt like a wild horse out of control.

From under the blanket, Benson's hand and gun came out and he fired once.

The shot barely missed Jimmy and ricocheted off some rocks down the street.

"Get his gun!" Zach shouted.

Jimmy, as hard as he could, smashed his boot down on Benson's gun hand.

The gun spun away in the dirt.

Benson screamed and bucked Truitt even harder under the blanket, but couldn't stand because Zach has his legs tied up.

C.J. stepped up, and with a swing of the shovel, hit Benson on the head through the blanket.

Now Jimmy understood why C.J. had wanted the shovel.

Suddenly, Truitt was lying on an unmoving pile of man and blanket.

Jimmy's heart was beating so fast, he could hardly breathe, and he was sweating like he had never sweated before.

Truitt pulled the blanket off and stood while Zach wrapped even more rope around Benson's legs and tied it off like he would a steer.

They had captured Benson.

Jimmy couldn't believe it.

Part Thirty-six
Now What?

"EVERYONE ALL RIGHT?" Jimmy asked.

"Yeah," they all said, but it was clear that Truitt was out of breath and more than likely bruised up from his ride on Benson's back.

Jimmy moved over and picked up the gun, holding the heavy hunk of metal in his hands.

More than likely, this was the gun that had killed his parents, shot his mother in the back, killed the family at Goose Creek, and the men in the desert.

Jimmy looked at the gun, then at the man out cold in the dirt of the street.

"Shoot him," C.J. said. "Don't let him ever kill anyone again."

"We wouldn't blame you," Truitt said, "after what he did to your parents."

"This man do something to you boys?" the barber asked from the door of his shop.

"Killed my parents," Jimmy said, his voice surprisingly calm for how his stomach was feeling. "Shot my mother in the back."

"Oh," the barber said.

"And then he killed a family back on Goose Creek," Zach said. "And some men in the middle of the desert, leaving women and children to die just so he could steal their money and stock."

The barber nodded. "You know, a lot goes on in this street that I just don't seem to notice."

Then the man turned and went back into his shack, cleaning, pretending to not look out the door.

Truitt laughed.

Jimmy was just glad that the barber wasn't going to try to stop them. Jimmy stared at Benson, then at the gun in his hands. He really wanted to kill Benson. More than he had wanted to kill anything or anyone in his entire life.

But he wouldn't do it.

He was still bothered by the man they had accidentally killed back on Goose Creek. Killing Benson would give him nightmares for the rest of his life.

And besides that, it wasn't the right thing to do.

He shook his head, still staring at the heavy gun in his hands.

"No, I'd be just like him if I killed him," Jimmy said. "For whatever the reason."

Jimmy unloaded the revolver and then laid it on a rock beside the barbershop. Picking up another large rock, he smashed the gun over and over, feeling the anger toward Benson with every blow.

The gun was shattered and bent and in pieces when he finally stopped.

"No one is going to be killed by that gun again," Jimmy said, panting at the work it had taken to destroy the gun.

"There isn't a big enough piece left to throw at anyone," Truitt said, laughing.

Jimmy turned back to see the rest of them all smiling at him. Along the street, a small crowd was gathering to watch.

To Jimmy, it didn't matter. Benson would never kill another person with that gun.

Continued next month...

USA *Today* Bestselling Writer

DEAN WESLEY SMITH

A Game
of Poker
with Aliens...
Never a Good Idea

WHO'S HOLDING DONNA NOW?

A game of poker with aliens... never a good idea.

Not that aliens cheat. Not that at all. They know how to win, and they want their winnings when they do win.

No matter the condition of the winnings.

WHO'S HOLDING DONNA NOW?

IT WAS AN ACCIDENT.

Nothing more. A simple accident. I saw the entire thing.

It was awful.

My name is Jacob O'Grady. I own Sandy's Restaurant and Lounge down on twelfth. It's a pretty good-sized place with low, wood-beamed ceilings and more beer signs on the walls than should be allowed in one place. No windows, and a constant smell of lingering smoke.

The polished oak bar had come out of an old saloon from downtown Boise I hear, but never took the time to trace it back. That bar was forty feet long and the center of the place.

I bought the bar six years ago from Sandy's wife after Sandy called some girl a whore. Turned out to be this big cowboy's special girl. The big guy didn't even waste time with Sandy.

Five shots. All hit Sandy.

That guy could shoot. Sort of impressive, actually.

Now I never insult no one. Main rule number one.

I have a lot of main rules. I got to just to stay alive.

Donna was like Sandy. She didn't learn so fast. Now it's too late. Or at least I think it's too late. I honestly don't know for sure.

Donna had long black hair, thick black eyebrows, and just a hint of a moustache along her upper lip. I thought she was good looking, with her long legs, model type figure, and real warm smile. I think the smile was why I hired her.

I suppose I should have warned her right off. But about the time I hired her, I still didn't really believe what was going on. And then after it got started, I was afraid to tell anyone.

Hell, who would have believed me if I would have said that aliens dropped by my bar every night. I'd have been laughed right out of the neighborhood, if not locked up in a funny white suit.

But I had aliens all right.

Three of them.

They looked human, at least on the surface. One seemed older than the other two, maybe in his fifties if he had been human. He had rough skin and dark, intense eyes.

The other two looked to be mid-thirties, also dressed in normal human clothes for men of this area. Jeans, work shirts, work boots. One had a thick, dark moustache and the other had blonde hair.

At first glance, a person couldn't tell they were any different than the other loggers or rock miners that came in here. They dressed the same, drank the same kind of booze, and stayed off to themselves. Damn normal-like. But I could tell they were aliens. I just knew.

I should have warned Donna.

Hell, I didn't know they were going to start playing poker. It fit right in, though, when I thought about it later.

Any night in Sandy's there's at least three poker games going. There's always the high stake in the back room, plus some pretty good smaller games going out in the main room.

The three aliens watched the games real close for about two weeks, drinking just enough to make sure I didn't toss them outside, but not drinking that much as to seem drunk. For all I knew, they couldn't get drunk.

Then one of them asked Donna for a deck.

Tell the truth, I didn't give it a second thought, even though by then I was pretty convinced they really were aliens, but their money was good and they sure didn't cause any trouble.

Donna gave them the cards. I remember real clearly because it was her second night and I had to show her where the decks of cards were stashed in the second drawer to the right of the cash register on the back bar.

The aliens worked at learning poker for about the next four weeks, never letting anyone join in, just playing their own game over in a corner.

Again, I didn't much care since they paid for their drinks and tipped Donna well.

They didn't ask many questions, but they asked enough around the room that I could figure out they didn't know much to start. But let me tell you, those three aliens were damn fast learners.

Damn fast.

Looking back, it's funny how things just sort of build up. Even them aliens playing cards would have been fine if Donna hadn't taken up with Cutbank Jones.

Cutbank was an odd bird. Long, kind of wiry, and just mean as hell. His eyes were so cold black that it used to make people squirm when he looked across a poker table at them. What Donna saw in him, I don't know. But one night I actually saw her make him smile. Amazing things do happen in Sandy's.

After the first few days, Cutbank came to think he owned Donna. About the only time she got away from him was while she worked. And even then, more times than not, Cutbank would be sitting in on one of the poker games and keeping an eye on her. He never let her get far from sight.

I meant to ask her one night if she needed help avoiding him, but just never got around to it before the night of the big game. I should have, I really should have. Regrets now in hindsight.

The big game started at about nine. The older of the three aliens got up and moved over to a table where Slim, Raymond, Cutbank, and Freddy were playing and bold-like asked if he could sit in.

No one seemed to mind, so after a few hands the other two aliens came over and joined the table, making it seven players.

All of them had the buy-in plus a little, and all seemed to play well, if not mechanical.

Eventually, Jones and Steven joined in when the high stakes game in the backroom got a little slow.

The entire thing made me nervous, but what the hell could I do about it? They were just customers, so I kept my mouth shut and made sure everyone had a drink when they wanted one.

Donna did the serving and the aliens tipped her well.

Cutbank treated her like trash. That not only annoyed me, but most of the men in the game. Donna was well liked. She just had that kind of smile.

For the first few hours, the game went fine and I was beginning to think the evening might just end up being a good one.

Cutbank held his own at the table. He might have been a nasty ass to Donna, but he could play a mean game of seven-card stud.

DEAD MONEY could be the start of a new thriller genre— the political poker thriller.

—*Sheldon McArthur,
former owner of
Mysterious Books in Los Angeles*

Available Now
**from all your favorite booksellers
in trade paper and electronic editions.**

Both Raymond and Freddy had tapped out and left, with most of their money sitting in front of the three aliens.

An hour later, Slim was gone and not long after that, both Jones and Steven.

That left only Cutbank on one side of the table and the three aliens on the other. Except for a few chips in front of Cutbank, the aliens had it all. And that galled the hell out of Cutbank. I could tell.

So could the few customers remaining in Sandy's.

The hand that started the problem was the hand that Cutbank drew into a straight, King high.

Two of the aliens folded right off, but the older one held on, betting twice what Cutbank had left in front of him, smiling all the time.

The rules in a game in Sandy's is that if you didn't have the money to cover the bet, you lost the hand.

At that point, I never saw a man get so red. For a minute I thought Cutbank was going to jump right across the table at the alien guy. But he didn't.

Being the good player that he was, he first studied his hand, then laid his cards face down in front of him, pushed what was left of his money into the center of the table, and then asked the alien if he could have a moment to cover the rest of his bet.'

Standard game policy in Sandy's.

The alien nodded and laid his hand face down on the table in front of him and scooted his chair back.

Again standard action. I had to admit, the alien had learned all the rules.

Cutbank nodded, his face still red, and then turned and scanned the bar. Not a soul there that would loan him a penny, let along the amount needed to cover the alien's bet.

His gaze stopped on Donna. She was standing beside the bar in the waitress station and she squirmed like a worm pinned to a hook.

Cutbank's eyes sort of lit up and he stood quickly and moved over to her.

I knew before he got there that it wouldn't do no good. Donna had had a good night, tip wise and all, but she didn't have anywhere near enough to cover his bet.

And it didn't take Cutbank long to find out.

She said she didn't have enough, but he could have what she did have. He called her something crude and then told her to get out of his way. He grabbed her drink tray and ripped open her money carrier. Maybe twenty bucks in there, plus change. Then he grabbed her and searched her pockets quick-like.

She was smart enough at that moment not to fight him. I'm sure he'd have beat her something awful if she had. Of course, none of the rest of us in Sandy's would have allowed that to happen.

She didn't have the money. As soon as Cutbank realized that, he tossed her roughly against the bar and then slammed his hand against the wall, cussing up a blue streak.

Right at that point, I really didn't blame him for being angry. Hell, I would have been with a hand like his and no money. But then I would have calmed down enough to throw in my hand and walk away.

Most men would.

But not Cutbank.

He went to three of the men in the bar, threatening them if they didn't help him. None of them had enough. He even glanced my way once but then thought better of it. He knew that he might threaten me out of the money tonight, but if he did, he'd never be welcome back in here again.

In a place like Sandy's, there are unwritten rules of the house. Break a rule and every other customer turns into my enforcer.

Cutbank liked Sandy's too much to go doing that.

But it turned out he didn't like Donna that much. He was across the room threatening old man Craig when he turned and saw Donna and the rest of the bar watching him. It was right at that moment that I knew he came up with the idea.

Quickly, he stormed back across the bar and grabbed Donna by the arm and dragged her off into the alcove near the bathroom. From where I was behind the bar I could see Cutbank talking and Donna shaking her head no. Once she tried to pull away from him, but he held her tight.

At that point, if she'd started putting up a fuss, three or four of us would have jumped in. But she didn't.

After a long minute of Cutbank talking real soft but intense at her, Donna's shoulders slumped and she nodded. Then she kept right on nodding. Satisfied, Cutbank pulled her over to the table and sat back down in his chair, leaving her standing beside him.

He smiled real snakelike at the alien and then announced that the other half of his bet would be Donna.

One night with Donna.

Let me tell you that caused a stir in the bar.

I wanted to object, but then remembered Sandy and how he had ended up and my main rule of not getting in the middle of something not my business.

Donna might work for me, but she had made herself Cutbank's woman and anything she did on her own time was her business. If she wanted help, all she had to do was ask and everyone in the bar would jump to help.

But she was just standing there, so no one moved.

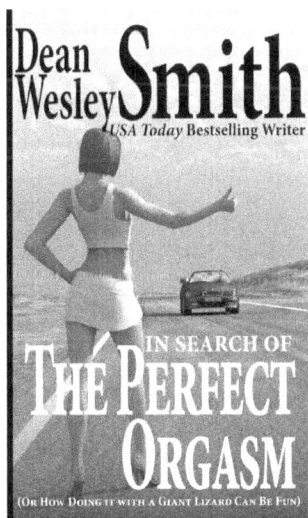

Some Classic Dean Wesley Smith Stories
Available at your favorite booksellers.

The alien was as surprised as the rest of the room. He glanced up at Donna and then back at Cutbank. Then he asked Cutbank to repeat what he had just said.

Cutbank did.

Then the alien did what any self-respecting man would do in that kind of poker game. He looked up at Donna and asked her if she agreed.

Right about then, I guess Donna had another chance to get out. If she'd have said no, not a person in the bar would have let her leave with Cutbank. She hesitated, but it wasn't a long hesitation before she said it was all right with her. Whatever Cutbank wanted.

The alien nodded and told Cutbank he accepted his call. Then the alien turned over his down cards.

Full house, queens over sevens.

Donna turned almost white as Cutbank slammed his cards into the pile of money and told the alien to deal the cards.

As the older alien pulled the money and the cards toward him, he asked just what Cutbank intended to wager.

Cutbank indicated Donna and again the alien looked up at Donna for her confirmation.

Donna nodded real slow.

Real slow.

All three aliens nodded in agreement and then they spent the next half minute or so discussing what a night with Donna was worth on the poker table.

I could tell that Cutbank was getting a little crazy right at that point. His voice was higher, his gestures quick and angry. I wanted to stop the game, close the bar and just go home and take a hot shower to wash off the stink of men like Cutbank and the women who let themselves be used. But another one of the unwritten rules of Sandy's was that no one ever interrupted a game. What went on in a game was between the men in the game and no one else.

So I stayed behind the bar and wiped out the same glass ten times.

The next hand was even sadder.

Cutbank again had a damn good hand. This time he had the full house, kings over sixes. Any respectable player would bet damn near the limit on that hand in seven-card stud.

Only this time, Donna was the limit.

The older alien that held the marker for one night with Donna dropped out early, but the other two stayed in. One of the aliens had four sevens.

Unbelievable hand.

Enough to make anyone crazy.

And that's what it did to Cutbank. Again he slammed his cards and his fist down on the table. Now his face was red and I could see clearly that he was sweating.

Donna looked as if she might faint.

But somehow Cutbank held his composure long enough to indicate another hand.

And once again Cutbank had a good hand. Three queens.

The two aliens who already owned nights with Donna dropped out when it came time to push forward their money. But the one with the moustache stayed in.

The alien had a straight, ten high.

That was all Cutbank could take.

He took one long look at the alien's cards, his face getting redder and redder, then slammed himself back and away from the table while reaching inside his coat. He yelled something about cheating and the next instant a forty-five was in his hand and swinging up at the aliens.

He never had a chance.

Quick as anything I have ever seen, all three aliens had small devices in their hands aimed at Cutbank.

The little guns (or whatever they were) looked like pocket calculators and made high-pitched whining sounds.

Cutbank staggered back under the blows of whatever the three aliens where aiming at him. His forty-five went off, the sound of the shot echoing around and around the room.

His shot, knocked off line by the aliens fire, hit Donna square in the chest sending her flying backwards into a table and then crashing sideways onto the wood floor.

Cutbank ended up slumped against the bathroom wall, very dead, but without a mark on him.

The alien with the moustache went quickly to inspect Cutbank while the other two and the rest of us gathered around Donna.

She too was obviously dead. Her pretty face was contorted into an expression of surprise. Blood formed a large pool under her, soaking her clothes, and giving the room a sick, copper smell that seemed to overwhelm the always-present smoke smell.

Quickly, the older alien said something in a language that sounded something like Spanish and Chinese rolled into one. The one with a moustache picked up Cutbank's forty-five and pocketed it while the blonde alien man attached a small box to Donna's arm.

I objected, telling them that they shouldn't touch anything until the police arrived. Murder was a serious thing, even if it was self-defense.

The older alien just shrugged.

He said that they had each won a night with Donna and they were going to take their winnings. I was going to object a little more strenuously, but suddenly

I caught a glimpse of one of those little calculator guns they had used on Cutbank and I thought better of it.

I guess everyone in the place at that moment thought better of it, because no one jumped in and tried to stop them.

Donna's body just sort of floated up off the ground until it was about waist high and then hovered there until the older alien expertly used Donna's foot to push her ahead of him out the front door while the blonde alien held the door open.

The one with the moustache followed and then the blonde alien just sort of nodded to the room and pulled the door closed behind all four of them.

Right at that moment, you could have heard a baby cry clear across town.

There were nine of us left and not a one said anything.

Finally, after I turned around and saw the big red puddle of blood and Cutbank very dead against the wall, I broke the silence by telling someone to please call the police while I made myself, and whoever else wanted one, a drink.

Of course, the police didn't buy the fact that three men just sort of zapped Cutbank and then floated Donna out, even with all of us telling somewhat close to the same story.

They did an autopsy on Cutbank and ruled that he had died of a heart attack. Made sense to me since there wasn't a mark on him. They didn't know what to do about the blood on the floor, so they didn't do anything and I mopped it up.

That all happened three days ago and now it's time to head to work. Tonight will be the forth night since they took Donna.

I don't know what to expect when I open up Sandy's. Sometimes I think Donna is just going to come walking back in the door live as can be.

And then sometimes I think that they just might dump her three-day-rotted body off after doing what they pleased with her for three nights.

That thought makes me sick, but it could happen. Sometimes you just never know.

I don't like to think that, so that's one of the reasons I've been covering for Donna the last three nights and holding her job open.

I can always hope.

———

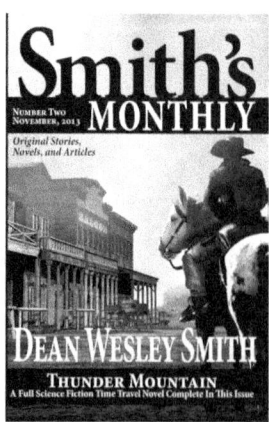

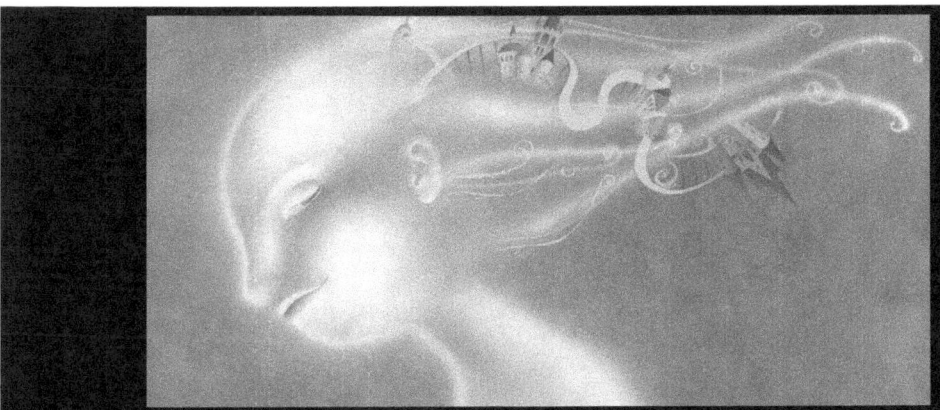

Poems by DEAN WESLEY SMITH

Heartburn

Mr. K. Berwick once said,
"You marry the person who is available
when you are the most vulnerable."

Two Nights ago, at five o'clock
I was vulnerable.
There was on one available.

So, I had a beer instead.
Beer always gives me heartburn.
A close approximation.

(First appeared in "An Anthology of New American Poetry" in 1976)

USA *Today* Bestselling Writer

DEAN WESLEY SMITH

THE ADVENTURES OF HAWK

Chapters 34-36

What Came Before…

Nineteen-year-old Danny Hawk, his uncle, and his best friend Craig, were in Cairo to look for his missing father. Danny had witnessed the death of his only contact in Cairo, Professor Davis, because the professor had Danny's father's journals.

Danny knows that the men who had killed the professor were now after him and the journals. Danny finds the journals and they decide to keep searching for Danny's father and try to rescue him. Along the way, Danny and Craig find some help from a street kid named Bud and twins from South Africa who had worked with Danny's father. They managed to escape the men chasing them over and over.

They finally decided to head out of Cairo. Beyond the headwaters of the Amazon, in the Republic of Congo, after a few more close calls, they hire a guide to take them into the jungle in search of a lost ancient city. Even into the jungle on the Trail of Elephants, they are followed. Then Danny barely escapes death when he falls through a floor in an old temple. The rest rescue him, but when they reach the bottom the men following them throw down the rope and trap them under the ancient city. But what they find next is amazing. An ancient council chamber.

And they find the fourth Hydra Journal entry.

HYDRA JOURNAL ENTRIES FOUND SO FAR
--The water flows uphill.
--The birth of a snake, the path of elephants.
--Under the teaming masses, the river becomes clear, the path muddy.
--From the highest city, power flows to the many.

So they head for South Africa where Ed and Ernie are captured. And if it is discovered who they really are, they will be executed. Somehow, Danny, Craig, and Bud manage to rescue them.

THE ADVENTURES OF HAWK

CHAPTER THIRTY-FOUR

October 3, 1970
Cape Town, South Africa.

THE FIRST NIGHT sleeping on the tops of the tall stacks of crates had been nerve-wracking. The crates were square, and Danny could barely lie side to side without his head or feet being near an edge. So all night he had a constant fear of falling asleep and rolling off.

He had managed to use a few of his clothes from his bag as padding and a pillow, but the rough surface of the wooden crate top still dug into his skin every time he moved. And any noise from outside the huge warehouse made them all sit up and hold their breaths in the dark. The dock was a busy place, day and night, so there were a lot of noises.

It had been a very long night.

After what seemed like an eternity, the sun finally came up, casting bright streams of light through the huge warehouse. From on top of the crates, the place looked more like a giant checkerboard, with the spaces between the crates dark lines. Since the tall stacks weren't much more than four feet apart, all of them had gotten used to jumping over the dark between the crates. It had twisted Danny's stomach the first few times, but now he knew it was nothing more than a really wide step to get from one to another.

Bud had vanished without a word just as the first light of day was starting to color the dirty windows of the warehouse. Now, suddenly, he appeared from out of the dark near Danny's crate.

"The British ship docked last night," Bud said. "They're just finishing unloading it now."

Danny had been worried a lot about how they were going to board tomorrow morning, in the light, with all the dock hands around getting ready for the ship's departure.

"I think," Danny said, "that when it calms down some around the ship, I should go talk with the Captain. See if we can board late tonight."

"Good idea," Ernie said. "Better than in the light."

"We can go on separately as well," Ed said. "Less chance of us being noticed that way."

"And I'm going with you to talk to the Captain," Craig said. "Less chance of a policeman paying attention if there are two of us."

"I'll make sure there are no police around before you go," Bud said.

"Good," Craig said. "I can't say I was looking forward to another night on top of this wooden mountain."

Everyone agreed to that, then talked softly for a while about what might be the best time to board if the captain of the ship allowed it. They decided that around eleven would be the best, since that appeared to be when there was a shift change of workers and thus the fewest number of people around.

For the rest of the morning, they all tried to sleep some more. Then, just after one in the afternoon, with the twins staying up on their crates, Bud gave the all clear.

Danny and Craig climbed down and strode out into the heat, headed for the ship, pretending to act like they belonged there and knew what they were doing.

There were a few dock workers a good warehouse distance away, but no one seemed to be anywhere near the British ship.

Danny felt really exposed out on the dock beside the huge ship, and even more obvious walking across the long plank way up to the ship's deck.

"Are we supposed to ask for permission to board?" Craig asked as they neared the edge of the ship.

Danny shrugged. "I have no idea, but I would think so."

"I don't see a doorbell," Craig said.

"Or even a place to knock," Danny said, looking both directions along the ship as they hesitated before stepping on board. He had a hunch they would be doing something wrong if they went on board without someone's permission, so he decided they would just stop and wait.

They stood there for a good thirty seconds, both of them looking around, not only for someone on the ship, but for guards with guns to come running in their direction along the dock.

No one seemed to notice them.

"Now I know what a target on a shooting range feels like," Craig said.

"Let's give it another minute, then board and find someone," Danny said. He was sweating in the hot sun and for the second time in two days, his hands were shaking.

At that moment, a voice with a clear British accent echoed down at them from up near the top of what looked like the bridge of the ship. "Permission to come aboard. Come to the top level."

Danny didn't see who shouted, but waved his hand in acknowledgement, then he and Craig boarded the big freighter.

The ship was long, with open holds in the front and back decks, and a three-story center area. Their footsteps echoed on the metal decking and it seemed even hotter on the ship than it had been on the dock, if that was possible.

"You ever get the feeling we're going from the frying pan into the fire?" Craig asked.

"In more ways than one," Danny said. "More ways than one."

CHAPTER THIRTY-FIVE

October 3, 1970
Cape Town, South Africa

INSIDE THE STEEL-PLATED structure, it wasn't any cooler. In fact, it seemed to be warmer.

"I hope our cabins have air-conditioning," Craig said softly as they climbed the metal staircase.

"Dreaming again," Danny said.

Craig made a snorting sound. "I used to dream of girls and football."

There was nothing Danny could say to that. Because his best friend had come with him, Craig had been shot at more than once, been trapped in a cave, had to jump off a moving ferry, and run from gunmen from the top of one building roof to another. Danny couldn't ask for a better friend, of that he had no doubt.

The upper deck had doors and windows open, and a slight breeze was blowing through the bridge area, cooling it a little.

"Come on in," a man in a blue uniform said from what looked to be the bridge area. The windows were huge along the front, and there was a giant wheel with a chair behind it square in the middle. The panels under the windows were filled with instruments the entire width of the room. And there was another big table along the back wall that held maps and charts. Hundreds of them from what Danny could tell.

"I'm Captain Townsend," the man said in a clear British accent. He smiled and extended his hand. "I assume you are two of my passengers to South America."

Danny and Craig both shook his hand as Danny did the introductions. The captain's hand was firm and calloused. He was shorter than Danny by a few inches and looked stout, as if he hadn't missed a meal in a long time. His uniform jacket was tight, and his tie slightly loose. Danny couldn't even imagine wearing a jacket and tie in this heat, but the captain didn't even seem to be sweating.

"Ya know," Captain Townsend said, smiling, showing a mouthful of really brown and twisted teeth, "I admire a man who has respect for another man's ship. So, what can I do for you boys? You know we don't set sail until tomorrow morning?"

"Yes, sir, we do," Danny said. "But we were hoping we could board later tonight, to stay out of the way tomorrow morning. We'd stay in our cabins and be no problem, I can assure you."

The captain looked first at Danny, then at Craig, no longer smiling. "The ticket master said you American boys were on the run from something. Now that wouldn't be serving your country, would it?"

Danny shook his head. "No, sir. We are both in college and not needed for military service."

Now the captain really frowned. Danny had a hunch he had clearly been ready to give them a long lecture on duty to a country.

"I don't much like taking on trouble on my ship. If not service, then what are you running from?"

Danny glanced at Craig, who just shrugged. Danny had no intention of going through the long story of the Hydra League, but he could tell the captain a little of the truth. Selected parts.

"I'm looking for my father," Danny said. "He disappeared in Cairo a number of months ago. We have information that leads us to believe he was taken to Peru. Four of my friends are helping me on this search."

The captain nodded and just waited for Danny to go on. This man was clearly very smart.

"Craig and I are from Washington State, and while in Cairo, we met Bud and the twins, Ed and Ernie. Bud is from Cairo and Ed and Ernie are from here. They are all about our age."

Now the captain was nodding, as if he was ahead of Danny's story, but still waiting.

"Ed and Ernie are black," Danny said, watching the captain's face. The man didn't seem to have a reaction, so Danny went on. "Their parents were killed by the South African government for protesting against apartheid. The government here is looking for them as well."

"For heaven's sake, son, why did you boys come back here then?"

"We were in Kenya," Danny said, changing the truth of his story a little to make it easier to tell. No point in telling him about a hidden city in the jungles of the Congo. "That was where we discovered we needed to go to Peru in my father's search."

Again, the Captain nodded. "And you had to change ships here? Now I see why you want to come on board tonight."

"Sleeping on a wooden crate in a warehouse can get tiring," Craig said, smiling.

The captain laughed. "I can see why it would. But you are putting you and your friends at great risk by telling me this."

He moved over a few feet and picked up a piece of paper. On it in big red letters was the word 'Wanted.'

The captain gave the paper to Danny. "It says there your two friends escaped from a dock jail yesterday, with the help of at least two white boys."

Now the captain was no longer smiling.

Danny felt his stomach clamp up into a knot. He forced himself to try to breathe, but he didn't get much of the warm air.

"Have I said lately how screwed we are?" Craig muttered, staring at the wanted poster.

Danny ignored his friend and squarely faced the captain, looking him in the eye. "Yes, sir, the twins were taken by port security because of their skin color and the fact that our last captain said they looked suspicious. If the government had discovered who they were, they would have been killed without trial. I was the one who broke them out of that cell."

"We all helped," Craig said, smiling a sickly smile.

"As I said, I don't like trouble on my ship," the Captain said. He stared at Danny for a minute. Then he nodded. "But I like the policies of this South African government even less. Half my crew is colored, or as they are wanting to be called now, black. My first mate has a dark skin color because he has a father from Pakistan. I hate even docking here."

He took the paper back from Craig and wadded it up into a ball and tossed it into a nearby garbage can. "Come on board tonight at eleven during dock shift changes," the captain said, his voice very serious. "Your cabins are numbered seven and eight on the deck below this one. Stay inside until we are at sea and someone comes for you."

"Thank you, sir," Danny said.

The captain nodded. "Just don't make me sorry I'm doing this."

CHAPTER THIRTY-SIX

October 3, 1970
Cape Town, South Africa

THAT NIGHT AT ELEVEN, Danny went on board first and alone, greeted by the captain. "I got most of my crew below securing the cargo. Make it quick."

Danny nodded and waved for the rest to come forward. The captain sounded as worried as Danny felt. That wasn't a good sign.

Craig came from the right and was halfway up the gang plank when Ernie appeared out of the shadows and came up the plank behind Craig. Both of them had disappeared with a quick thank-you to the captain when Ed appeared and came on board, followed quickly by Bud. It all took less than a minute.

"Stay hidden until we come to get you," the captain said to Danny as he turned away to let Danny follow Bud inside.

The cabins were warm, but not unbearable. Ed and Ernie took one with only two bunks, Craig, Bud, and Danny took the other one that had three.

As Danny closed the door, Bud dropped onto the bunk. "I hope prison beds are this comfortable."

"I don't like this," Bud said, walking around in a circle in the middle of the room like a caged animal would walk. "We are trapped here, trusting the honor of a British captain."

"If we're going to get out of this country," Danny said, "we don't have a choice."

None of them slept during the next six hours. Danny just sat on a bunk facing the door, expecting it to be opened at any moment by a South African policeman with a big gun.

Bud alternated between pacing and sitting on the floor in the corner. Craig just lay on his bunk staring at the ceiling. They didn't talk. They felt like they didn't dare.

It was still two hours from sailing when the door did burst open, but it wasn't the South African police, but the captain. "Quickly, bring your things. You have to hide."

Danny scrambled to his feet, grabbing the case with the copies of his father's notebooks and his clothes bag, then went out the door behind the captain, a half step ahead of Bud.

The captain said the same thing to the twins, then without waiting to see if he was being followed, went down the hallway to a staircase and then started down.

He didn't stop at the main deck, but kept going down the tight, circular metal staircase.

Danny lost track of how far they went down, but clearly they were going down into the cargo hold.

At the bottom, the captain shoved open a hatch and went through, waiting until all five boys had followed him.

The inside of the freighter's cargo hold was almost as large as the warehouse, and just about as tall. Lights were strung along the ceiling and they gave the place a dim, eerie glow.

Parts of the cargo hold were stacked with the same kind of crates they had spent the night before on. They were all well tied down to the walls and each other. It seemed the big wooden things were standard shipping crates for this area of the world.

The captain pointed to the large stacks of crates secured against a bulkhead. "Climb up on top and stay very silent and out of sight, no matter what you hear. We're done loading this area, but there will be inspectors walking through."

With that, he ducked back through the hatch toward the stairs and slammed the hatch closed.

Thirty seconds later, they were all on top of different crates and had their gear stored on the bulkhead side.

Up that high in the cargo hold, the temperature was higher than it had been outside on the deck. Danny didn't much like the idea of them being trapped down here, but again, he could see no choice.

On the crate beside Danny, Craig stretched out staring at the deck over him, his head resting on a folded up shirt.

"How much did you say you paid for these tickets?"

All Danny could think to say was *Hopefully not with our lives.* So instead, he said nothing.

Continued next issue…

Now Available
from all your favorite booksellers
in trade paper and electronic editions.

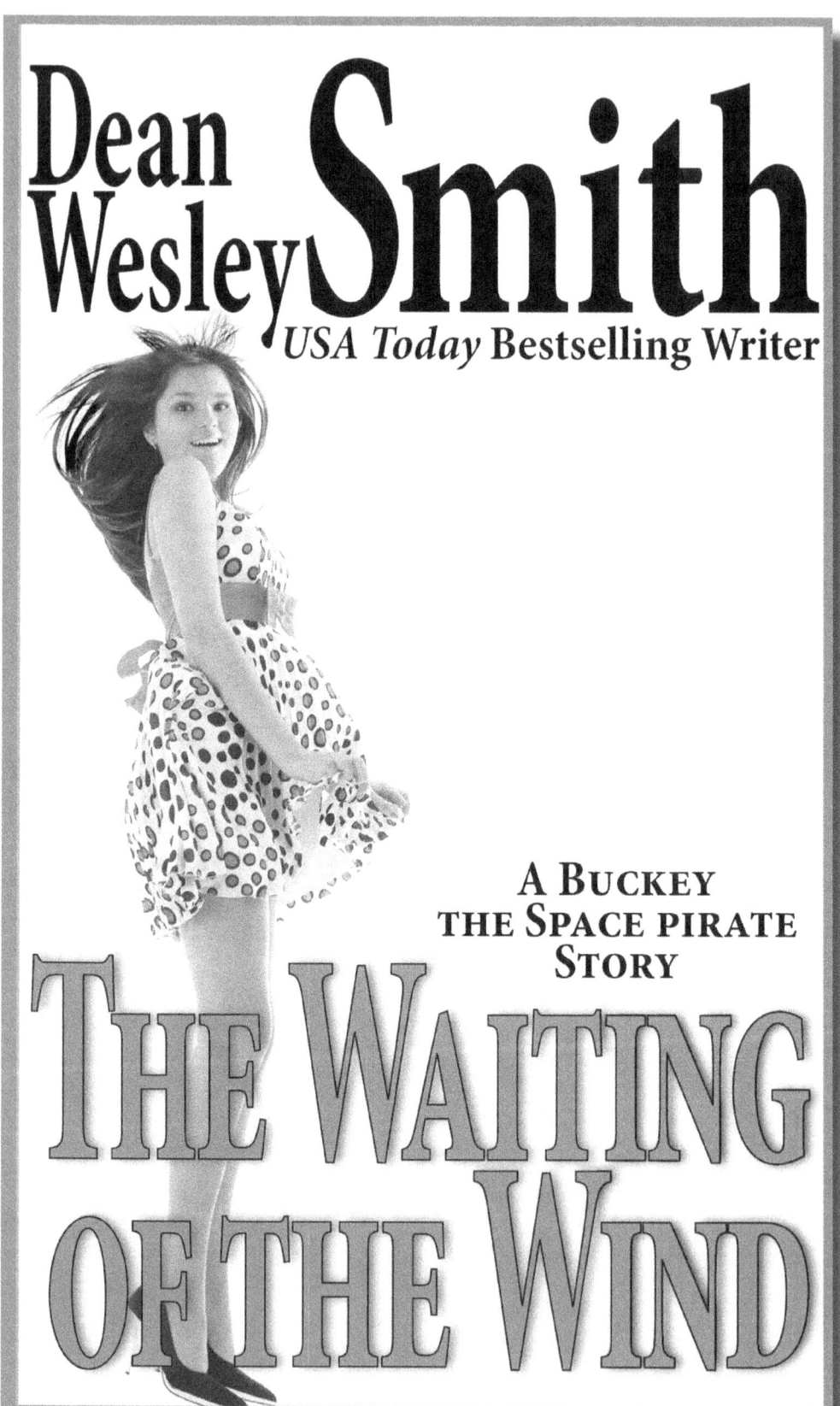

Dean Wesley Smith

USA Today Bestselling Writer

A BUCKEY
THE SPACE PIRATE
STORY

THE WAITING
OF THE WIND

When Buckey the Space Pirate decides to take a creative writing course, of course he turns for help to his best friend, Fred the talking oak tree.

Fred knows the English language better than any human alive. But Fred is still an oak tree, and oak trees do have their quirks when it comes to writing.

THE WAITING OF THE WIND
A Buckey the Space Pirate Story

FIRST ATTEMPT

"I knew the wind was waiting for me. The wind always did. It was my fault for falling in love with the wind. For letting the wind fall in love with me. If I had just worn panties that breezy day in April, this never would have happened. Or jeans instead of that light cotton dress. But it was such a beautiful spring day, the kind of day that makes a person want to feel free, and I wanted to feel completely free.
"And the wind noticed."

"WHAT DO YOU THINK? Nifty opening to the story, huh?"
Fred, the fifteen-foot oak tree, said, "You write well for a space pirate, Buckey."
Oh, oh, not a good sign when an oak tree damns with faint praise.
I could feel the sweat dripping down my back from the heat. I was wearing cutoffs and a tee-shirt to stay cool against the eighty-five degree afternoon temperature and was using what little shade the oak tree gave me as well. But Fred was so darned skinny, I had to move the lawn chair and glass of lemonade every fifteen minutes just to try to stay in his shadow.

And now he clearly didn't like the story I was working on for class.

I had had on my Buckey the Space Pirate science fiction convention costume (sword, plumed hat, and black tights) the first time Fred talked to me.. Or at least the last incarnation of Fred talked to me. So he still called me a space pirate and Buckey, even though that wasn't my name and he knew it.

Fred is a talking oak tree and I'm sort of his dad. But since Fred can travel back along the lines of oak trees in his family for millions of years, I mostly feel like a kid in front of my own kid.

A time-traveling and talking oak tree can make a person feel very small if he wants to.

The previous Fred (who stood in the old park downtown and was cut down because they needed to widen the road) told me how he came to be able to actually talk to humans. On the night before his death he suggested I do the same thing to save him and give him the skill to once again talk to humans. It seemed he was the only oak tree in all of creation that could and if I didn't help him, the skill would die with the chain saws.

So after I was convinced that it just wasn't someone playing a practical joke on me, I used a prophylactic for what it was supposed to be used for, then put a seed from the first Fred in the rubber and planted everything in my mother's backyard.

The new little Fred started talking about a year later and we've been best friends ever since. Which is why I spend so much time in my mother's backyard. I know, weird for a college kid, but at least I don't live in her basement anymore. And since I can't seem to find a girlfriend at the moment, I don't have much else to do.

I took a drink from the lemonade my mom had made for me and glanced back at her house. I had told my mom that I needed to work on a summer school writing project for my creative writing class I was taking, so I might be talking out loud some. The creative writing class in the summer sounded like an easy way to get some credits and get part of the English credits I needed for my degree in history out of my way.

And besides, with what I could learn about history from Fred, I was going to need to learn how to do the books I was going to get rich writing about little-known facts in history. Fred actually showing me history, real history, was why after three years I had switched my major to history from political science.

Today Mom had just shrugged when I said I would be out back. She was getting used to me being in the back yard at all times of the year talking to a tree. I know she worried about me, but at least I wasn't in jail, and as far as she was concerned, that was a victory in its own right.

"Come, on Fred," I said to the oak tree. "It wasn't that bad."

"For a space pirate, I suppose not," Fred said again, his voice sort of surrounding me as it always did. His voice was growing deeper with each month of growth. Pretty soon he would be back to the old depth of voice from the first Fred I met.

I glanced at the spiral notebook in my hand. That first paragraph I had read to him wasn't so bad. I was sort of proud of it to be honest.

"So what's wrong with it?"

"I could illustrate with a limerick," Fred said.

"No limericks," I said, being firm. "Just tell me what's wrong."

Fred loved limericks and most of the time they were just flat rude. Over the last few years I had come to hate them, although I had to admit some of the ones Fred made up stayed with you. And if I let Fred get going on limericks, any real thought of conversation would end completely.

"Besides the anthropomorphism of the wind and the overuse of passive voice, nothing."

"Coming from a talking baby oak tree," I said, "that's an amazing criticism."

"Everyone knows the wind can't talk," Fred said.

"Everyone knows oak trees can't talk either," I said.

But looking at the paper, I knew he had a point about the passive structure. My professor had spent an hour of her time talking on just that alone.

So I turned the page and tried again.

SECOND ATTEMPT

I knew the wind waited for me. The wind always did. My fault for falling in love with the wind and for letting the wind fall in love with me. I decided against wearing panties under my light dress that breezy day in April. A mistake. But the beautiful spring day opened my mind, made me mad for the desire to be free in all ways. I wanted to feel completely open to everything.

And the wind noticed.

I LOOKED UP at the tender green leaves of the young oak tree shading me from the hot afternoon sun. "Well?"

Fred said nothing.

"You have to admit, no passive verbs in that one. And it's shorter as well."

"Less pain on the reader," Fred said. "Always a good thing."

I knew this conversation wasn't going to go anywhere. Fred seemed to know more about the human language than any human I had ever met. I had no idea why I thought I could write to meet his tastes. After all, I was just a beginner.

But being a sucker for punishment I went on. "So, what's wrong?"

"Setting would be nice," Fred said. "Right now you just have some woman jabbering about getting goosed by a gust of wind. Boring pretty much describes it. But I do have a limerick that might spice up the piece."

"No limericks," I said. "I need to finish this for a grade in this writing class."

"You would be better served to spend your days in your Buckey the Space Pirate costume taking gratuities for saving young damsels in distress. But since you are not likely to take up such a noble occupation, try to write it again and I will listen again."

I nodded and went back to work on the third rewrite of the opening of my story.

THIRD ATTEMPT

From the top of the rocky cliff of Lover's Leap, I could see out over the green, deep valley below and the river that gave it life. I knew the wind waited for me. The wind always did. My fault for falling in love with the wind, for letting the wind fall in love with me. I decided against wearing panties under my light cotton dress that breezy day in April. A mistake. But the beautiful spring day opened my mind, made me mad for the desire to be free in all ways. I wanted to feel completely open.

And the wind noticed.

Now I stood naked waiting for the wind to take me to the sky so we could be together, drifting over the beautiful green valley and the winding blue river..

"Brooke, no!" Rich shouted from behind me as he climbed the dusty trail toward me.

I READ IT to him again.

"Wow, characters, conflict, and a setting," the little oak tree said. "I'm impressed."

I knew for a fact he wasn't. Oak trees have a level of sarcasm that has few matches in the human race. I suppose that comes from standing in the same place for hundreds of years and letting their minds roam through time. If I had to do that I'd be sarcastic as well.

And completely crazy.

"Come on, Fred. Honestly, I need a grade here. Help me out."

"All right. First, how about better names. In all the fantastic names humans have taken through time, you pick an English woman's name that means stream and a male's name that implies money. Dull. Find names that add layered meaning to your story."

"Says a tree named Fred."

"Short for Friedrich, which means peaceful ruler."

I looked up at the young oak tree. "Why did you shorten it?"

"There was a time in my early years in the downtown park when a German-sounding name was not a welcome thing, so I decided to change it."

"Oh, that's right, you were around in the park for World War Two," I said.

"And The Great War," Fred said. "Besides, would you have listened to me if I said my name was Friedrich?"

"If I remember right, I couldn't shut you up that first time we met."

"I was just trying to entertain your date in my last days."

"By calling one of her body parts, a part I was very interested in exploring, larger than a punt? You call that entertaining?"

I was still mad at him for that.

"I was enjoying myself," the little oak tree said.

The sun seemed to get hotter even through the thin shade from Fred's leaves.

I took a long drink from my lemonade. Most of the ice had melted, which meant I had been out here in the sun more than long enough.

"So if I change the character names, will it pass?"

"Oh, I would think so," Fred said.

"Thank you," I said, closing my notebook and climbing out of my lawn chair.

"But a nice limerick would help you so much more."

"I have to learn how to write on my own," I said. "Not copy down your words. That won't help me at all."

"A Space Pirate with morals," Fred said. "Who would have known? I tell you, saving the fair damsels in distress would be a calling for you."

"Getting a degree in history and getting into a good graduate school is the only calling I care about at the moment."

"Suit yourself," Fred said.

"See you later." I turned for the house.

"Do come back and read me your finished story," Fred said. "I so want to learn how the woman with no underwear used her private regions to fly with the wind like Dumbo. My kind of story."

I just shook my head. As I said, oak trees can be very, very sarcastic.

Then behind me Fred started into a limerick.

"There was a woman of Kings
Who ate all three meals of beans..."

"Don't go there!" I said as I walked away. "I can still hear you."

For a moment the little oak tree remained silent. Then as I had almost reached the house, he started into a new limerick.

"There was a woman quite stewed,
whose clothing was found very strewed,
and if I'm not mistaken,
the wind did the takin'
and left her on the rocks most screwed."

As I reached the back porch I shouted back at the young oak tree, "Passive construction, no characters, and setting would be nice."

For the first time in two years, I got the last word on the oak tree.

USA Today *bestselling writer Dean Wesley Smith returns with a second novel to the world of* Dust and Kisses *from the first issue of* Smith's Monthly.

Together, Callie and Fisher work to discover the secrets of a galaxy that have been hidden in plain sight, even from the powerful humans who had rescued millions. And in the process, they just might change everything.

Now Available
from all your favorite booksellers in trade paper and electronic editions.

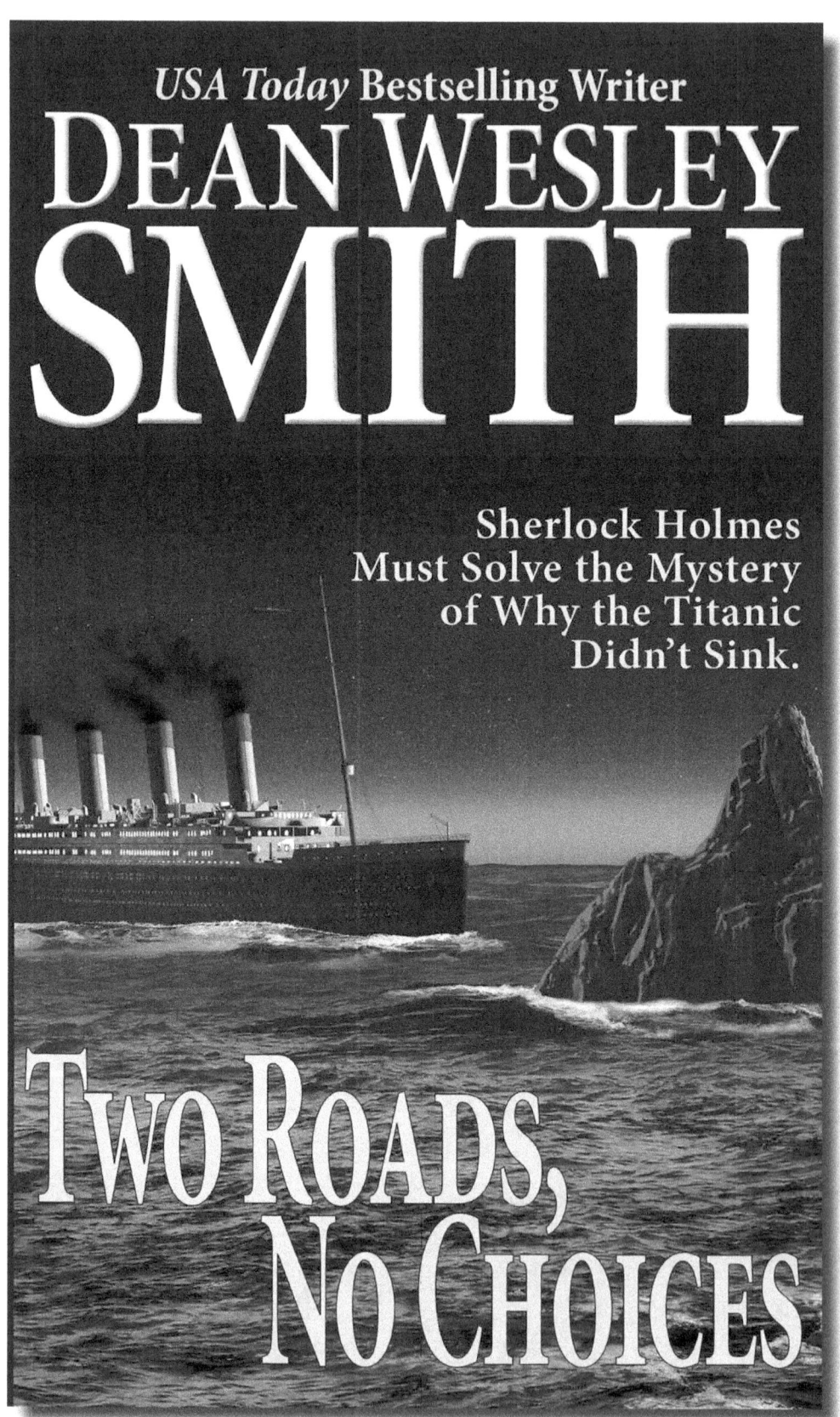

USA *Today* Bestselling Writer

DEAN WESLEY SMITH

Sherlock Holmes
Must Solve the Mystery
of Why the Titanic
Didn't Sink.

TWO ROADS, NO CHOICES

The Titanic oceanliner barely escapes disaster when it rams an iceberg on its maiden voyage. Sherlock Holmes and Watson know that. The news covered it.

Then two strangers appear to ask Sherlock Holmes an impossible question: Why didn't the great ocean liner sink?

First published in Sherlock Holmes in Orbit *from DAW Books, edited by Mike Resnick and Martin H. Greenberg, and written with permission of the Doyle estate.*

TWO ROADS, NO CHOICES

One

THE HAND ON my shoulder seemed rough, brusque in its rush to wake me. As I roused myself from the warm comfort of my quilts and rolled to focus on the worried face of Holmes, he said "Dress quickly. And for extreme cold. We have visitors here, possibly to take us for a voyage."

Before my sleep-fogged mind could muster a response, or even a simple question as to where we would be traveling, he turned and left me to the quiet of the late-night hour.

I finished with my toilet and dressed as quickly as I could, for such awakening by Holmes had portrayed in the past a need for haste on a new case. And since my friend had taken very few cases as of late, this new adventure must be extraordinary in nature. That thought had my hands shaking with such excitement that I took two attempts to fasten my vest.

As I emerged into the main room, I found Holmes in his favorite armchair, his fingers in a steeple as was his habit when waiting patiently. He had started a robust fire to take the chill from the room and the orange light flickered across his features.

Across from him sat two strangers and immediately I was struck by their strange dress, the cut of their jackets, and the look of their hair. The one on Holme's left and closest to the door had strikingly blonde hair, green eyes, and a handsome face that showed no scars. He was also clearly the taller of the two, even though they were both sitting. At his feet was a large brown case that had the appearance of being very heavy.

His companion had long, almost shoulder-length brown hair and wore an outer coat that he had opened to the warmth of the fire, revealing on the edges of the coat a form of metal fastener with small teeth running along both sides of the opening. I had read of such a fastener before, but never seen one in use. The man had a dark complexion and seemed to be of Italian or Eastern decent.

I was shocked that Holmes had offered neither of them tea or coffee and was about to correct the oversight when Holmes said, "Oh, good, Watson. Now we can start." He indicated that I should take a chair near the hearth and I did as he instructed.

He turned to the gentlemen as I sat and nodded. "Okay, please explain who you are, why you are here, where you are from, and what you want from me."

Both of the men had been staring at me in a seemingly nervous fashion, as if I were someone they had known for a long time, yet were embarrassed to greet. I knew from what Holmes had said that he had kept them from telling their story, even so much as their names, until I was present. He did that on occasion when he felt the need of a second pair of eyes and ears. Somehow, in a standard Holmes fashion, he must have deduced that they had wanted us to go on a trip and that it would be to a cold climate. Even though I had no idea how he came to such a conclusion, I would wait until later to ask him how he knew such details.

Holmes leaned forward in anticipation and for some odd reason I found myself just able to contain my own excitement.

The short, dark-haired man cleared his throat, glanced at me and then looked directly back at Holmes. "My name is Carl. Doctor Carl Frederick. This is Doctor Henry Serling." He indicated the blonde man, who in turn nodded at both of us.

Doctor Frederick's accent seemed to be American, yet of no region that I was familiar. I would have to ask Holmes later if he knew the regional source.

Doctor Frederick went on. "Slightly over two months ago a new White Star Liner left port from Southampton."

Holmes nodded. "Yes, the RMS. Titanic."

Doctor Frederick nodded. "I'm glad you are familiar with it."

"It would be hard not to be, considering the coverage it received. It seems to be one very magnificent ship. Exceptionally lucky that it did not meet a tragic fate on that first voyage. Even an unsinkable ship meeting an iceberg can sometimes lose the battle."

Doctor Frederick glanced nervously at his companion and then said, "I don't think luck had anything to do with it."

Holmes gave him a very sharp look. "I'm afraid, Doctor, that I do not understand your comment."

Both of our guests seemed almost embarrassed, as if what they were about to say would seen so outrageous, so disgusting that Holmes would toss them into the street. I had seen that look a number of times when a person was about to confess something to Holmes. This time both men stared at their hands, then at the floor, then back at their hands.

The fire crackled and what seemed like a long time passed until finally the blonde Doctor Serling took a deep breath. "Carl, we agreed." His voice was also clearly American, but again very odd.

Doctor Frederick nodded slowly, clearly making a decision. He looked Holmes squarely in the eyes. "The Titanic was supposed to have sunk. Slightly over fifteen hundred lives were lost when it did."

I thought that someone had punched me below the ribs at that moment and I suddenly knew the taste of disgust. It never occurred to me to question that the men were crazy, but their words instantly proved them so and suddenly I felt worried for the safety of Holmes and myself.

But Holmes seemed to take the statement of the possibility of such an immense disaster as a fact. He leaned back in his chair, exhaling slowly, but never taking his gaze from Doctor Frederick. As his friend I could see the thought had him shaken, but he remained composed as always.

The fire popped and flared for a moment as Holmes said in a very cold voice, "Go on."

> ## *"We need your help in solving why the Titanic did not sink."*

Again Doctor Frederick glanced at his companion. Then he half shook himself and turned to face Holmes squarely. "We need your help in solving why the Titanic did not sink."

Holmes did not even blink at such an absurd idea and when I started to object he held up his hand and stopped me. "And who might you represent?" he asked. "I assume you are not from owners of the liner or any government agency. What is your interest?"

Doctor Frederick almost laughed. Then he became very serious again. "Our lives. Our very future and that of this time, actually. You see, you will not believe me, but we are from the future. Actually, just over a hundred and two years in the future. But, I'm afraid we are from a future where the Titanic sank."

Holmes nodded. "I assumed you were not of our time from your clothes and your language the moment you stepped into this room. He nodded to Doctor Serling. You are also wearing some form of lense on your eye that I have never seen before."

Doctor Serling smiled and nodded. "They are called contact lenses. They take the place of glasses."

Both visitors seemed taken aback by Holmes calm acceptance of their bold statement that they were from the future. I, on the other hand, was not as willing to take their word. Such fancy imagination was the domain of an early evening of pleasant reading of H. G. Wells, not of the middle of the night on Baker Street.

But Holmes waited for a response. "You have still not answered my question."

Both Doctor's glanced at each other until finally Doctor Frederick seemed to understand Holmes's question. "If you mean our employer, then I suppose that originally would have been the state of California. We were both faculty at the University of Southern California, Physics Department. Our specific research into time travel was funded mostly by the United States government."

Holmes nodded, as if he understood everything they had been saying, as I suppose he might have. "Why the interest in the Titanic?"

"In our time the Titanic, and the night it sank," Doctor Frederick hesitated with that statement, then went on, "are a thing of immense interest. It wasn't until September of 1985 that the wreck of the great ship was found. Since then hundreds of expeditions have been launched to the site of the wreck. It seemed only logical that one of the first time travel expeditions would go back to the night the Titanic sank. Here, let me show you something."

He motioned for Doctor Serling to open the large case and Doctor Frederick extracted a large, colorful book. As he handed the book to Holmes I noticed the word TITANIC stamped on the front cover in red. A beautiful painting of the great liner sailing the open seas filled the cover.

"That book was originally published in 1992. We brought it along as resource material. Little did we imagine that it would be put to this use."

Again the room grew quiet except for the crackling of the fire as Holmes inspected the front and back of the large and obviously heavy book and then opened it and started slowly thumbing through.

"Flip to page 196. That section is about the discovery of the wreck. There are photographs and such."

Holmes did what he was told and then spent the next few minutes moving through the book, his keen eyes missing nothing. I had a great desire to stand and move to his side to look at such a book, but I held my place, as I know Holmes would have wanted me to do. But as the minutes wore on the task of remaining in my chair became very difficult, to say the least.

Finally Holmes closed the book and placed it on the stand beside his chair. "Since it is obvious that a tragedy such as this book portrays would have a large influence on the future, can you tell me what that might be?"

Doctor Frederick shook his head negatively. "I'm afraid not. You see, the future we came from no longer exists. At least to us. The only way possible to move forward in time for us and our machine is to a homing beacon, for lack of a better way to describe it. I could tell you about the future where the ship did sink, but—"

Doctor Serling broke in. "Let me try to explain what has occurred. With every event in history there are two or more possible futures leading from that event. Such as forks in a country road." He glanced at Holmes and Holmes nodded, so he went on. "On the night the Titanic sank the logical two main futures are a future where it did and one where it did not. Of course, there are many other possible futures where only a hundred were killed, or ninety-nine. And depending on who was saved and who wasn't, those lives lost or saved may or may not allow the futures to blend back into one. In our time we call these different worlds parallel dimensions or universes."

I caught myself shaking my head at the insanity of this man's words, but Holmes clearly was giving the man his full attention, so I said and did nothing, even though my instinct was to toss them both into the street.

"So what happened?" Holmes asked. "Did you change the past, causing the Titanic to not sink?"

"No." Both Doctors spoke at the same time and both were emphatic, as if Holmes had asked them if they had committed a mortal sin.

"We arrived, "Doctor Frederick said, "on the Titanic about two minutes before it struck the iceberg, and did nothing but watch. However it quickly became obvious that history had changed. We were unable to return to our time and ended up having to hide in unoccupied cabins until the ship sailed into New York."

"Was it possible," Holmes asked, "that your machine simply moved you over onto a different 'road' as you put it?"

Doctor Serling seemed clearly impressed with Holmes. "We considered that, but we don't think so. If that was the case we feel our homing device would still be functioning. But it isn't. We clearly went back to a fork in the road of history and are now traveling down a different road. Someone or some thing altered our world's history so that the world we came from no longer exists to us."

Holmes nodded. "And you want me to help you find out who altered history. Who stopped this"—he tapped the book—"from happening?"

Both doctors nodded slowly.

Two

"THIS IS BEYOND the imagination," I said, no longer able to hold my tongue. "I have heard some crazy stories in my time but—"

Holmes held up his hand for me to stop and then turned to the gentlemen. "How would you propose I do this task?"

Doctor Frederick pointed to the large case. "In here is the machine that moves us through time. Come back with us to the night of the Titanic hitting the iceberg."

"What?" I said.

But Holmes nodded. "Can you then bring us back to this point?"

Doctor Frederick shook his head negatively. "Not exactly. We can leave a homing package here, but time will flow at the same pace as the time you spend on the ship. If we are there for an hour you will return here in an hour."

Holmes again nodded, then turned to me. "Watson, dampen the fire. And fetch our heaviest coats. We are going for a short trip."

"But you can't really imagine—" For the third time tonight Holmes stopped me with a sharp look and a hand gesture.

"My dear Watson. We have a case at hand." He was clearly seeing something I was missing and willing to let these two have enough rope to prove their insanity.

I sighed rather loudly, but then nodded and did as I was instructed. Holmes and I then donned our coats as Doctor Serling seemed to type on some sort of instrument inside the case, clicking like the sound of a dog scampering across a hardwood floor. Then he placed a small blue-green cube on the table on the top of the large book and nodded for Holmes and myself. "We are ready. Please step close."

Holmes did so immediately and I followed reluctantly. My mind was starting to worry at the possibility of this actually occurring. Yet the thought was so utterly preposterous that I couldn't hold the reality of it.

As I stopped beside Holmes, Doctor Serling tapped a small button inside the case.

For a moment nothing registered. It was as if someone had turned off the lights and the fire and all the sounds and feelings of the world.

Then as quickly as it left the world was back.

In my mind we were still standing like fools bundled against the cold inside the warm Baker Street address. But then Holmes said, "Interesting" and stepped toward the wooden rail to gaze out at the black night.

"What in the devil—" The icy cold wind sucked the words from my mouth. I could not only feel the cold, but smell and taste it. Intense, biting cold mixed with the salty smells of the open sea. I spun around to quickly look in all directions as the wind messed my hair and pulled open my coat sending shivers through my torso. We were clearly on a large ship, somewhere near the bow. The width of the ship was almost that of a city block and a towering wall of metal rose both forward and aft of our position.

"We are on the forward well deck near the starboard side," Doctor Frederick said to Holmes.

Holmes only nodded as his intense gaze took in every detail. I on the other hand fought to keep my late dinner in my stomach. The very fact that we stood here on this cold wooden deck challenged every

principle I believed and lived by. I must be dreaming. Holmes had not woken me and any moment this would all be a fleeting memory of a long night of troubled sleep.

Overhead a bell started ringing insistently. I glanced up at the tall pole and could barely see the light from what seemed to be a crow's nest. Words floated down to us through the night air. "Iceberg right ahead."

Doctor Franklin turned to Holmes. "That was lookout Fleet talking to Sixth Officer Moody who is on the bridge." Franklin pointed toward the stern and up. "All right on time."

Holmes only nodded. He seemed to be listening intently to the sounds of the night, the water slapping against the sides of the huge ship, the low rumble of the engines. After a moment he nodded and then leaned out over the rail to watch the iceberg approach.

I moved over beside him and did the same, the cold wind hitting my face and hands with a much harder intensity. Out of the shadow of the well deck, I suddenly realized just how fast the ship had been moving and that realization combined with the blast of cold wind took my breath away.

I stood back for a moment, then again leaned out into the wind, peering into the black where the ship was headed. It took me a moment to understand that the dark shape, darker than the night, as if someone had punched a hole in the air, was a huge wall of ice, far wider and bigger than the ship. Fear twisted my stomach and for a moment I forgot the intense cold on my skin. I could see no way that a ship of this size could turn fast enough to avoid a collision.

Yet I continued to watch with fascination as every moment seemed to stretch.

It was a sick fascination, as if watching a horrible fight where someone was being badly hurt, yet unable to turn away.

As my eyes watered and the tears seemed to freeze on my checks, I watched.

Slowly the ship turned, just enough, and just at the last second. The bow somehow slid by the leading edge of ice.

There was a faint rumbling lower in the ship and a distant scraping sound.

The huge gray wall was suddenly beside us and it seemed as if I could reach out and touch the rough ice. Yet I knew that if I did the razor-sharp edges would have cut my hands.

Holmes and I instinctively both took a step away from the rail and watched the mountain slide past the ship. When it was far beyond the stern of the ship and again fading into the black of the night Holmes turned to Doctor Frederick. "So what do you observe is different?"

"Nothing from our three times back here since we became stuck. However, the records we have said that this part of the deck where we are standing was originally covered with ice from the berg as it scraped past."

Holmes nodded.

"So we are only talking a matter of feet," I said, "maybe even inches between saving this ship and having it sink?"

It was Doctor Frederick's turn to nod. "In this world, as I am sure you read in your newspapers, the ship sustained damage, but the watertight compartments held the ship afloat until it could get to New York. In my universe the damage was too extensive and the watertight compartments did very little."

Behind us ten or twelve hearty men emerged from a door, the yellow light casting a long bright streak across the deck. They were clearly interested in

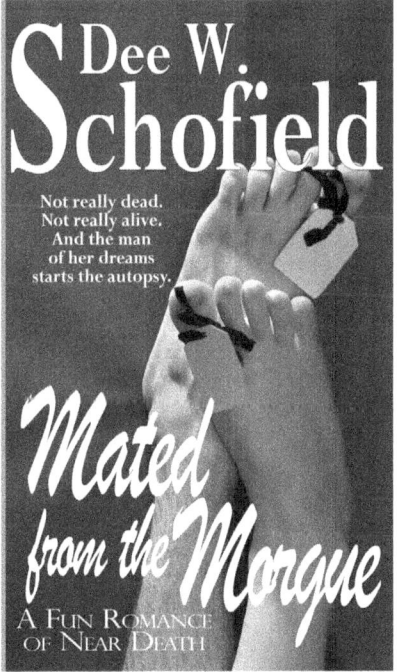

what had happened and why the engines had stopped. They talked loudly among themselves and headed toward both rails to gaze into the night. I again leaned out and looked to the stern. The iceberg was now barely visible, a gray mountain looming in the night.

Holmes turned to Doctor Serling. "Is it possible to see these events again?"

Doctor Serling nodded. "Actually, yes. We can move up, and back in time, to the boat deck."

I looked at Holmes and then at Doctor Serling who was again working in the case. "You mean that we can be up there on the boat deck at the same time we are, or were, here this time watching? I mean—" I stopped. I was totally confused and again my fear returned.

Doctor Frederick nodded and pulled his coat tighter around himself. "Yes, but there are limits. We have never been able to get close enough to ourselves in experiments to see our earlier, or later, self. But that has not been from lack of trying." He laughed. "Time travel is still new to us. We really can't explain some of the paradoxes. We just know they exist and somehow the universe stops certain things from happening."

"So," Holmes said, pointing up at the leading edge of the boat deck. "I will not be able to go to that position up there and look down at myself here, unless I am, or was, doing it now. Correct?"

I glanced up, but a later version of Holmes was not standing there, much to my relief.

"That would seem to be the rule," Doctor Serling said. "Ready?"

Holmes nodded.

"What about the passengers?" I asked, but to Doctor Serling that question didn't seem to matter.

The cold, the salt-filled air, the feeling of the wooden deck under my feet all went away for a moment.

And suddenly we were standing next to a lifeboat about halfway down the boat deck, again on the starboard side.

Without a moment's hesitation Holmes strode to the starboard side of the ship and looked in the direction of the coming wall of ice.

I glanced around, relieved that no passenger was within sight to witness our arrival. "I have no desire to get used to this mode of travel," I said, pulling my coat around me tightly in a vain attempt to hold out the wind. "How fast is this ship traveling?"

"Over twenty-two knots," Doctor Frederick said.

"Far too fast," I said.

Doctor Frederick only grunted as the alarm bell started its insistent noise from the direction of the bow. He and I moved to join Holmes at the starboard rail leaving Dr. Serling with the heavy case.

Again we watched as the iceberg took its collision course. I found myself unable to take my gaze from that huge, growing mountain. That same sick desire as before kept my gaze frozen into the cold wind until finally, at what seemed to be the last moment, the ship slowly turned, shifting the iceberg to the starboard side of the liner.

With a fairly loud scraping the cold gray wall slipped past. No one said a word this time and again Holmes seemed to be listening.

I, on the other hand, was suffering to again keep my nerves in control. I took a few quick steps back from the towering wall of ice as it slid past. There was something about this entire event that felt ghoulish, as if we were robbing graves.

I shook that thought from my mind and instead thought of the warm fire at Baker Street.

Three

THE MOUNTAIN FADED into the distance behind the ship as Holmes stood at the railing, not watching it but instead deep in thought. I had no idea what he might be thinking. I just knew I wanted to be off this ship and back in my warm quilts, if that was not where I was still.

"Once more," Holmes said, turning and moving back over to Doctor Serling. "Only this time could you be somewhere near the bridge?"

Doctor Sterling seemed to think for a minute and then nodded. "Yes, I think I can get us to the boat deck on the port side. That was a deck above where we were on our first visit. That would be close enough for you to move to the port door of the bridge and watch what was happening."

Holmes nodded. "That would be satisfactory."

Serling went to work. A number of first-class passengers now occupied the deck, staring toward the stern after the retreating wall of ice. But Serling and Frederick paid them no attention, as if they were nothing but harmless ghosts.

Serling typed in his case and suddenly the night again vanished.

And just as suddenly returned.

We now stood on the other side of the ship, on an empty boat deck, slightly closer to the bow.

Holmes immediately started toward the door of the bridge. I struggled in vain to remove the thought from my mind that I was not only standing here at this moment, but also at two other places on this same ship. It was enough to make a sane man crazy and I was sure that insanity was where I was heading at a speed faster than the ship.

"You only have one look," Doctor Frederick said. "We won't be able to repeat this again."

Holmes glanced over his shoulder. "I understand perfectly, Doctor."

Just as Holmes stuck his head around the edge of the open bridge door the warning bell rang out through the night air.

Again we watched as the iceberg loomed closer and closer, only to be swept past the starboard side. Being on this side of the deck I felt less threatened by the entire event. Or possibly I was just growing used to it. Another thought I put quickly out of my mind.

Holmes never took his head away from the open door to even once glance at the iceberg. As the ship slowed and drifted in the black waters he turned to us. The look on his face was one that I had never seen before. It was almost as if he had seen a true ghost.

"Holmes, are you all right?" I asked as he rejoined us.

"I need one more time here," he said. "Can you get me close enough to the main engines to watch them during the time of the collision?"

Again Doctor Serling thought for a moment while the cold cut through my coat as if it wasn't there. I had experienced many cold London nights, but none anywhere near as cold as this.

"We'll have to go back five minutes sooner to give you the time," Doctor Serling said. He worked in the case for what seemed to be a long minute.

Then again without warning from him the world and the deck and the cold wind vanished. It would at least be courteous for him to give us a moment to prepare.

This time Doctor Serling had placed us in a fairly narrow hallway lit by electric lamps at intervals along the walls.

I leaned against the polished wood and took a deep breath of the warm, coal-smelling air. It was a relief to be out of the wind and the cold, but the thought of being inside a ship about to hit an iceberg had me on the edge of a slight panic.

"Through there and down the circular stairs," Doctor Serling said, pointing to a wooden door at the end of the hall. "The engine room will be down there. You only have a few minutes."

Holmes nodded and didn't waste a moment striding the distance to the door and disappearing through it.

I opened my coat to allow the warmer air to flow around my torso. Doctor Serling adjusted a dial inside his case and then sat on the carpeted floor. Doctor Frederick just paced.

Finally he stopped and turned to me. "Do you think he can solve this?"

I gave a slight, very half-hearted laugh. "If there is something to solve, I am sure he can. But I do not exactly understand what you are asking of him." I stared at Doctor Frederick and then said quietly, "If you ponder it, I am not sure you understand either."

"We are asking him," Doctor Frederick said, gesturing at the walls around us, "to simply put history right. This ship belongs on the bottom of the Atlantic. It needs to be there for history to return to normal."

I simply watched him as he started his pacing again. I knew it would do no good to remind him of the hundreds of people he said would die tonight if that occurred. In the background we could hear the seemingly distant rumble of the engines and occasionally a noise of a passenger from somewhere nearby. But otherwise the hallway remained silent until a fairly loud scraping and grinding filled the air.

I held onto a smooth edge of wood paneling and took deep, controlled breaths until the noise stopped. The engines dropped silent and then there was only quiet. Again my mind filled in the comparison between the silence of a graveyard, or the silence of the dead of night, before even the birds are moving.

Frederick looked at me and I returned his stare saying nothing.

At the end of the hall the door opened and Holmes rejoined us. "We can go back to Baker Street now," he said, his voice sounding tired and removed of all energy.

I glanced first at Holmes and then at the Doctors as they looked at each other puzzled.

"Did you solve our problem?" Doctor Frederick asked.

Holmes did nothing but shake his head. "The fire would feel comforting against the chill."

After a moment Doctor Serling bent to the case at his feet, made a few adjustments and suddenly the hall was gone, replaced quickly by the familiar surroundings of Baker Street.

Four

WITHOUT REMOVING MY heavy coat I bent to the fire and soon had it roaring again, its yellow flame overpowering the lamps.

I finished and turned to the room. Holmes had removed his coat and was again in his chair. Only it was very clear he was deep in thought. Both our guests understood his mood and both were respecting it.

I removed my coat and hung it in its place, then moved back to the chair near the fire. The heat cut into the oppressive cold of the night and the feeling that the ship had been haunted. Haunted by not only our own ghosts, but more by the fact that many people might have died that night. In my years with Holmes and as a doctor I have witnessed many close calls and many deaths. Yet none to my memory had shaken me as much as standing on the deck of that ship tonight.

Holmes stirred and picked up the book beside him. "Does this book have an account of the collision?"

Doctor Frederick nodded and Holmes opened the book and went to work studying and quickly reading. We remained silent and I spent the minutes holding my hands out in front of me so that the cold could be forced out by the warmth of the flames. The memory of being on that ship would, in time, fade into a seemingly bad vision and nothing more.

Finally, Holmes laid the book back down and sighed. "I'm afraid there is nothing I can do to help you gentlemen."

"What?" Dr. Serling said. "You mean you *won't* help us."

"I didn't say that," Holmes said. "I said I *can't*."

"But—" This time it was Dr. Frederick's turn to stop his companion.

"Mr. Holmes," Dr. Frederick said, "Are you saying you do not know what caused the switch in history?"

"Basically, yes. That is what I am saying." Holmes patted the book. "The details outlined here are exactly what occurred on that ship, except, of course, the ship we visited tonight didn't sink. I can think of a thousand factors that would have caused such a difference."

"Such as?" Doctor Serling said. He was not disguising the panic and the fear in his voice at all.

"Such as someone or something turning the iceberg just a fraction of a degree." He made a helpless gesture. "I would not think such a feat possible, yet I did not think travel through time possible until this evening either."

Before either Doctor could say a word Holmes went on. "The switch might have occurred much earlier in the evening. As the Captain ordered the increase in speed, the implementation of the order could have been delayed just a few seconds, which would again allow the iceberg to be in a slightly different position at the time of the collision, thus making the damage lighter."

It was clear that Holmes's words were being understood by our guests. Finally Doctor Serling sighed. "It was a hope. Nothing more."

Doctor Frederick nodded slowly, his shoulders slumping. "A crazy stupid hope, at that."

Doctor Serling stood and moved to Holmes, who also stood. With an extended hand the Doctor said, "I would like to thank you for your attempt and your time. It was generous of you."

Holmes only nodded and shook the Doctor's hand. Then Doctor Serling turned to me as Doctor Frederick moved to shake Holmes's hand.

"Where will you be going?" I asked as he took my extended hand.

"We left a homing beacon in a hotel room in New York. We will return there and do our best to not influence the future too much."

"That seems like a very logical plan of action."

He smiled at me. "It would seem we have very few other options at the moment."

He turned and moved back to the large case as Doctor Frederick shook my hand and then moved over beside the case.

Holmes picked up the large book and handed it to him. "You might want this."

Doctor Frederick shook his head. "Please keep it as a gift. At this point it is nothing more than a work of fiction."

"I will treasure it," Holmes said and tucked the book under his arm.

Doctor Serling nodded, reached inside the case and suddenly they were both gone.

The crackling of the fire was the only sound as I stood staring at the empty place where they had been.

"Quite something, isn't it?" Holmes said.

I turned and watched as Holmes almost dropped into his chair, the exhaustion heavy on his strong shoulders. He laid the book on his lap and stared at it as if it were a monster to be tamed.

I poured us both a hot coffee and a snifter of brandy and then dropped into the chair across from him. He continued to stare at the cover of the book, not even offering his thanks for the drinks.

"It seems," I said, "that the night wore on you as much as it did myself."

Holmes only nodded.

I took a sip of the brandy, letting it warm the deep cold inside. "It is lucky that you did not find the answer to their problem."

Holmes looked up at me and for the first time I saw his eyes, watery and burning with an almost insane gaze. "My dear Watson," he said, his voice low, barely in control, a state that I had never witnessed in Holmes. "I knew exactly what caused the change."

"What!" I almost came out of my chair, my coffee spilling a hot stain down my pants.

He nodded slowly. "I lied to them. Actually the solution was simple." He tapped the book but made no motion to continue.

"Please, Holmes. I must know." I was sitting on the edge of my chair, facing him.

He grunted and then for the first time reached for his brandy. After a long sip he looked me square in the eye. "It is the knowledge of nightmares."

"But they will be my nightmares," I said.

He looked at me and then slowly nodded. "I first read the answer in here. It said that at the time of the sighting of the iceberg the First Officer William Murdock ordered the engines 'full speed astern' and put the helm 'hard to starboard.' Now, such a move would cause the ship to turn to port."

I nodded. I knew enough sailing to understand that basic principle.

"But," Holmes said," putting the engines full speed astern made such a huge ship much more difficult to control and thus the turn was just slightly slower. The ship would then strike the iceberg in a direct manner, thus causing enough damage to cause it to flounder."

"I am at a loss," I said. "Is that what happened? Why did the ship stay afloat?"

"No," Holmes said. "The engines remained full speed ahead, thus giving the ship just a fraction more ability to maneuver, thus allowing it to only graze the iceberg."

"So First Officer Murdock somehow changed his order? But how?"

Holmes shook his head. "No, he ordered full speed astern just as the book says. When I heard him give that order was when I first knew that our guests were correct. That ship should have sunk that night." He took another drink from his brandy.

"That was why you needed to visit the engine room?"

Holmes nodded. "The man on the telegraph between the bridge and the engine room at that moment was not from our time. He ignored the order and thus saved the ship. And changed the future it would seem."

I stared at Holmes. "How could you know he was from a different time?"

"Simple, really. Just as Doctor Serling wore what he called contact lenses, so did the man on the telegraph in the engine room."

I sat staring into my brandy, letting what Holmes had told me sink in. Finally I gathered enough nerve to ask the question I knew Holmes was expecting. "If history really was changed by someone from the future, why didn't you set it right?"

Holmes almost laughed. "I had the opportunity to do so. Remember what Doctor Serling told us about there being more than one future from every decision?"

"Forks in a road," I said.

Again the insanity seemed to burn like a flash fire in Holmes eyes as he fought for control. "We are simply on the branch of the road where I did not stop the person from the future."

He gulped down the last of his brandy, studied the crystal snifter for a moment and then with all the force he had he threw the glass into the fire where it shattered and sent sparks flying.

He leaned back into his chair and closed his eyes. His hands gripped the large book in a death grip, his knuckles white. Softly he said, "On that other road I stopped that man, doomed a great ship, and killed over fifteen hundred human beings in the process. I know that road exists. I know I walked it."

My head was spinning from the very thought of what Holmes had suggested. I took a sip of my brandy and stared at the light reflecting off the shattered fragments of Holmes's glass. "You mean," I finally said, "that on that other world we are sitting talking about how you stopped that man and the deaths it caused?"

Holmes nodded very slowly.

"But you could have never done that." I wanted to shake him, wake him from his crazy thoughts.

He opened his eyes and I saw they were almost empty of energy and life. "My dear Watson. I most certainly could have. And in that other world, on that other road, I most certainly did."

He closed his eyes again and sank farther into his chair, as if a huge weight was pushing him down.

And I finally understood what that weight was. My friend had had the future of the world on his shoulders tonight. More weight than any man should be forced to carry.

Even if that man was Sherlock Holmes.

~

DEAN WESLEY SMITH

USA Today BESTSELLING AUTHOR

AVALANCHE CREEK

A THUNDER MOUNTAIN NOVEL

Returning to the time travel western world of Thunder Mountain, USA Today *bestselling writer Dean Wesley Smith weaves his most complex story to date.*

In one timeline, to help with an advanced math problem, Bonnie and Duster Kendal hired Brice Lincoln.

In a second timeline, to help with an advanced math problem, Bonnie and Duster Kendal hired Dixie Smith.

When Brice and Dixie finally meet in the past, instant attraction. And instant problems.

A time travel western that stretches acrss timelines from the Idaho Wilderness to an old Boise hotel with a very special room.

AVALANCHE CREEK
A Thunder Mountain Novel

For Robert and Florence Smith,
my dearly-missed grandparents.
They taught me to love Idaho and the wilderness of Monumental Creek.
He worked the mines and she cooked in the mining camps.
Together they survived the winters and the fires and the floods and the avalanches.
Thanks for giving your grandson a real appreciation of the wilderness.

Chapter One

July 7th, 2016
Brice's Timeline

BRICE HENRY LINCOLN sat in a padded deck chair, his feet up on the wooden railing, staring out over the fantastic beauty that was the Idaho Primitive Area.

As far as he could see there was nothing but range after range of high mountain peaks and incredibly steep-walled valleys. All were covered in deep green pine or brown rock faces. The summer sky was a deep, dark blue and there wasn't the slightest sign of a cloud.

He could tell that it would end up being a warm day.

The hot, dry smell of high-mountain pine trees was already filling the air, a summer smell he had grown to love his entire life, from his early family days camping every summer on the shores of McCall Lake to his hikes in the Boise National Forest when he was home in Boise.

That smell and the feel of the hot, dry mountain air told him he belonged here.

Brice sipped at his Diet Coke. He had finished a wonderful breakfast of ham and eggs and hash browns a half hour ago and was just waiting. He was dressed in a long-sleeved blue dress shirt with his sleeves rolled up, Levis, and New Balance tennis shoes.

He had no doubt that if he spent too much time out in the high-mountain sun today, he would burn, even though he had a pretty good tan from running for exercise every morning back in Boise.

At twenty-eight, he spent far too much time in front of a computer, so he also made sure he got a set amount of exercise every day.

And a nap.

He flat loved naps. Twenty minutes and he was ready to go again.

Where he was sitting on the deck of the Monumental Lodge, he was at over eight thousand feet in elevation. The sun was far more intense up here and the air a lot thinner.

He had spent the night in one of the fantastic rooms of the Monumental Summit Lodge, sleeping on a real, old-fashioned featherbed under a soft quilt. He had kept one window open letting in the cool night air, and he couldn't ever remember getting such a wonderful night's rest. He could sure get used to being up here in these mountains, of that there was no doubt.

The only sounds as he sipped his Diet Coke were a few birds in the trees, a slight wind through the needles of the pines, and some faint rattling of breakfast dishes behind him.

There was no one else but him on the huge, open wooden deck that ran along the east side of the lodge. The lodge was a massive log structure straddling this high mountain saddle. It had steep shake roofs, massive logs polished to a shine by time and weather, and forty guest rooms. Only for six or so months in the late spring, summer, and early fall were those rooms full.

The road up here was closed in the winter and only the owners stayed on. But when the narrow, winding road up the side of the mountain opened in the spring, the lodge seemed to always be full.

The massive main room inside the lodge behind him was a jaw-dropping sight, with the towering ceiling and massive polished logs. The dining area filled a corner of the huge room, serving food on what seemed to be fine china.

The furniture in the main area and lounge looked like it was right out of the late 1890s and every detail stayed consistent with that period. He had no idea how anyone had managed to build this place back over a hundred years before.

And maintaining it in the brutal winters of this area had to be an ongoing fight of epic proportions. It had to take real money to do that.

In front of him, down over a thousand feet, was one of the great tourist attractions of the state.

And absolutely the hardest place in the state to get to.

Back in 1909, just a few years after

this hotel was finished, the entire mining town of Roosevelt was flooded out of existence by a massive landslide that blocked the canyon and backed water up over the town.

From the pictures he had seen, some log buildings could still be seen down through the crystal clear lake water, and the logs from the broken buildings had jammed the area where the stream had finally gone over the mudslide.

Brice had talked to a lot of people who had seen the place and all of them were awed by it. He had also heard rumors that on clear nights you could still hear the pianos playing from the old saloons. He didn't believe in ghosts, but he knew enough history of the place to almost believe that.

Finally, today he was going down to see that town. Except for not looking forward to the drive down the narrow road across the cliff face to get down into the valley, the adventure ahead had him excited. Since he had always heard about this place, but it was so remote, he had just never made the time to come here.

And his parents could never afford a room in this lodge. They could barely afford the time off to pitch tents on the shoreline of McCall Lake for a week.

And during all his years of college, he had no chance, time or money to get up here. But now, his bosses, Bonnie and Duster Kendal had wanted him to see this lodge and the lost town under the lake. He sure hadn't turned them down when they offered. He had no idea how they got rooms here in the peak of the tourist season, but somehow they had managed.

Bonnie and Duster were two of the greatest mathematicians working today. Both had graduated, as he had, with doctors' degrees in higher theoretical mathematics. He had come out of Harvard, they both had gone through Stanford.

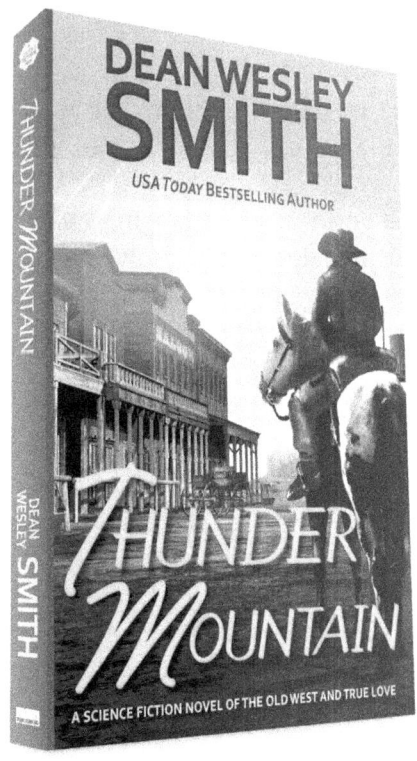

But they didn't teach and do research as he had been headed to do until they had hired him. They worked theory, on their own dime, writing papers and letting their discoveries out for all to have and work from.

And some of their work was so far out on the edges of modern mathematical theory, even he had a hard time grasping it. Which kept him very challenged.

And he loved a mathematical challenge. Far more, he was sure, than he would have loved teaching.

Not only were Bonnie and Duster two of the great mathematical minds on the planet, they were two of the nicest and most beautiful people Brice had ever met. Bonnie looked to be about thirty and was tall, with long brown hair she always kept pulled back. When she walked into a room, heads turned.

Duster was tall, even taller than Brice's six-foot. Duster had short brown hair and piercing dark eyes. He seemed to always be wearing expensive long-sleeve shirts tucked into Levis and cowboy boots. He also often wore a long oilcloth duster and cowboy hat that made him look like he had stepped out of a western pulp novel.

Once in a while Bonnie even called him Marshal. Brice had never asked why.

Bonnie and Duster both seemed far, far, far older than their early thirties age. Around them, Brice often felt like a child, even though he was only five years behind them.

But they were fantastic bosses. And they liked to laugh more than anything, which he appreciated more than he wanted to admit.

They had hired him, moved him back to his home town of Boise, given him more money than he could ever imagine making doing research for some university, set him up in a large office overlooking the Boise River, and said he had an unlimited budget to hire assistants when the job required it.

Brice had no idea where they got their money and he didn't ask, but they sure never worried about it. That seemed below them.

After he had gotten set up in the office, they gave him the most challenging work he could have ever imagined. His job for the last year had been working in the theory and the mathematics of alternate timelines.

He had finally been starting to grasp some of the concepts Bonnie and Duster were working at just in the last two months, and both of them seemed very happy with that.

Now clearly, he was helping them move forward in their research and they seemed overjoyed. And they had no problem letting him take credit where and when he wanted to.

He actually never cared for credit, so on that score he was like them.

This was a dream job and he kept hoping it wouldn't end soon.

He sat back, sipped his Diet Coke, and stared out over the beautiful mountains he loved so much. After Bonnie and Duster finished their breakfast, the three of them would pile into Duster's big Cadillac SUV and head down to see the lost town of Roosevelt, Idaho.

Something Brice had wanted to do since he was a kid.

So right now the excitement of the coming day was making him feel like a kid again.

Chapter Two

July 7th, 2016
Dixie's Timeline

WINIFRED DIXIE SMITH held on tight and stared out the window of the back seat of the big Cadillac SUV as Duster Kendal expertly worked it down the steep road along the cliff face and into the Monumental Valley.

A thousand feet below her, she could see the tops of the tall pine trees and the start of Monumental Creek. One slight miss, or if something happened to the road, the fall would wipe out three of the great minds in mathematics in one tragic accident.

Normally, she wasn't afraid of heights at all. But with the edge of the road and the thousand foot drop seemingly only inches from her, she now wished she had sat on the passenger side of the back seat so all she could see would be the side of the cliff face and the wonderful view ahead of the steep-walled valley.

Dixie never used her real first name and was often called a "pixie" by friends because she stood barely five-four. She had bright red long hair and large, round, brown eyes. To make the pixie resemblance even stronger, her skin was light, with a lot of freckles. She had slathered on more sunscreen today than she ever had before, and at this high altitude, she was going to be lucky to escape only with a slight burn.

The pixie look had served her well in school, especially in some of her graduate level mathematics classes. It caused people to underestimate her and she often left someone who did that flatfooted. Now,

this high in the air, for the first time she wished she was an actual pixie because if she remembered right, they had wings and could fly, just in case Duster missed a turn.

She was fairly certain the big Cadillac SUV couldn't fly.

She had been excited about seeing the submerged town of Roosevelt, Idaho, since she had heard about it for the first time last year after moving from Phoenix to Boise. But she had also heard about how bad this road was going in.

All of that had been accurate and not exaggerated in the slightest. There was no real good way to actually describe how remote this was and how truly frightening this road was.

The road seemed to be no wider than the car and at times she swore Duster almost scraped dirt on the inside hill. The road was dirt and had some pretty nasty bumps in it that made Dixie very glad she was strapped down tight and holding on for dear life.

Bonnie Kendal sat in the front passenger seat, not seeming to be concerned in the slightest about the road. And her husband, Duster, was an expert driver, clearly, and was only using one hand on the wheel to take the SUV down the cliff road. If Dixie had been driving, she would have inched along with both hands glued to the steering wheel and sweat rolling down her face.

On second thought, there was no amount of money that could have made her drive this road period. A person had to know her limits and driving this road was one of those limits.

"How was your stay last night in the lodge?" Bonnie asked, turning slightly to talk with Dixie as if they were just driving a freeway.

Thank heavens the question hadn't been a mathematical one, because Dixie had no doubt her brain would not have been able to deal with that while worrying about falling a thousand feet.

"It was wonderful," Dixie said. "Thank you again for showing me that fantastic place."

And it had been something out of a dream. The Monumental Summit Lodge had no comparison she had ever seen. The entire place was made out of logs and the ceilings in the main room towered overhead. The stone fireplace, even in the summer, had a fire going, and the furniture was straight out of the 1890s and stunning. When she had walked in the huge front door of the place, she had felt she had been transported back in time to 1890.

Even the plates and cups in the dining room were period china.

And considering the mathematical theory she had been working on with Bonnie and Duster over the last year, she found that almost funny. They had been working on the mathematics of time travel and alternate time lines. And they had been making progress.

Bonnie and Duster had hired her right out of Princeton, after she finished her doctorate. She had been living in Phoenix with her parents until she landed a research and teaching job at a major university. But since Bonnie and Duster were known as two of the great minds of mathematics, and had offered her an obscene amount of money to go to Boise to work for them, she had accepted.

And hadn't regretted a moment of it so far.

Of course, if this Cadillac slipped off this road and fell a thousand feet down the cliff, she was sure she would regret the decision for a few seconds.

"You like the featherbed?" Bonnie asked, smiling.

"I got lost in it and the wonderful quilt," Dixie said, smiling. "Never slept so well in my life. That lodge is amazing. Who built it?"

Bonnie smiled. "Now that's a long story that we'll tell you over lunch."

Duster just laughed.

Dixie had no idea what was so funny about the construction of the lodge, but clearly they both were close to it since they had been able to get two rooms in the lodge at the height of the tourist season up here.

Bonnie turned back around to watch ahead and Dixie forced herself to look out at the mountains and the fantastic view and not look down.

Fifteen minutes later Duster bounced the big Cadillac over a bridge and across the valley floor. And for the first time in thirty minutes, Dixie actually allowed herself to take a full breath.

She had never been one for carnival rides and being scared. She was more a hiking and camping girl. And about as high as she ever wanted to be was on the back of a good horse.

"Is there another road out of here?" she asked.

"Nope," Duster said. "Nothing but hiking trails out of here. This is primitive area. The only reason this road is here at all is because of a patented mining claim that allowed the road to be grandfathered in when they changed this to a primitive area."

"It's not as bad going back up," Bonnie said, not turning around. "Besides, we have dinner and room reservations back in the lodge tonight and we can't miss that."

Dixie only nodded to herself and put the drive back up that cliff out of her mind. She would enjoy this beautiful valley on this fantastic summer day and take the road when it came.

Chapter Three

July 7th, 2016
Brice's Timeline

BRICE REALLY ENJOYED the ride along the smooth dirt road on the valley floor. Even though the valley was very narrow in places between the towering slopes of trees and rocks, it still seemed a magical place as the big Cadillac wound through the tall pine trees.

At one point, Duster had taken the Cadillac around a corner and straight ahead was a ruin of a huge mill tucked against one side of the valley. It was nothing more now than a massive pile of tan and weathered boards, twisted and fallen. Brice was shocked at how large it had been as the road passed the ruins within ten feet.

"That mill never got started," Duster said. "They built the building, but the actual stamp mill never got brought in before the mine ran dry, so they chopped all that wood and never used any of it."

Duster pointed to long piles of logs cut about four feet long and neatly stacked about head high winding through the trees in all directions. The top layers were nothing more than decayed wood, and some of the piles had huge trees growing out of the middle of them.

Brice had to admit that the piles of cut wood, now tanned and deteriorating with age, looked very, very creepy.

"So all these trees have come up since?" Brice asked. "This valley had no trees from the looks of how much lumber was cut."

"Darned few," Duster said. "Over a hundred years of growth will make for some tall trees, even in these harsh conditions. No one needed to cut any of them down after the town went under and the mines played out."

Brice nodded and just sat back and watched the scenery. They passed the remains of a few more old log cabins and he could see more ruins tucked against the far side of the valley.

Then suddenly the valley opened up to about two football fields wide and Duster pulled the Cadillac off into a parking area with four other SUVs, all empty. Clearly the occupants were exploring the area somewhere.

The road went directly across the valley, over a low bridge, and then up a side valley.

"The lake and remains of the town are down the valley about a mile's hike from here," Duster said. "No road in there."

He stopped the car in the shade and turned it off and all three of them got out into the warm morning air.

Again the smell of hot pine trees hit Brice. The only sound was water running over rocks in the stream. Otherwise the valley was in complete silence.

The ridges towered over them. He couldn't imagine being trapped in this valley for an entire winter.

"How many people lived in this valley when the town of Roosevelt was in its prime?" Brice asked.

"At one point," Bonnie said, "over ten thousand people were living and working in this valley. Less than a few hundred ever stayed over for the winters, though."

Brice couldn't imagine ten thousand people in this small, steep-walled valley. It must have been damned noisy at times.

Bonnie and Duster both took out lawn chairs from the back of the SUV and a small table and started to set them up in the shade.

"You're not going to the lake?" Brice asked as he watched them.

"We've seen it," Duster said, his voice kind of low, which Brice had come to know after a year meant that Duster was upset about something.

Bonnie took Brice by the arm and walked him toward the trail leading along the left side of the canyon, handing him a cold bottle of water as they walked.

"Take a look at the town," she said, "go across the logjam and on down the trail about a quarter mile to the cemetery. Then come back and we'll have lunch. We have some things to talk about."

Brice looked into the intense eyes of Bonnie and then nodded. "How long?"

"If you take your time and enjoy it, about two hours. We're fine here. Don't rush."

He nodded.

With that Bonnie turned back to Duster.

Brice watched her for a few steps. His two bosses were sometimes very strange people. But he liked and trusted them and he wouldn't trade his job for anything.

He turned and headed down the wide trail toward the lake that had buried a town over a hundred years before. The excitement of finally seeing it had his stomach twisting.

This valley was the real past, not the theoretical mathematical past. And sometimes he just needed to get away from the numbers and see the actual reality.

Chapter Four

July 7th, 2016
Dixie's Timeline

DIXIE KNELT BESIDE the metal plaque attached to a stone near the old Roosevelt Cemetery. The tall trees around her kept the area completely in shade, and below her about fifty paces, Monumental Creek tumbled over rocks, the only sound in the valley.

Bonnie stood about twenty paces back up the trail toward the lake. Duster hadn't wanted to come with them, saying he had seen it before. Bonnie didn't want Dixie going alone, so she had walked with her.

And Bonnie's answers to Dixie's questions about the valley and the old town were stunning in the detail. Dixie could tell that this valley was really something special, and when she stood on the side of that crystal blue lake and looked down through the water at the remains of a few buildings still there, she felt a great sense of loss.

She wasn't sure why.

"How many people died in the landslide and flood?" Dixie had asked after looking down into the water for a time.

"None," Bonnie said. "Numbers of people died in this valley before the town went under the water, but it took five or six days to back the water up over the town and the valley clear back up to where we are parked."

"That far?" Dixie had asked, stunned.

Bonnie had nodded. "Monumental Creek is bringing down sand and mud and slowly filling the lake. In another hundred years this will be nothing more than a meadow."

Then Bonnie had led her across the logjam of the remains of old homes that blocked the stream at one end and up a wide trail about a quarter mile to the cemetery.

The metal plaque said simply,

In Memory of the Thunder Mountain Dead
of Whom Thirteen are Known
to Rest in this Cemetery.

There were ten names there and three unknowns. The plaque had been put there in 1949 and clearly someone still maintained the small cemetery since a large rope showed the outline of the cemetery and a few graves had headstones still. Most graves were just depressions in the dirt.

One name was a Smith, with W.D. initials. She would have to do some research on that person when she got back to see if it was a distant relative of hers. That would be interesting to find out. She did have some Smith relatives in the Idaho area in the past. Her mom down in Phoenix kept that kind of information. It would be fun to find out.

Dixie stood and again she felt the immense sadness of the area sort of settle over her like a blanket. She was never a sad person. She always figured life was too exciting to be sad and too much fun. So this felt very strange to her.

She want back down the trail to Bonnie who was watching her.

"Ready to head back for some lunch?"

Dixie only nodded and then with one more look back at the small, roped cemetery and metal plaque on the stone, she turned and followed Bonnie up the trail.

This entire valley was amazing. Exciting to explore and sad at the same time.

By the time they had hiked back along the lake and up the trail the mile to where Duster waited, the excitement of being in the wilderness and exploring the past had completely pushed aside any feeling of sadness.

She was really coming to love Idaho and the huge mountains and the beauty of it all. And a year ago, she hadn't expected to when she moved from Phoenix.

Chapter Five

July 7th, 2016
Brice's Timeline

BRICE GOT BACK to Bonnie and Duster just under two hours after he left. He had found the lake amazing and the small cemetery depressing. Even though he knew from studying this place as a child that no one had died in the big landslide and flood that buried the city of Roosevelt, it still felt just amazing and creepy.

There were a couple of campers tucked off in the trees above the lake, their red tent bright against the natural colors of the trees and rocks. He had decided after seeing that tent that there was no chance he would ever camp near this lake.

The valley was wonderful, the area fantastic, but camping near a lake with an old mining town under it was just too damned strange for him. Even if it didn't have ghosts.

Bonnie was working to set out a lunch on a card table and after a few minutes, just before she was almost ready with everything, Duster patted Brice on the shoulder.

"Come with me," he said. "Something I want to show you before we start lunch and our conversation."

Duster, wearing his long brown oil-cloth coat and brown cowboy hat, even though it was warming up, walked into the road and toward the bridge over Monumental Creek. It wasn't much of a bridge, more like some logs framing in a culvert that the stream went through.

Duster got to the middle of the bridge and turned and looked back up the valley.

Brice stood beside him and looked back up the valley as well.

The huge Monumental Lodge dominated the ridgeline, even from a few miles away. It was a stunning building, sitting there like that, filling the saddle between two large mountain peaks.

"Amazing place, huh?" Duster asked.

"It is," Brice said, letting Duster lead the conversation.

"I've stood in this very spot and that lodge was not there," Duster said, simply.

"I've lost what you mean," Brice said, turning to look at his boss.

Duster had a very, very serious expression on his face as he stared up at the huge lodge on the ridge.

"I built that lodge in another timeline," Duster said. "And when I returned to this timeline, the lodge was here. And that's what we have had you working on for the last year, trying to help us figure out how that could happen."

With that, Duster turned and started back toward Bonnie and lunch, leaving Brice standing there, staring at the lodge, trying to even grasp what Duster was talking about.

Or more likely joking about.

Chapter Six

July 7th, 2016
Dixie's Timeline

DIXIE MANAGED to not say anything or ask any question about Duster's wild statement that he had built that lodge in another timeline until Bonnie got all of them sandwiches and some fruit and bottles of water on the folding table.

They were sitting in the shade of some tall pine trees and only the sound of the stream and a faint breeze through the trees disturbed the silence of the valley.

Dixie had spent the last year working the math, with Bonnie and Duster, on the likelihood of various timelines and what was possible between such timelines, if they existed.

But that had all been theory.

Mathematical theory.

Not building a lodge.

Dixie took a bite of her sandwich, which Bonnie had had the kitchen in the lodge prepare. Dixie had ordered a prime rib sandwich with light horseradish sauce on it on a thick bun. It tasted wonderful and she let herself slowly chew on the sandwich before saying anything.

Bonnie finally broke the silence.

"What Duster told you is true," she said. "We built that lodge in another timeline because we had always heard of a big lodge being there, but in this timeline, it didn't exist."

Dixie put the sandwich down on her paper plate and stared at Bonnie, trying to even grasp why they were saying what they were saying.

"When we returned to this timeline," Duster said, "there it was."

"We figured that alternate timeline forms of us," Bonnie said, "came to this timeline and built it while we were in another timeline building the same thing."

"But the math we had up until that point didn't back that up," Duster said. "We have the reality. Now we need to just back it up with equations, with numbers that explain the reality."

"Before we talk math," Dixie said, trying to get her mind to settle down and just think, "explain to me how you can move into the past in another timeline. Not the math of it, the physical ability of it."

Bonnie nodded. "Good question and one we expected. On the way back to Boise we'll show you all that. But in your equations, didn't you see that all timelines could be reflected in a physical location? In fact, didn't you find that all timelines *should* be represented in a physical manner?"

Dixie forced herself to sit back and think.

Bonnie and Duster went back to eating, not pushing Dixie, giving her the time, which she appreciated because right now she was worried that her wonderful bosses and her job were about to vanish into moments of insanity.

When she had started working for them, the level of progress in mathematics of alternate timelines had been very advanced, as she would have expected from two of the great math brains on the planet. She didn't understand exactly their fascination with the topic, but they were paying her and that was their interest, so it had become hers as well.

She took a deep breath of the clear mountain air and let it out slowly. Dixie's assignment for most of the last year had been to go over all of Bonnie and Duster's previous work, checking everything for mistakes. She had checked the mathematical aspects of time being expressed in a physical location that existed in all timelines at the same time. A sort of nexus or hub of time.

Math said a nexus or hub existed, at least in theory, tying all dimensions and timelines together in a physical location.

Dixie sat forward and looked first at Duster, then at Bonnie. "Are you telling me you discovered the nexus for time?"

Bonnie nodded and smiled.

"By accident, actually," Duster said. "My great-grandfather stumbled into the physical area of it in this timeline while digging a gold mine."

"That's what we can show you on the way back to Boise," Bonnie said. "But you checked our math and proved mathematically that it needed to exist, right?"

Dixie nodded. She didn't want to, but the math didn't lie. She had just thought it all theoretical.

"Actually, we found it and then came up with the math to prove it was there," Duster said. "We didn't believe it for years, either."

"Even after you see it," Bonnie said, "you'll have trouble believing it."

"But assume for the moment we're crazier than loons," Duster said, smiling at her. "Let's just talk math and what you have done in the last few months to advance our work."

Bonnie nodded and indicated that Dixie should take another bite of the prime rib sandwich.

Dixie did, then took a drink of cold water, then another bite as they all ate in silence. The sandwich was wonderful, the mountain valley beautiful and even comfortable in the shade. And so far she hadn't gotten too much sun, so her skin was fine.

She forced herself to just calm down and let the food and cold water and beautiful day ground her.

"So over the last two months," Bonnie said, "you have shown mathematically that with the infinite number of alternate timelines that exist, when we decide to go to another alternate timeline, an almost infinite number of our counterparts make the same exact decision."

Dixie ignored the travel aspect and went back to her calculations in her mind. She nodded after a moment. "With any decision, an infinite number of our counterparts would make the same decision if it really was a decision. And an infinite number of alternate timelines would split from that decision."

"Your work also proved, at least to me and Bonnie," Duster said, "that an infinite number of those alternate timelines would then flow back and merge if the decision point had no lasting impact on the larger universe."

"Correct," Dixie said, nodding again. "But you have already checked my work on all of this. Why tell me this here and now?"

"We need you to take your work to the next level to really help us," Duster said.

Dixie wasn't sure what he meant by the next level. So she kept silent.

Bonnie nodded. "When we returned from the alternate timeline past where we built that lodge, we returned to a timeline where the lodge had always existed for us in our lives. It had been built."

"Our memories shifted," Duster said. "We remembered both timelines, one where that lake and town were a forgotten part of Idaho history, and the lodge didn't exist and another where that lake is a major tourist attraction and that lodge exists."

"You are saying your memory is of two timelines, two alternate histories?" Dixie asked, not believing it. "I don't think that would be mathematically possible."

"We agree with you there," Duster said, nodding. "But convince our memories. And it's not just the two of us, either. There were six travelers who helped build that lodge and all six remember the previous timeline just as clearly. It is a fact."

"So somewhere, our math is wrong," Bonnie said. "Or we haven't found the right calculation for it yet."

Dixie really wanted to ask who the others were, but knew that would derail the focus of the conversation, so again kept silent. She could ask that later.

"We need you to help us figure out mathematically how that is possible," Bonnie said. "Since it happened."

"We are not only giving you a raise on your job if you decide to stay with us after all this," Duster said, "but we will make you independently wealthy if you agree to help us."

"Your job is about to change dramatically," Bonnie said, nodding. "Once we show you the focal point, the nexus of time and show you that it exists and that you can move into alternate timelines from it, your entire life and belief systems will change as well."

"In other words," Duster said, smiling, "we trust you and need your fantastic mind on this task. Maybe, between the three of us, we can actually advance the understanding of time and space."

"And help us figure out a mathematical reason why we can remember that lodge not being there," Bonnie said. "We were raised in a world where the lodge was there, and we were raised in a world where the lodge was not there. That should not be mathematically possible."

"Yet here we sit," Duster said, shrugging.

Dixie took a deep breath and let it out. They had just tossed a lot of things at her. She was going to need time to think.

"But realize," Bonnie said. "You can decide to walk away right now if you would like. And honestly, as crazy as all this sounds, I wouldn't blame you."

"I honestly think you would be crazy to stay," Duster said. "Considering everything we've just said. But you have to admit, it's a hell of a mathematical challenge."

"And we want you to stay," Bonnie said. "We flat need your help. In all the country, we couldn't find a better mathematical mind than yours."

Dixie nodded. "Being needed feels great, I have to admit. And the challenge would be great. But give me some time to think about it and ask a few hundred really stupid questions before I give you an answer."

Both Bonnie and Duster laughed and Bonnie pointed to Dixie's half-eaten sandwich.

"Might want to finish that," Bonnie said. "We have dinner reservations at seven and that's a good six hours and a scary car ride from now."

All Dixie could do was nod and take another bite of the wonderful-tasting prime rib sandwich.

Duster stood and took his chair and went out onto the road to the middle of the bridge and sat down facing up the valley and the lodge. His oilcloth duster draped around him, his cowboy hat tipped back slightly.

He was clearly a man used to being alone with his own thoughts, Dixie could tell that. Typical for most mathematicians and she was no exception.

Dixie took another bite of the sandwich, letting her mind roam back through the assumptions she had proven mathematically over the last year.

After a minute, Bonnie stood and started cleaning up.

Only the sounds of the water over the rocks and the light breeze through the pine needles broke the silence.

Dixie finally finished as much of the sandwich as she could and moved it aside. Everything they had told her, except the memory of being in another timeline, was possible mathematically.

Physical travel to another timeline was another matter.

As Bonnie picked up Dixie's plate, she said, "I know we sound crazy, but we really aren't."

Dixie looked up at Bonnie, into her dark eyes. "If I hadn't done a year of math working with you both to prove what you just told me was real, I would be looking for a way to walk out of this valley right now."

Bonnie nodded. "And honestly, I wouldn't have blamed you in the slightest."

Chapter Seven

July 7th, 2016
Brice's Timeline

AFTER LUNCH, BRICE had gone for a walk, heading back down the trail to the lake. He had passed a couple coming out who looked sunburned and were smiling.

"Wonderful valley, isn't it?" the woman said to him as he stepped out of the trail to one side to let them pass.

"Beautiful," he said.

But his mind was a long ways from the valley and the warm afternoon. He was just letting his mind drift back over everything Bonnie and Duster had told him, including the new job offer and actually showing him the time nexus. If that actually existed, he wanted to see it more than anything else.

But now his mind was going back over a year's worth of work for them. They had just told him that his work for that entire year hadn't been theoretical, but actually real.

That changed the perspective on everything.

He had proven mathematically that the same person could not exist twice at the same moment in the same timeline. So in reality, he could not go meet himself in another timeline. Time and the very math of time would not allow that to happen.

And Bonnie and Duster had already proven, and Brice had confirmed with his calculations, that any decision, no matter how small or by whom, split off an alternate timeline. Most of those timelines merged almost instantly back with the main timeline it had split from. But sometimes a decision kept the timelines branching into infinite numbers of timelines.

Brice really needed to see the physical aspects of the time nexus because mathematically, alternate timeline Bonnies and Dusters should not have been able to accidently stumble on this world to build that lodge. That had to be influenced by the physical nature of how they were traveling to other timelines.

With that alone, Brice had about a hundred questions he could think of.

He found himself again just above the small lake that covered the old mining town. In some alternate timelines,

the town had not been destroyed by the flood, the landslide hadn't happened, or had been smaller or diverted.

That timeline was an infinite number of timelines sideways from this timeline.

He understood the numbers, the scale, and the math of it all.

He sat down on a large rock looking out over the lake and just let his mind keep working over the last year.

He had become an expert on the mathematical theory of alternate timelines, thanks to Bonnie and Duster and their work. But with one simple crazy conversation over sandwiches, he realized how little he really did know yet.

His basic decision to stay with this job, or go teach, would cause major timeline shifts he was fairly certain. Most people made decisions and caused nothing more than side ripples that were reabsorbed into the main timeline. But he had proven with mathematical equations that getting married and having a child tended to start theoretical alternate timelines since the child moved forward through time and had children and so on and so on.

So the question was, could he really go teach, knowing this was here, even if he didn't believe it?

The answer was clear. Of course he couldn't.

He had spent a year with Bonnie and Duster: Brice liked them and he trusted them. Brice needed to see this through. It was too much of a challenge to not stay with them.

Brice stood and with one last look at the lake, he turned and headed back up the valley. He wouldn't tell them his decision until dinner.

And then, if they really weren't crazy, tomorrow he would see the nexus of time, where mathematically an infinite number of timelines were expressed in a physical form of some sort.

The idea of that just twisted his stomach. He couldn't even imagine it outside of the mathematics that said it existed.

And he trusted math.

He just didn't trust his own imagination.

Chapter Eight

July 8th, 2016
Dixie's Timeline

DIXIE STARED OUT the window as the big Cadillac SUV headed along the Snake River. Dixie and Bonnie and Duster had gotten an early start out of the lodge and had reached Cascade, Idaho, in just under three hours. They had stopped for a quick lunch, then gone toward Boise and then cut over toward the border with Oregon at a small town called Horseshoe Bend.

From Cascade to the Snake River had taken just under two hours. Duster had told her their ultimate goal was an old mine above an old ghost town named Silver City.

From what Bonnie said, they were about an hour away, so they would reach the old mine around two in the afternoon.

It had been an amazing beautiful drive, down out of the central Idaho mountains, then across the large Treasure Valley to the Snake River, and now they were headed into a mountain range on the southwest side of the state called the Owyhee Mountains.

Dixie had loved it all.

Idaho was such a spectacularly beautiful place in its ruggedness. But the closer they got to the blue-tinted mountains ahead, the more her stomach twisted.

Dixie had told Bonnie and Duster last night over a wonderful dinner in the big lodge that she wanted to stay and keep up the work, and she wanted to see the time nexus.

They both had seemed very pleased and Duster had offered a toast.

"To the future," he said.

"All of them," Bonnie had added.

And they had all drunk to that.

Dixie had decided at dinner that she didn't want to ask questions about what she was going to see until she saw it. She had decided she had just wanted the mathematics she had worked on over the last year to speak for itself.

She had a thousand questions, and both Bonnie and Duster had agreed with Dixie's idea to hold the questions.

"After you see the place," Bonnie had said, "we'll answer any question you might have. On anything."

So they had enjoyed the meal, talking about the lodge and the fantastic mountains and history. Bonnie and Duster seemed to know a great deal about the area's history and their stories were always wonderful to listen to.

And because of the cool night air coming in through the window and the deep featherbed, Dixie had managed to get a good night's sleep even with the worry about the next day.

When Duster turned off the paved highway onto a wide and fairly smooth dirt road that headed up into the mountains, Dixie finally couldn't hold the questions anymore.

"Can you give me some history on how you found this place?" she asked.

Bonnie nodded and indicated that Duster should tell the story.

"My great-great-grandfather was a prospector in the first boom of the Silver City area. He dug a gold mine on the side of Florida Mountain to the west of Silver City. For a time he had a good gold vein and then it pinched off. He dug a little farther and gave up."

Duster had the big SUV moving at around fifty up the wide and fairly straight road. He clearly drove it a lot, and Dixie wasn't anywhere near as nervous as when they went up the narrow, winding road to the lodge.

"After a few years, my great-great-grandfather reopened the mine and dug, hoping to hit another vein," Duster said, "but instead he hit a large cavern. He worked it a little more off the big cavern until he broke into an even larger cavern full of crystals. That was when he boarded the mine up and went to Boise to have a family."

"Crystals?" Dixie asked.

Bonnie nodded. "Each timeline is represented by what looks like a rose quartz crystal."

Dixie couldn't even begin to imagine that. "How big is this place?"

"Infinite," Duster said.

"The crystals that are nearest where his grandfather broke in are just one tiny area of timelines, and there are billions there and more forming all the time."

"We believe it moves off into other dimensions of a sort," Duster said, "but haven't been able to mathematically confirm that either."

Dixie didn't know what to think, other than her stomach was clamped into a knot.

"The mine stayed boarded up and in the family. My grandfather showed the mine to my father," Duster said, "who then showed it to me and Bonnie after we finished at Stanford with our doctorate degrees."

"We spent the next four years living in an apartment behind my parent's home in Boise," Duster said, "doing nothing but studying the place and doing some of the basic math calculations that you have checked for us this last year."

"I would call those far from basic," Dixie said.

"Those calculations got us to the idea of using the power of a crystal to actually shift timelines into the past," Duster said.

Dixie decided to not question that. After she saw it, she might be able to put the math on the reality and see what they did. But right now questions on that topic would just confuse her even more.

"How many people know about this place?" Dixie asked.

"Duster and I, six historians and an architect and an interior designer we hired to build the lodge. So you will be the eleventh person."

"Not counting my mother and father," Duster said, "who don't like this place and want nothing to do with it. They have no idea what we've been doing up here and don't want to know. They moved to Arizona a year ago and seem happy there."

Dixie was shocked at the mention of an architect and interior designer. "Are you telling me Ryan and April know about this?"

Dixie had met them numbers of times in and around Bonnie and Duster's office. They had their own design firm down near the Boise River, but always seemed to be in and out with Bonnie and Duster.

Dixie had liked them a lot. She had never met a couple so much in love and who laughed as much as they did.

"They designed and built and furnished that lodge," Duster said.

"It still looks almost exactly how they built it," Bonnie said. "Or at least how their counterparts from another timeline built it."

With that all Dixie could do was sit and stare out the window as Duster took them higher and higher into the mountains.

And the wide road got narrower and rougher.

Chapter Nine

July 8th, 2016
Brice's Timeline

FOR BRICE, the last part of the drive into the mine had been flat horrifying. Duster had left the narrow dirt road right after a bridge over a mostly dry creek and started up what looked to be nothing more than a game trail.

And Duster didn't slow down because the hillside was so steep. The big Cadillac just bounced over ruts and holes, eventually turning a sharp left and heading across the hill through the trees.

Brice held on for dear life through the bumps. And when the car turned to go across the side of the steep hill, he desperately wanted to climb to the other side of the back seat. He was behind Duster and Brice felt the car was about to tip over and roll down the steep hill. But at the same time there was no way he was going to unbuckle his seat belt.

So he just leaned to the inside of the car and held on tight and hoped as Duster bounced them through the trees going across the steep slope, finally pulling into a grove of scrubby pine trees, the nose of the car pointing upward.

"We walk the rest of the way," Duster said, shutting off the car and climbing out.

"Fun ride, huh?" Bonnie said, glancing back at Brice before unbuckling her seat belt and climbing out as well.

"I'm up for walking down," Brice said as he managed to catch his breath and release his grip on the side of the seat. His hands were shaking as he climbed out into a warm blast of thin, mountain air.

As with the town of Roosevelt under the water, he had always wanted to visit the ghost town of Silver City, but again had never made the time. Now about a thousand feet down the hill below him he could see the remains of the old mining town in the bottom of the valley.

There looked to be only about twenty buildings left standing and two buildings had some cars parked in front of them.

"Not much of a town left, is there?" Duster said as he waited for Brice to calm his nerves and look around.

This area was much, much drier than the Monumental Lodge area and the hot smell of sagebrush mixed with the hot pine smell. Brice loved both smells.

"We walking very far?" he asked, figuring he would need some sunscreen if they were.

"Nope," Duster said. "Just across the hillside there. Watch your step on the trail. It's a long ways down."

Duster led the way, followed by Bonnie.

Brice fell in behind them.

He had been stunned that ten other people knew about this place. That means Bonnie and Duster had led eight others like him to this old mine. He would have to ask them later if they were as scared as he was feeling.

They reached the flat top of an old mine tailing. The remains of an old shack still barely stood to one side in front of a boarded-up mine. It was clear that the earth had caved in behind the boards.

He didn't know much about mines, but he knew for a fact there was no way they were going into a mine that way.

Had Bonnie and Duster just been playing an elaborate mind game? That didn't seem like them, but at the moment this looked like a bust.

"What we are about to show you has to remain between us and the few others who know about this place," Duster said.

"We trust you or we wouldn't be showing you this," Bonnie said. "You can quit and leave at any point, but the non-disclosure agreement you signed when you came to work for us must remain in full force. Understood?"

"Not sure who would believe me anyway," Brice said. "But I understand."

Duster laughed. "That's what they all say."

He took what looked like an old skeleton key from his pocket and looked around.

Bonnie did the same. "Clear," she said after a moment.

Duster nodded and turned toward a huge rock near the mine entrance and twisted the head of the key.

The face of the rock slid back, showing a door behind it that clicked open.

Brice was impressed. In a million years he never would have thought that rock moved.

"Just some of the many, many security features we have installed," Duster said as the three of them went in the door to a small room.

Duster hit a large red button and the door closed and the rock outside slid silently back into place.

It took a few seconds in intense blackness before the lights came up and a big metal door opened into a mine tunnel.

It had huge timbers and the remains of a small-gauge mine-car track running up the middle.

Lights hung from the ceiling clicked on, showing the mine leading off into the mountain.

Brice stepped out into the tunnel and looked around at the big timbers. He was about to ask if it was safe when he noticed above the timbers how everything had been reinforced. A major earthquake wouldn't knock this place down. It looked old, but was far from old. Another security feature in case someone got in here.

Bonnie and Duster had started down the mine tunnel, so he followed, feeling the air temperature cool the deeper they went.

As the mine tunnel and tracks curved to the right, Duster just walked straight ahead and through the rock wall and timbers.

"Hologram," Bonnie said, stopping and waiting for him. "Give me your hand and close your eyes and I'll get you through it."

She took his hand and disappeared into the wall. Just as his face was about to smash into the wall, he closed his eyes.

Nothing.

After a step he opened them again as Bonnie let go of his hand and looked back down the mine tunnel.

"More security protections," Duster said. "And if anyone got that far, I would have been notified and set off even more protections from anywhere on the planet."

With that Duster turned and kept on going down the mineshaft, again walking through what looked like the end of the tunnel.

Bonnie didn't wait for Brice this time and vanished behind Duster.

Brice managed to keep his eyes mostly open and his hands in front of him as he walked through the wall.

That was just downright creepy.

On the other side of the hologram was a huge cavern. The lights had come up showing a massive number of shelves filled with supplies and racks and racks of various clothing all looking like it was right out of a period costume party.

The ceiling of the huge cavern was rock and a good fifty feet overhead and the floor was smooth and hard.

"I need something to drink," Duster said, heading through the cavern toward a back corner. "Anyone else?"

"A bottle of water would be nice," Bonnie said.

Brice nodded as he looked around, staring at the huge space and all the supplies.

"Make that two more," she said, following Duster.

Brice turned and followed them both past a wall of rifles and pistols, all looking like they were fresh out of a museum, yet looking almost new.

In the back area of the big cave was what looked like a modern living room, with couches and chairs on a large carpet and a huge modern kitchen with a dining table that could hold at least ten. The cave floor in the kitchen had been tiled.

Duster dug into the fridge and then laughed as he pulled out three bottles of water. "Ryan and April were here and left us dinner for the evening."

"I wonder why they didn't stick around," Bonnie said.

"They have a great-great-grandkid playing in a softball league, remember?" Duster said.

Brice was about to ask how that was possible, then just shut his mouth and took the bottle of water. He would just add that to the thousand other questions he was sure he was going to have.

"So this is the first big cavern your great-great-grandfather found?" Brice asked.

"This is the place," Duster said. "We use it now for storage and meals and such."

Brice took a drink of the bottle of cold water.

"Might want to leave that on the table," Bonnie said, setting her bottle down as well. "We'll be right back anyway."

Brice took another drink, set the bottle down, and turned to follow her and Duster back across the cavern. A huge metal door was locked on the far side of the cavern. It looked like it had filled in a mine tunnel.

Duster opened it quickly and on the other side was a dead-end mine tunnel.

"Yet another hologram," Duster said and walked forward and right on through.

"Do not touch anything in this room except the ground," Bonnie said.

Then she walked forward and vanished through the wall.

He followed her, again managing to barely keep his eyes open as he stepped through the hologram that looked like a solid stone wall.

Beyond it, the huge cavern took him a moment to even see.

He took about five steps over the smooth dirt floor and then just stopped.

A long wooden table with a small wooden box set to one side of the cavern. The wooden box had some wires running from it.

The cavern had to be as large as some huge professional basketball arenas.

Every inch of the massive cavern was covered with millions and millions of quartz crystals of all size and shapes. All of them seemed to be glowing with a light of their own, giving the room a soft, clear light. It was as if every crystal had a light behind it.

Never, in all his life, had he seen anything so beautiful.

Crystals seemed to grow in clumps and in some areas massive numbers of crystals seemed to almost form shapes jutting from the walls and down from the distant ceiling.

To one side of the huge room was an archway that seemed to lead off into another massive cavern of crystals and beyond that more and more and more caverns into the distance.

"Every crystal you can see is a major alternate timeline very close to our timeline," Duster said.

"Millions and millions of microscopic timeline crystals are forming around each major crystal every second," Bonnie said, "and then being absorbed back into the timeline if the decision does not change anything major. If it does, then the new crystal grows and might eventually be a major timeline as well."

"It's real," Brice managed to say.

"It is very real," Bonnie said. "The math does not lie."

"Math never lies when you do it right," Duster said.

With that Brice just sat down in the dirt, staring at all of time on the walls around him.

Chapter Ten

July 8th, 2016
Dixie's Timeline

DIXIE MANAGED to climb back to her feet after a few long moments of just sitting there staring at the massive cavern of crystals. Never had she imagined anything so beautiful. It was like she was standing inside a diamond.

She moved over to where Bonnie and Duster stood beside the big wooden table.

"Remember to never touch a crystal," Duster said. "We're not sure what would happen and we don't want to find out. Luckily my great-great-grandfather wore gloves when he worked and broke through into here."

Dixie nodded.

"This is the machine we invented to jump timelines," Bonnie said, indicating the big ugly wooden box on the table with a dial on it and some wires leading out of it.

To Dixie it sure didn't look like much more than what a kid could bang together in a garage.

"Not much to look at," Duster said, "but it gets the job done."

"What exactly does it do?" Dixie asked.

Duster picked up the two cords. "We attach one end of these two cords to a crystal on the wall and the other to the machine right there where the electrical terminals stick out the side. Whoever is touching the machine is transferred to that timeline for the date set on the dial above the terminals."

"We can only go as far back as the mine is open," Bonnie said. "So we're limited to the late 1870s. We tend to like 1878 the best, since Silver City is past its first boom, yet still has a lot of supplies."

"That's also just after my great-great-grandfather boarded the place up for the last time," Duster said.

Suddenly part of the math that Dixie had worked on concerned the variance of time and matter.

"How long did it take to build that lodge?" Dixie asked.

Duster shrugged. "A couple of years."

Bonnie smiled. "Starting to apply the math you've been working on, huh?"

Dixie just nodded.

"You can stay in another timeline as long as you want," Duster said. "You can age and even die there."

"But you will only be gone from this timeline for two minutes and fifteen seconds," Bonnie said. "And if you die in another timeline, you return here very much alive."

Before Dixie could ask another question on that impossible fact, Duster said, "Look at it this way. The power of the machine only allows one hundred and thirty-five seconds in this timeline to pass. When you are in the other timeline, you become a part of that timeline. By your very arrival there, you change that timeline and more timelines branch off."

"You can have children, raise a family, die of old age in the other timeline," Bonnie said. "Your family and everyone you influenced stay in that timeline when you return. Only two minutes and fifteen seconds elapse here."

"How many other timelines have you visited?" Dixie asked, trying to get her mind to form even a solid thought.

"Hundreds and hundreds," Duster said.

He pointed to the wall of crystals closest to the table. Dixie could see small hairband-like bands on many of the crystals. "April suggested we start marking crystals we have attached to, but that's only been in the last year or so."

Dixie had to ask, even though she wasn't sure she wanted to know the answer.

"How many years have you two lived?"

Duster shrugged and looked at Bonnie. "You still keeping track of that sort of thing?"

"I stopped about a year ago when we went past a thousand years," she said. "Counting it just made me feel old."

Before Dixie could even catch her breath, Duster put on a pair of thick leather gloves and attached the wire ends to a glowing rose crystal on the wall that seemed to be a major one and had to be a good ten inches long.

"Bonnie, why don't you take Dixie on a little test run and I'll start working on that meal April and Ryan left us."

Dixie wanted to scream and run from the room.

"It will be fun and we'll be right back, I promise," Bonnie said. "Just touch the box."

Dixie touched the smooth polished wood on the side of the box. It wasn't hot or cold. Just wood.

Duster adjusted the dial on one side of the wooden box and then Bonnie touched the box beside Dixie with her bare hand and picked up one of the wires leading to the wall with a glove-covered hand.

Duster attached one wire to the box, then smiled at Dixie. "See you in two minutes and fifteen seconds."

Bonnie attached the other wire and Duster vanished.

"Where did he go?" Dixie asked, the panic filling her voice.

Duster had just vanished from the big crystal room.

How was that possible?

The big wooden table was still there, the wires were attached to the wood box, but no Duster.

"He didn't go anywhere," Bonnie said, smiling and putting her arm around Dixie to both give her support and turn her toward the now closed metal door leading back into the cavern. "We did. Welcome to 1878."

Chapter Eleven

October 14, 1878
Brice's Timeline

BRICE LOOKED at Duster. Bonnie had just vanished out of the crystal cavern.

"What do you mean we moved? What do you mean 1878?"

Duster laughed. "Don't worry, it freaked me out beyond words the first few times I jumped timelines. Bonnie is still back in July in 2016 in our home timeline."

Duster pointed to the wire leading from the machine over to a crystal on the wall. "We are now in the timeline contained in that crystal. If we change something, other timelines will start forming because we are now a part of that crystal's timeline."

Brice managed to nod, but he wasn't really believing what Duster was saying.

"Come on, I'll show you," Duster said, heading toward the now-closed metal door that led out into the other

cavern. The lights in that cavern came up as they entered. Brice noticed his bottle of water was not on the table where he had left it.

Brice followed him to a rack of clothes where Duster grabbed a long coat off the rack for Ryan and a cowboy hat. "Slip this on in case anyone spots us."

Brice did as Duster headed for the mine tunnel leading to the entrance.

Brice just stumbled along behind him, doing his best to even form a clear thought.

And failing.

Brice prided himself in thinking clearly in emergency situations, but this was something different. Duster was trying to get him to believe that all the work Brice had done in theoretical math and alternate timelines had actually been about a reality.

Brice was a mathematician.

He didn't deal in reality.

He dealt in theory.

At the entrance to the mine, Duster showed him the scope that let Duster check out the hillside for people close by. Brice looked through it as well and could see no one.

It looked strange out there. Almost dark, and with gray overcast.

Duster closed the door and hit the big button to open the outside door.

The blast of intense cold air caught Brice by surprise and snapped some thinking back into place.

There was a moderate wind and it was snowing lightly as they stepped out onto the flat area of the mine tailing. The old shack now had windows in it and an ore car sat between it and the boarded up mine entrance.

"The Cadillac is parked over on that hillside in 2016," Duster said, pointing to a barren ridgeline with no car that in one hundred and thirty-eight years would hold a stand of trees.

Duster moved over to the edge of the mine tailings and pointed downward.

It took Brice a moment to realize what he was seeing through the blowing snow.

A thousand feet below him, Silver City was a live and flourishing town, with hundreds of buildings. Many of the buildings had lights coming through windows and smoke from chimneys mixed with the blowing snow.

"That's still a pretty rough mining town at this point in history," Duster said. "Just in the middle of its first boom phase."

The cold air made Brice pull the long coat in tight around his body.

He had no idea how this was possible. None.

Brice looked around. The big rock was closed back up, the old mining shack looked like it had only been built a few years before. The boards over the mine were fresh and the dirt they were standing on looked recently dug, not settled and packed by years of weather.

And below Brice was the booming town of Silver City, Idaho. A place he had read and heard about as a ghost town his entire life.

Only the town below was far, far from a ghost town.

"How about we head back in and get that food Bonnie's started on," Duster said. "Damn cold out here."

"That's real?" Brice asked, pointing down the hill at the town.

"Very real," Duster said. "This is 1878, identical in all ways to the 1878 of our timeline. Maybe in this timeline someone got stuck in traffic and in our timeline they didn't."

"No differences at all?" Brice asked as they turned back to the rock and Duster, with a quick look around, opened it.

"I've been into the past in hundreds of different timelines," Duster said, "and never once saw a difference from ours, until I returned to our timeline after building the lodge and someone had built it in our timeline as well."

Duster stepped through the door.

Brice followed with one last look around at the blowing snow and the barren hillside where the Cadillac should be parked in trees.

He had about a thousand questions, he was sure.

As soon as his mind returned and started to actually work again.

Chapter Twelve

October 14, 1878
Dixie's Timeline

"THESE THIN COTTON dresses are far too light for this weather," Bonnie said. "This is dangerous. Ready to head in?"

Dixie had been shivering for the entire time they had been out in the snowstorm, but she wasn't sure if it was from the cold or the shock of what she was seeing. Bonnie had had her put on an 1880s style dress over her clothes without buttoning it in the back.

Bonnie had done the same thing, saying it was just in case someone saw them from a distance.

Dixie just couldn't believe they were actually going out of the mine into 1878, but she was still numb from Duster disappearing in the big crystal cavern.

After Bonnie checked to see if anyone was nearby through a scope and showed Dixie how to use it, she had opened the door and they had stepped out into blowing snow.

And out there Dixie had seen things that didn't seem possible, such as a real town where a ghost town had been before. And no trees where the Cadillac had been, and the cabin looked much newer and still had windows.

Bonnie quickly checked around for anyone watching and opened back up the rock and they stepped back inside.

For a moment they were in pitch darkness before the light came up and the door to the mine opened.

"Wow, was that cold," Bonnie said. "Duster could have dialed us in a summer month just as easy."

"It wouldn't have been as believable," Dixie said, following Bonnie down the mine tunnel and into the mountain.

"Maybe not," Bonnie said, "but it would have been warmer."

They quickly put the dresses back on the rack, then headed back out into the beautiful crystal cavern.

Dixie was still shivering from the cold and was blowing on her hands when she followed Bonnie into the big glowing cavern.

She made it two steps before stopping and just staring again.

"Come on," Bonnie said. "Hot drinks are waiting for us in our timeline in the future."

Dixie nodded and got herself moving and over to the table.

"Put your hand on the box," Bonnie said.

Dixie put her hand beside Bonnie's hand.

Bonnie pulled a wire from the box, then quickly slipped on some leather gloves and removed one wire clamp from the crystal.

"I'll label it later," she said.

She came back over to the box and unhooked the other wire, then took Dixie by the arm. "Let's get something warm, what do you say?"

"Where is Duster?" Dixie asked.

"He better damn well be two minutes and fifteen seconds into making us some food and something warm to drink."

"Oh," was all Dixie could say.

She was still shaking and she still wasn't sure if it was from the cold or information overload.

She had just taken a round trip to 1878.

In another timeline.

How in the hell was that even possible?

She knew the math she had worked on for the last year said it was possible.

In theory.

But reality was another matter all together.

Chapter Thirteen

July 8th, 2016
Brice's Timeline

BRICE FOLLOWED DUSTER out of the crystal cavern and into the storage cavern. Part of Brice's mind wasn't allowing him to accept what he had just seen, and the other part of him was slowly getting excited.

He had just traveled in time, traveled to another alternate timeline. How incredible was that?

But it couldn't really have happened.

It just couldn't.

Bonnie was in the modern kitchen area of the big cavern, working at the counter with her back to them.

There was a steaming mug of hot chocolate in front of one chair at the big table and Duster took that chair and wrapped his hands around the mug. Brice's bottle of water was still sitting where he had left it.

"Wasn't sure if you wanted some hot chocolate, tea, or coffee," Bonnie said, glancing over her shoulder at Brice. "Coffee is going to be instant."

"Hot chocolate sounds great," Brice said, sitting so he could face Duster and Bonnie across the big wooden table.

The hot chocolate smelled wonderful and rich and Bonnie took a mug of steaming water out of the microwave and stirred in a spoon-full of mix and set it in front of him. Then she went back over a cabinet, took out a pack of small marshmallows and tossed it onto the table in front of them before going back to what she was doing.

"Hard to imagine we need hot chocolate to warm up in July, isn't it?" Duster asked.

Brice still felt chilled to the bone from the short trip outside. "It is," Brice said, dropping some marshmallows into his cup and then blowing on it to cool it all a little before sipping the rich, thick drink.

It warmed him some, but not all the way yet.

"So, ask anything you want," Bonnie said without turning around.

Brice looked at the two of them. Clearly they had lived a very, very long time, as they had said, in different timelines. So there was one thing right off that bothered him more than anything else.

"So why exactly did you hire me?"

Duster laughed and Bonnie just shook her head without turning from the sandwiches she worked on.

"Not the question we were expecting," Duster said. He sipped on his hot chocolate, then set it down. "We hired you because of that lodge appearing in our timeline. We are clearly not seeing the math of how that can happen."

Brice nodded. "Mathematically, from everything I have been working on with your original calculations, it can't happen."

"Exactly," Bonnie said, turning and putting a sandwich in front of Duster, then Brice. "We hired you because we wanted fresh eyes, a fresh mind on this problem."

Brice sat back, holding the hot chocolate in his hand. "Each crystal out there is the physical manifestation of a timeline. At least from the math you two have worked out and I checked."

Both nodded, but said nothing, letting him go on.

"Even though it may seem like a lot," Brice said, "there are a finite number of crystals in that one cavern. All of the crystals in that room are worlds that are very, very similar, down to almost every detail."

"Indistinguishable," Bonnie said, nodding.

Brice was now, as far as he was concerned, back working in theoretical form. For the moment he was going to let the fact that he had actually traveled to another timeline just sit.

"So the math is firm on the fact that if someone in this timeline attached to a crystal in that room," Brice said, "and the same person in another timeline did the same, a new timeline would form that would allow both to go to that timeline, and not meet themselves."

"Yes," Bonnie said. "And we tried once to stay past our own birthdates and we found ourselves back here. The time-line spit us out, in other words. Time does not allow the same person, in any form, to be duplicated in a timeline."

Brice nodded. "From the math you both knew that would happen, correct?"

"We wanted to test it," Duster said, nodding.

Brice took another sip of the hot choc-olate. He was finally starting to warm up.

"So you hired me to determine the math that explains why you could re-member the lodge always existing and the lodge not existing at the same time. Correct?"

Both Bonnie and Duster nodded.

"We were stumped and still are," Duster said.

Brice forced himself to take a deep breath. Having two of the greatest math brains to have ever existed say they were stumped was something to hear.

"We think you are on the right track," Bonnie said. "That's why we wanted to show you the reality of all this, to maybe help you jump to the answer."

"It's going to take a bit for the reality of this to settle in," Brice said, indicating the cave around him.

"Yeah, it would at that," Bonnie said. "Duster, how about you take Brice back to say 1901 Boise for a late sum-mer and early fall? Boise is always so beautiful in the fall. That will give Brice time to think. The Idanha Hotel is wonderful."

Brice knew the Idanha Hotel. It was a classic landmark in Boise and it had been renovated and saved a few years back. It had been built in 1900, so it would be in its first full year of operation. It was a stunning place renovated, at least from the outside. Brice could only imagine what it looked like in 1901.

"There's no need to do that," Brice said.

Duster laughed. "I got a guy who gets shot in Flagstaff in October 1901 that I wouldn't mind trying to rescue in a few timelines. So we go back in the middle of August and that will give me enough time to get to Flagstaff."

Bonnie laughed. "Whatever you want, Marshal," she said. "But leave Brice in Boise, at the Idanha Hotel, to think on his own and get used to the past and the idea of all of this."

"How's that sound?" Duster asked, turning to Brice. "You up for a couple months in a fancy hotel, getting used to the reality of all that math you've been working on?"

Brice nodded, but his stomach clamped up tight at the very idea.

"Finish your sandwiches," Bonnie said, pointing to the half-finished sand-wich in front of Brice. "I'll make you some traveling food while you get ready and I'll do the dishes and clean up while you are gone."

That startled Brice even more. He could spend a few months in the past and only slightly over two minutes would pass here.

He would only age a few minutes.

He knew that from the math he had done.

Damn, reality was confusing at times.

Chapter Fourteen

July 8th, 2016
Dixie's Timeline

DIXIE WATCHED as Duster appeared touching the wooden box on the table in the vast crystal cavern. He took a glove and carefully undid one wire only from the box, then stepped away, leaving the wires all attached to the same crystal on the wall.

He carefully adjusted the dial on the machine just slightly.

"Two horses are tied up outside the shed and saddles and some extra supplies are in the mine shaft near the door," Duster said. "The horses should be fine there for a couple of days. They have enough food and water. And the weather is good, not too hot."

"Thank you, dear, for doing that for us," Bonnie said, kissing Duster.

"My pleasure," Duster said.

Dixie just shook her head. After agreeing to go with Bonnie to spend a few fall months in a Boise hotel in 1901 to get used to all this, Duster had offered to jump back ahead of them and get them a couple of horses and supplies. In 1901 Silver City was in sharp decline and it would be difficult to get horses.

Dixie was surprised. It seemed they had figured out a way to time their arrival into the past timelines to the day. And it was easier and safer for a man in 1901 to buy horses and supplies than a lady.

So in the two minutes and fifteen seconds they had waited in the crystal cavern, Duster had spent part of a summer in 1901.

Bonnie said that more than likely he spent it playing poker and drinking at the Idanha Hotel in Boise, since he loved the place. And he said he had made reservations for them.

Dixie was shocked that Bonnie said something like that so calmly. But after being together for maybe upward of a thousand lived years, they clearly understood each other.

Dixie only hoped that some day she would meet a person that would understand her. So far, her love life had consisted of a few boyfriends who eventually got bored and left after a year and a few short-lived flings. Not much else, since school had kept her so busy and focused.

Now, because of all that work, she stood in an underground cavern that seemed to be the very nexus of time dressed as a woman from 1900. She was wearing riding clothes that a woman of the time would wear, with black leather pants, a very puffy white blouse, and riding boots.

Duster and Bonnie had hoped she would come along on this and had ordered her a wardrobe of period clothing, from underwear to make-up and hair products and hats to keep her shaded. It all surprisingly fit very well.

At five four, finding clothes that fit was often a challenge for her.

They were going to let her take sunscreen and normal sports bras and her own underwear along with period underwear, plus a few other pieces of clothing, but the modern stuff had to remain very hidden.

Bonnie planned on getting Dixie settled in the Idanha Hotel in Boise, then go on down to San Francisco for a few months. She hadn't said why and Duster hadn't asked. He did say he would try to do some of the dishes while they were gone.

Dixie would have diaries from the times that women used to write in and would be able to make notes the entire time. Bonnie told her to write down everything to make it real when she got back.

Dixie couldn't imagine actually living for a full two months, yet only have a few minutes pass.

Really hard to grasp that concept just yet.

Dixie stood beside the big table in the crystal room, studying everything. The wires from the machine were still hooked up to a crystal about six feet up the wall near the table. When Duster had returned, he had only taken off one wire from the machine. So they were jumping back into the same timeline he had just left, only a day after he left.

She understood the math and theory of that as well, but again the reality of it scared hell out of her.

"Got your keys?" Duster asked.

Dixie nodded. Duster had given her two keys to the mine and had shown her where the spare was hidden up the slope if anything happened to Bonnie. The plan was that if Bonnie didn't return to Boise by October 15th, Dixie was to come to Silver City, not let anyone see her climb to the mine, and pull a wire from the machine. That would bring both of them back, no matter what had happened to Bonnie.

So that would leave Dixie alone for about two months in 1901 in Boise, Idaho, since they were going back on August 10th.

"Ready for an adventure?" Bonnie asked Dixie, smiling.

Dixie managed to nod, or at least she hoped she did. Her mind was on auto-pilot and her stomach was twisted in a knot.

"Touch the box," Bonnie said and Dixie did.

"Have fun," Duster said, smiling at them.

"Back in a few minutes," Bonnie said and hooked up the wire.

Duster vanished and Bonnie stepped back from the machine.

"Let's go see if we hit the right time and those horses are there," Bonnie said, turning and heading for the door to the cavern that was standing open.

Dixie stepped back and forced herself to take a deep breath. She wasn't sure if she wanted to know if it really was August 10th, 1901.

Chapter Fifteen

August 15th, 1901
Brice's Timeline

BRICE FOLLOWED DUSTER along the trail down the hill away from the mine. Duster had spent part of the morning telling Brice all the tricks to getting back to the mine without being seen in case something happened to him.

And he had given him two of the strange-looking skeleton keys to the mine and showed him how to find the hidden key up the hill above the mine.

Then they headed along a trail away from the mine. Both had on the long oilcloth coats, cowboy hats, jeans, and cowboy boots. They both had packed saddlebags over their shoulders.

Brice was surprised that even though the day was hot, the light oilcloth long coat seemed to keep him cooler by keeping the sun from him. The saddlebag was packed with money, some gold, and a few changes of clothes. Everything else he would buy on the way to Boise or in Boise after he got there. Duster was funding the entire trip and didn't seem worried at all about money.

"I'll explain all that to you at some point in the future," Duster had said, waving off his money questions when Brice saw how much money he was carrying in his saddlebags in hidden pockets. "You're here to just rest, think, and try to figure out why we can remember that lodge being built."

It took them about two hours to hike down to a small ranch where Duster bought them two horses and saddles. So it was only a little after two in the afternoon when they headed up the hill and out of the Silver City valley.

It had been a while since Brice had ridden a horse, and after the first hour he asked Duster if they could walk for a while.

Duster had just laughed and agreed. "Takes some getting used to."

They alternated walking and riding, not seeing hardly anyone else, until they were down on the Snake River right before dusk. Brice felt like he had been through a beating, and every muscle in his back and legs ached.

Duster quickly showed Brice how to take care of the horses for the night, then started a fire and got them the two sandwiches Bonnie had made and packed for them. After eating in mostly silence, they both rolled out the bedding they had brought on either side of the fire.

The ground was hard, but Brice didn't care he was so tired.

He put his head on his saddlebag and the next thing he knew Duster was working the fire to get some coffee brewing and the sun was starting to color the sky in the east.

Duster managed a decent cup of coffee somehow over that fire and they again ate sandwiches and packed food. "No point in cooking for just the two of us," Duster had said.

Brice walked around and stretched while eating and sipping the coffee and by the time they broke camp, he was feeling a little better.

They rode for an hour, walked a half-hour, rode for an hour, not really stopping for anything. They ate as they walked and talked, Duster mostly pointing out landmarks that would allow Brice to get back to Silver City from Boise on his own if he needed to.

In 1901, the road system was fairly well developed for farm wagons, and farms dotted the landscape along the river edges and up on the flats on the other side of the river once they got across on a ferry.

Just before dusk they rode into Caldwell, Idaho, and gave their horses to a stable to take care of for the night.

Compared to the Caldwell that Brice knew, this town was nothing more than a small farming town tucked in a shallow valley. But it did have a small hotel that Duster paid for rooms in.

For the second day, Brice was so tired he could barely walk. He had prided himself on being in good condition, being a runner, exercising regularly. But he was in good condition for 2016, not 1901. And none of this seemed to bother Duster at all.

"There should be water and towels in your room," Duster said as they headed up the stairs, carrying their saddlebags. "Wash up and meet me near the front desk in fifteen minutes and we'll get some dinner. And bring that saddlebag."

Brice nodded and fifteen minutes later he found himself across the street from the hotel in a small restaurant with check-ered cloth table coverings and cloth nap-kins and silverware. He felt better at least getting one layer of the dirt off.

They mostly ate in silence, since there were people close to them at another table. But Brice had to admit, the rib-eye steak was about as good as he had ever tasted. And the fresh bread seemed to melt in his mouth.

He had made a comment about how good the food tasted and Duster had just laughed. "Wait until you get to Boise."

He hadn't said anything else.

The next morning at sunrise, after a breakfast of eggs, ham, and coffee, they were again saddled up and heading toward Boise.

To Brice, it flat didn't matter that he had slept on a feather bed in a small ho-tel or on hard dirt next to a river. He had slept like the dead both times.

And felt just as beat up the next morn-ing.

He had really, really been kidding himself when he thought he was in good condition before this trip. He was a com-puter math geek and this trip was point-ing that out clearly.

And painfully.

Chapter Sixteen

August 13th, 1901
Dixie's Timeline

DIXIE COULDN'T BELIEVE that they had finally made it to Boise. She had never considered herself out of shape, but after the first day walking and riding, she felt like an entire football team had run over her in band practice.

She had thought she was good at rid-ing horses, but it became quickly clear that it was one thing to ride a horse for thirty minutes or an hour in a modern saddle on flat ground, another thing com-pletely to ride a horse over rough ground with a 1900's saddle.

Parts of her body hurt she didn't know could hurt.

And after sleeping on the hard ground and a second day of travel, the torture was just getting worse. The water to clean off and the good dinner and the feather bed in the hotel in Caldwell had helped some, but not a lot.

She and Bonnie had talked a lot about the problems a woman had in 1901 as they walked, and the problems Dixie was going to have as a small woman. For the first bit of time Dixie would need to just stay close to the ho-tel in Boise and one or two restaurants until she became more comfortable with everything.

Boise in 1901 was very civilized and law-abiding, but it was still the Old West. Women would get the right to vote in Idaho in a few years, one of the first states to do so. So women had respect, but still being careful was the key.

They also talked about how memory was permanent from these trips, not physical aspects. Bonnie stressed that a few times and wouldn't go any farther than "You'll see."

After the two days of riding and tor-ture, Dixie had every plan on staying mostly in the hotel and just thinking while Bonnie was down in San Francisco.

She had remembered seeing the big stone Idanha Hotel over the last year, but it had been one of those old buildings in downtown Boise she had paid little inter-est to. So she really knew nothing about where they were heading or where she would be staying.

But no matter where she ended up staying, she really, really needed to let the reality that she was in the past in a different timeline sink in. Until that happened, she had no real hope of actually helping Bonnie and Duster with the math issues of what had happened with the big lodge.

A lodge that wouldn't even be built for a year or two yet.

The day was warm and they had been riding along the Boise River for a number of miles on a wide wagon trail before finally reaching the center of town.

Families in wagons had passed them going in the other direction and a number of men had passed as well, tipping their hats as they went past. Bonnie had told Dixie to not look directly at the men, but just nod in return.

"That's the Idanha Hotel," Bonnie said as they rode into the edge of the larger downtown area, pointing to a massive red brick and stone building that seemed to tower over the other buildings. It also had four turrets with flags on top of them and Dixie could only imagine the rooms in those rounded turrets.

"Wow," was all Dixie could say.

Bonnie smiled. "Wait until you see the inside of the place. Duster loves staying there and playing poker, since there's a major poker room in the basement. I like it as well, but it's not as nice as the places I stay in San Francisco."

Again, Dixie decided to not ask why Bonnie was going there. Instead Dixie just studied all the stone and wooden buildings making up the downtown area. Most of them were two stories tall and the center of the town seemed to be along a wide street she remembered as Main Street.

They took their horses to the stable behind the hotel and left them there, taking their saddlebags and moving around the edge of the building to the front entrance on the corner with Main Street.

The road was still dirt and very wide, but very smooth and not really dusty, which surprised Dixie. The sidewalk was mostly stone and around town there were many, many bicycles leaning against buildings and very few horses other than ones pulling large wagons.

The downtown area seemed to hum with a slow-moving business.

All the men seemed to be dressed in dark suits with vests and the woman were all in long cloth dresses, other than a few who were also dressed in leather riding pants as she and Bonnie were.

There was no doubt, standing there on those stone front steps, that Dixie was in the real past. Even the heat and the smells of the horses coming from different directions made it seem very, very real.

Bonnie took Dixie's arm and turned her toward the front door. They went up the front stone stairs and through two massive wooden and glass doors. Inside, the huge space took Dixie's breath away. The floors were a mosaic Italian marble tile, and the towering ceilings were polished oak layered in between stone columns.

It was designed to just flat be stunning and it stunned Dixie.

A number of comfortable-looking seating areas with couches and chairs were scattered through the large lobby on area carpets, giving the place a comfortable feel. Light streamed through the huge windows on two sides making the inside almost as bright as the summer day outside.

Numbers of men sat reading papers, and a few women sat knitting around the lobby. Again all the men wore dark suits with vests and most of them had watch chains hanging from the vest pockets. The woman all wore long dresses that clearly had petticoats under them.

On one side of the lobby to the back was a metal cage that seemed to be an elevator with the name Otis stamped above the door. Dixie had no idea elevators had been invented in 1901, let alone had made it to Idaho.

A grand marble staircase curved upward near the metal exposed elevator. It was wide and bright and six people could stand on one stair and not touch.

An ornate oak front desk ran along one wall on the far side of a massive field of marble tile with two men in suits behind it. On the wall behind the desk were a massive number of mail boxes for each room.

"How many rooms does this place have?" Dixie whispered to Bonnie as they walked across the tile toward the front desk.

"One hundred and forty," Bonnie said. "All wonderful."

The two men at the front desk smiled at them and greeted them.

"We have a reservation," Bonnie said. "I assume for two suites. The names are Mrs. Bonnie Kendal and Mrs. Dixie Smith."

Dixie was shocked for a second about how Bonnie had given her name, but then realized that having a pretend husband more than likely made her safer.

Both men smiled again and nodded. "We were expecting you. Both of your suites are ready and paid for completely."

Duster had clearly set all this up ahead.

They both signed the huge ledger, Dixie making sure she signed it Mrs.

W.D. Smith and beside her Bonnie nodded and said nothing.

The man behind the desk gave them their keys and told them their room numbers on the sixth floor. Then asked where their luggage might be to take to their rooms.

"It will be coming along in a few days. It was delayed, so we plan on doing a lot of shopping between now and then," Bonnie said, laughing and smiling at the two men. "So thank you, we are fine."

Dixie was impressed at how smoothly Bonnie said exactly the right things. Women of the time were expected to travel with large trunks and a lot of clothing.

Still carrying only their saddlebags, they turned and headed for the staircase and elevator.

"We don't plan on riding that, do we?" Dixie asked.

Bonnie laughed. "Not a chance. Safety brakes are still a thing of the future."

"Oh, thank you," Dixie said.

The climb to the sixth floor was actually fairly easy. Maybe she was starting to get in better shape after the last two days.

Or maybe she was just too tired to care anymore. That seemed more likely.

Chapter Seventeen

August 17th, 1901
Brice's Timeline

BRICE WAS STUNNED at everything about the big Idanha Hotel. The ornate lobby, the fact that it had an elevator, and now the suite he was to stay in on the sixth floor. For the time he was going to be in this suite, this must be costing a fortune. Yet Duster planned on keeping his corner suite on the sixth floor the entire time he was gone as well.

When Brice had asked him why, Duster had shrugged and said simply, "Never know when I might get back."

The hallway at the top of the stairs on the sixth floor went off in two directions. It was carpeted with a flower-patterned carpet of blue and orange that actually fit the décor of oak columns and patterned wallpaper.

Each door was of solid oak and sconces dotted the walls between each door, clearly electrical. The hotel had named all the rooms on the sixth floor instead of numbering them. Each name was screwed on the door with a decorative bronze plaque.

Brice's suite was on the south corner of the building and was called Lost River. The suite had a large living room area that extended out into the turret area with a view through the tall windows that looked out over parts of the growing town and the city.

The ceilings in the room were a good twelve feet high and a faint blue-flowered wallpaper covered the walls.

Since it was a corner room, lower parts of the windows opened on both sides of the room allowing a breeze to go through the room and keep it surprisingly cool.

An oak writing desk was tucked to one side of the living room and a large oak table filled the turret area. Brice had a hunch he would be using that table a great deal over the next two months.

The bed was a huge four-poster made out of polished oak that dominated the bedroom part of the suite and off that room was a washroom with a sink, a large metal tub, running water, and a toilet with a water tank high on the wall. For some reason that toilet actually in the room surprised Brice.

He clearly needed to learn a lot about when things were invented and what was new. In all the years of math, it had never once dawned on him that he needed to learn details of history for his future job.

Duster had left him to wash up and get settled in his room. Since Brice didn't have many clothes, just one suit and vest, there wasn't much to hang up or put in the big chest of drawers in the bedroom.

He stripped down to his underwear and used the sink and washcloth to wash off the trail grime as best he could. Later tonight he would take a bath to really get clean.

Then he dressed in his black jeans, a dress shirt, a vest, and his suit jacket. He actually looked exactly like every other gentleman on the street, which surprised him.

He left his cowboy hat and oilcloth duster on the hanger near the front door.

He pulled on clean socks and his cowboy boots and was just standing when Duster knocked at his door. Duster's suite was called Game Lake and was down the wide carpeted hallway on the west corner of the building.

Brice opened the door and Duster came in.

Duster had on a suit jacket as well and a dress shirt, but he also wore his cowboy hat and oilcloth duster, open down the front.

Duster just seemed comfortable with that look.

"Saddle bags?" Duster asked.

Brice pointed to them on the top of an oak table near the door. Other than unpack some clothes and empty out his trail food supplies, he hadn't done anything with them yet.

"Carry about fifty dollars on you at all times and one of the keys," Duster said. "Remember how far a simple dime goes in this time period."

Brice nodded. Duster had given him that talk on the way here yesterday and he had already pulled the fifty dollars.

"The gold and the rest of the money you need to hide," Duster said. "Nothing worse than being back here and out of money, trust me."

Brice looked around, but the only places he saw right off to hide anything would be the obvious places.

"Dig the money and gold out and divide it up into three parts after you take out the fifty dollars," Duster said. "If you need to cash in the gold, there's an assay office down the street a few blocks."

Brice took the money out of the hidden pocket of his saddlebag and spread it on the table. The pocket was designed into the saddlebag by Duster and was invisible to almost all searches.

"Leave a third in the saddlebag in the pocket," Duster said.

Brice did that and Duster took the saddlebag and draped it over a chair near the bed in plain sight.

"Since it's empty, not a lot of use to some thief and easy to identify." Duster pointed to Brice's initials that were stitched in clear letters on both sides of the saddlebag. "So no one would take it."

That made perfect sense to Brice.

"Grab another third of that and follow me."

Brice did as he was told, carrying a good five hundred in bills and some gold about the size of his large finger. From what Duster had told him, the money he was carrying would buy a couple really nice homes in this time period.

Duster pointed to the sink attached to the wall in the bathroom. "Take a look up under there."

Brice got down on his knees on the blue tile of the bathroom and looked up at the underside of the sink. It was molded metal in the shape of the sink and not finished on the underside.

"See the lip around the edge?" Duster asked.

It took a moment for Brice to see it, but then he spotted how the front and side edges of the sink were curled up under the sink to give the sink a rounded bottom look, even to someone sitting low in the bathtub.

That rounded bottom edge that was turned up formed a nice gutter. Brice put the money in under that edge on the bathtub side of the sink, making sure it was tucked down tight.

"That's pretty nifty," Brice said, standing and brushing off his knees.

Duster nodded. "Both crooks and regular people don't know that's there, so never use it."

"So what do I do with the last third?" Brice asked.

"We give it to the front desk to put in the safe," Duster said. "They would expect us, as men of means renting these suites, to do exactly that. And also, anyone watching knows we have left no money in our room, so no point in breaking in."

"I'm guessing all this came from hard knocks early on," Brice said.

"More than I care to remember," Duster said. "So let's go give this money to the front desk and I'll show you the best steaks in all of Boise about three blocks from here."

"Sounds perfect," Brice said, realizing he really was hungry.

He was finally starting to relax a little and realize just where he was. And that he was going to live for almost two months here in this room, in this town, in this time, in this timeline, while only two minutes and fifteen seconds passed.

Chapter Eighteen

August 15th, 1901
Dixie's Timeline

AFTER DIXIE WASHED up and got ready to go out for dinner in her one good dress she had packed in her saddlebag, Bonnie had shown her how to hide two-thirds of her money and on the way to dinner they had checked the other third with the hotel front desk.

Bonnie had Dixie carry at least fifty dollars, but only ten of it in her purse, the rest of it in a garter under her dress. It was not a good idea for women to carry a lot of money in this time period, and ten dollars was almost too much, since dinner was going to cost them about fifty cents each in the hotel dining room overlooking Main Street.

Besides that, they would just charge the meal to their rooms.

Dixie's suite was in the north corner of the building and was called Avalanche Creek while Bonnie's suite was in the east corner of the sixth floor and was named Dutch Flat. For some reason, numbers didn't suit this hotel.

The view from Dixie's windows over the town and part of the valley was flat amazing. She had relaxed after getting cleaned up and seeing the wonderful suite. It would not be a hardship at all to stay for a few months in this suite and work on really understanding the math problems that Bonnie and Duster faced.

Bonnie said it was amazing how at times, simply sitting and thinking added more insight into a math problem than hours crunching numbers on major computers.

Dixie agreed with that.

The dining room of the hotel was a large, high-ceilinged room of cloth-covered tables and high chairs and waiters with tuxedos. Of the forty tables, only about a third were occupied during the dinner hour and no one was close enough to them that they had to worry about being overheard.

Plus the evening was warm, so Dixie decided that after Bonnie left she would have dinner in her room with the cross breeze between the windows.

They talked about some of the things Dixie needed to be careful of, and a few times with a waiter close by Dixie had to whisper a question to Bonnie about what was standard behavior for eye contact for a woman in this time in a restaurant, what was the right fork, or when to eat and not eat, including where to place her napkin.

It was one thing to eat in a formal restaurant in 2016, another to eat in one in 1901. But somehow she managed to not make any major mistakes and Bonnie assured her she would be fine.

After a wonderful dinner of fresh-caught mountain trout and creamy potatoes in a rich garlic sauce, Dixie felt almost human.

Back in the suite, Dixie took a long bath. The staff brought in three heated containers of water and it felt heavenly.

After her bath, she barely managed to crawl into bed before she fell asleep, the big featherbed holding her like a mother holds a child.

The sun streaming in the big windows woke her just after dawn. She managed to get her long red hair up on the top of her head and dressed in her riding clothes before Bonnie got there.

After a wonderful breakfast of ham and eggs served to them in Bonnie's suite by the staff, they went shopping and bought Dixie a full wardrobe of dresses and shoes and petticoats.

Bonnie didn't buy anything for herself, saying that she would do so when she reached San Francisco. And she told Dixie that she should save the clothes and they would take some of them with them to the mine to take back for future trips into the past.

That was the first time that Dixie had thought about going into the past more than this once. It sort of startled her and she decided she would think about that after the next two months.

She had a lot of things to think about. More than she could have ever imagined.

Chapter Nineteen

August 18th, 1901
Brice's Timeline

DUSTER HAD LEFT early in the morning, heading out to Arizona.

For the first two hours, Brice had just sat in his room, feeling panicked and very much alone. Duster had done everything he could to help Brice get ready, including helping him shop for more men's clothes of the time.

And for two days they had eaten in a different restaurant every meal, getting Brice used to the different places close to the hotel.

Now, Brice was alone in the past, in a different timeline, and he had to admit, scared to death.

Finally, after a couple of hours, he started to get hungry. He knew he needed to get some lunch. He had decided that for the first day or so he would just stay in the hotel and get used to things. He and Duster hadn't even eaten in the hotel restaurant, but Duster had said it was good food.

Right now Brice decided that he needed to stay in the hotel, do some thinking, take some notes, get his nerves back.

Brice checked his pocket watch. It was almost eleven and the dining room downstairs would be opening for lunch soon. He and Duster had bought him a few journals that would be suited for a man taking notes. Duster also bought him a couple of the nicest fountain pens and refilling ink. And a few pencils as well.

After a few tries, Brice discovered, to his surprise, he liked the feel of the fountain pens. So he made sure one pen was full of ink, then took it and his journal down the six flights of stone stairs to the main lobby and into the dining room.

The big dining room was wonderful and comfortable and surprised him with its feel. It had very high ceilings and high windows framed in polished oak. The tables were covered in fine linen tablecloths and each table had a single flower in a crystal vase in the center.

A large fireplace dominated one wall, but wasn't lit. More than likely that fireplace in the winter kept this room very comfortable.

The higher parts of the windows had been opened which allowed the air to move through the room, keeping it fairly cool even though the day outside promised to be warm.

Brice took a seat near the window on the Main Street side, his back to the wall and out of the sun. Not only from there could he see anything in the restaurant, but he could also watch the traffic on the boardwalk outside and in the wide Main Street.

He opened his journal and titled the page with the date, August 18, 1901, and his location and the time. Then he closed the journal and placed the pen on top of it and just sat back.

He really, really needed to calm down. But in all his life he had never felt so alone and helpless. He felt more like he had been dumped in a distant country.

This traveling in time and crossing timelines was very real. And the world around him was very real. The only thing that made it different than his timeline was his presence and Duster's presence.

And if neither of them did anything to really change this timeline, it would remain the same as their own completely.

Of course, with infinite amount of timelines, in some timelines he and Duster would change something.

But that didn't really matter. With an infinite number of timelines and every person making thousands of choices every day, no one timeline was the right timeline. Brice knew that from his math.

But hard to convince his surface mind.

A waiter soon took his order for a beef sandwich and an iced tea with real ice chipped off of stored ice two stories down in cool cellars under the hotel. It was expensive, but as Duster had convinced him, they could afford it without a problem. Brice needed to act like a man of means.

You don't stay for a few months in one of the most expensive suites in the new state and not act the part.

Brice was about to open his notebook again when a very short, and very stunning woman with bright red hair and light skin came into the restaurant alone.

She had her hair up and never even looked around, just straight ahead.

One of the waiters bowed slightly to her, and she smiled and nodded her thanks.

The smile about took Brice's breath away.

He watched her every move as the waiter showed her to a table on the far wall, directly across from Brice, and held the chair for her until she was seated.

She couldn't be any more than a few inches over five foot tall, and from what Brice could see, her hair was held fashionably on the top of her head with some decorative barrettes made of some sort of bone.

She also looked uncomfortable and slightly unsure of herself.

She had been carrying a small journal and a fountain pen and placed both on the table in front of her.

Then she took a deep breath that made Brice catch his breath.

He couldn't remember when he had had a reaction to just seeing a woman like this. He had had his share of girlfriends through college, but most had found him dull, since his focus was on his studies so much.

And he had never been much of a drinker and he found parties boring to the extreme. So what few women in college who had made it clear to him that they were interested soon dropped their interest after a couple months of fun sex.

So this reaction to a woman was unusual for him.

And then he realized exactly where he was.

It was 1901.

This woman had been dead in his timeline for half a century, if not more. She was more like the age of his great-great grandmother.

And besides that, he would have no idea how to meet a woman of this time.

He just shook his head and opened the journal and marked down his thoughts.

He hoped she was staying for at least a few days. Her beauty from a distance would give him the distraction he needed to get calmed down and thinking about math.

Chapter Twenty

August 18th, 1901
Dixie's Timeline

BONNIE HAD LEFT two days before, heading to San Francisco, and today was the first day Dixie felt brave enough to even leave her room and go down and eat in the hotel dining room on her own. She had decided that lunch would be the safest and less crowded of the times. And so far she had been right. Only a few people were in the dining room and she didn't look at them.

She had been taking her meals in her room and just letting herself relax and watch the town and the street below her window. She hadn't gotten her mind clear enough yet to even think about the math problem at hand, but she had a hunch that given a little more time, she would be bored enough and settled enough to do just that.

She reached the dining room shortly after it opened and was greeted by a wait-er that remembered her from the number of times she ate here with Bonnie.

Dixie asked for a table facing the restaurant with her back to the wall and he showed her across the room to a wonderful table that also allowed her to see Main Street outside the big windows.

The dining room was still cool, but she could tell that by dinner it would be too hot to eat here. Until the weather changed, she would take breakfast and lunch here, but not dinner.

She placed her journal and pen on the table in front of her and took a deep breath to get herself to relax. Then she looked around at the others in the dining room with her.

An elderly couple clearly of means sat together near the front windows not talking. Two men were engaged in a hushed conversation at another table, more focused on what they were saying than anything else around them.

And against the far wall directly across from her sat a man with short brown hair and chiseled features that took her breath away. He was bent forward slightly writing in a journal. He had on a clearly expensive suit and wore it like he had been born in it.

Her breath seemed to catch in her throat and she could feel her heart start to race. Not out of fear, but out of excitement just looking at him.

She stared at him for a moment, stunned at how strong her reaction to him was. She had to force herself to just take a breath. And she could feel her face getting flushed.

She had never felt that kind of reaction to just seeing a man before, let alone a man who, in her timeline, had been dead for more years than she wanted to think about.

Bonnie had given her no pointers at all about meeting men in this time period. And just the idea of that scared Dixie more than she wanted to admit. She wasn't any good at meeting men in her own time. What would she talk about with a man born in the eighteen hundreds?

But still, she had never had that kind of reaction to just seeing a man before. She flat couldn't look away from him, and didn't want to.

The waiter approached the man and set down a glass of tea with real ice chips in it. Bonnie had her order that as well every time they had come in here because it was a status thing. Ice in the Old West in the summer was expensive.

So clearly the man had a lot of money.

He glanced up at the waiter and smiled and Dixie damn near fainted. The man was more handsome than anyone she had ever seen. And his smile showed perfect, white teeth and reached his eyes, as if he smiled often.

Then he did what she had not expected. As he took a sip of his iced tea, he looked at her.

She had no idea what was appropriate, but she just couldn't look away, and it seemed he couldn't either.

Finally, after what seemed like too long a time, and yet was far too short a time, she forced herself to look down at her leather journal. She could see out of the corner of her eye that he almost spilled his tea trying to put the glass down.

She knew her face was flushed red and that he could see it since she had such damned white skin.

What was happening? How could she fall at first sight for a man in 1901?

Did jumping timelines cause sane judgment to fly out the window?

Chapter Twenty-one

August 19th, 1901
Brice's Timeline

AFTER THE EYE contact with the stunning woman across the dining room, Brice decided that for dinner his best option was to just avoid the dining room in the hotel and any chance of seeing that woman again. He couldn't believe how attracted to her he was.

Never had he felt anything like that.

And when they held each other's gaze, he felt excited and scared to death at the same time. He desperately wanted to just walk over to her and introduce himself, but he had no doubt that alone might get him kicked out of the hotel.

He was way over his head even talking with a woman from this time period, let alone being interested in one.

They had both spent the rest of their lunch writing in their notebooks and avoiding any sort of eye contact. Clearly she had found him attractive as well.

That seemed very dangerous for her in 1901.

One thing was for certain, though. She had certainly taken his mind from being alone.

For dinner he went down the street to a steak restaurant, but the next morning he went down to the hotel dining room just as they opened at six in the morning and took the same seat he had from the day before.

The huge dining room was almost chilly from the cool summer evening and the open windows. It felt great, since yesterday evening he had found himself stripped down to his shorts with the windows open in his suite to stay even slightly cool.

And he had taken a cool bath, without any hot water from the staff, and that had felt good as well.

The entire time, as he was trying to focus his attention on the math problem he faced, he couldn't get the face of the woman from his mind. He hoped she would be at breakfast.

And he hoped she wouldn't be at the same time.

Since he was one of the first in the door, she was nowhere to be seen. He felt the disappointment and was surprised at that feeling. In fact, he was amazed at himself for having this reaction to a woman, especially a rich woman from 1901.

Ten minutes after he sat down and ordered his coffee, she appeared, again alone, and was shown to the same table directly across from him.

As she sat down and took her napkin and placed it in her lap, she looked up and saw him and actually jerked.

He smiled and nodded to her and she smiled and nodded as well before looking down at her journal. He could tell that her face had flushed again, just as it had yesterday, and that made him smile even more.

Again, over breakfast, they both wrote in their journals, and he only once caught her looking at him.

When he finished breakfast of ham and eggs and a wonderful soft toast, he got up and looked directly at her and smiled and nodded.

Then he left, amazed that he could even walk straight because his stomach was so clenched up around his breakfast. He had no idea how many rules of impropriety he had just broken, but he didn't honestly care.

At lunch they did the same thing, nodding and smiling, but looking quickly away. And he worked in his journal as she worked in hers.

He had not yet gotten to even thinking much about the math problem that Bonnie and Duster had assigned him.

But what he was working out, mathematically, was the chance that he could meet and spend time with this woman over and over in different timelines.

His math said it was possible.

In fact, his math said that he could live here until he died of old age and only have two minutes and fifteen seconds pass in his own timeline.

So meeting the red-haired short woman was helping him get focused on the math of time and different timelines, but just not on the right problem.

Chapter Twenty-two

August 22nd, 1901
Dixie's Timeline

AFTER FIVE DAYS, Dixie was pleased the handsome man had not left the hotel yet. It seemed that he was staying for a time as well, but she had no idea where in the massive hotel.

During breakfast and lunches in the dining room, they had gotten into a routine of nodding and smiling at each other as they both ate and worked in journals.

One evening, while eating dinner at the table in her room, she had seen him leave the hotel and cross the street. He had the stride of a man in complete control and in shape. And he wore a cowboy hat and oilcloth long coat over his suit just as Duster did.

She had spent two days going back over math that she had already checked for Bonnie and Duster about time spent in the past. Because of this man that now really interested Dixie and she figured it was a good place to start.

Bonnie and Duster had told her that the amount of time spent in the past didn't matter, and that even dying of old age didn't matter, since only two minutes and fifteen seconds would pass in the original timeline no matter what happened in this timeline.

And Bonnie had said that she had stopped counting when she and Duster went past living a thousand years. For the first time, Dixie was starting to understand the reality of that, not just the math.

But since her brain worked in numbers, she had to put that math back in her head. She could have a relationship here in the past, live here for years if she wanted, and when she returned to the crystal cave in the old mine, Duster would still be doing the dishes.

So the idea of what she did here not making a huge difference was making her relax some around the handsome man. And now she was hoping she might actually get a chance to meet him. She didn't know how, but she was relaxing enough to be open to the idea now.

She had always thought that romance novels where a woman went into the past and fell for a man there were very silly. But this man seemed so different than the others around her. And he had great teeth, something many of the men she had seen so far did not have.

In fact, his white smile just flat seemed out of place.

If it took going into the past for her to have a reaction toward a man, then she would spend far more time in the past.

And thanks to Bonnie and Duster, she could.

And another thing she found interesting. She didn't really miss her computer. She was enjoying working the math out with a fountain pen, going slowly, being deliberate. She often did her best thinking at whiteboards, and this journal seemed to be functioning like a whiteboard for her.

At breakfast, she went down at her normal time and the handsome man was sitting at his normal table. He glanced up and nodded and smiled at her and her heart actually felt like it might pound out of her chest as if she had run a good five miles at top speed.

The waiter was not close, so she took a deep breath and walked toward the handsome man.

He looked shocked as she approached and managed to scramble to his feet.

"Winfred Dixie Smith," Dixie said, extending her hand. "But everyone just calls me Dixie."

She was happy that her voice didn't crack.

He took her hand, smiling, but with worry in his eyes. The feeling of his skin against hers sent shockwaves through her.

He bowed slightly and said, "The honor is mine. I'm Brice Henry Lincoln, Brice to my friends."

Damn, not only did his touch send shivers through her, but his voice was perfect and sexy.

He finally let go of her hand and she felt slightly disappointed.

"I felt we should finally meet," she said, "since our schedules seem to match for a few meals each day."

"I was hoping for that as well," he said.

He glanced around at the almost empty dining room. "I am not sure what is appropriate, so forgive my brashness, but would you care to join me for breakfast? That is, if you are dining alone this fine morning?"

She looked him directly in the eyes. She could see they were a dark green and she could see he was concerned that he had overstepped his bounds.

She took a deep breath. "I am alone and I would love company for breakfast."

There, she had done it. Dixie wasn't sure if Bonnie would be proud or not.

Brice quickly moved around and held a chair for her across the table from him.

She nodded her thank you and sat down. She placed her journal and pen on the table and noticed it was very similar to his. Then she motioned to the waiter.

When the waiter approached, she said, "I will be joining Mr. Lincoln for breakfast. I would like my normal."

"Very well, Ma'am," the waiter said, nodding and turning away.

When she looked back, Brice was staring at her and smiling like a teenaged kid on a first date.

And with that she smiled back at him. And damn it all to hell, she could feel that she blushed again.

Sometimes she really hated having light skin. It gave far, far too many of her thoughts away.

And right now, the thought of getting to know this handsome man from 1901 was on the top of her mind.

And getting to really, *really* know him wasn't far below the surface of her mind as well.

Chapter Twenty-three

August 22nd, 1901
Brice's Timeline

BRICE HAD ALMOST passed out from sheer panic when he saw the beautiful red-haired woman walking toward him. Somehow he had managed to get to his feet and do his best impression of a gentleman.

Her touch had sent electric shocks through his entire body and she was even more beautiful up close than she was from across the room. He had no idea how that was possible.

She also had a beautiful voice and a perfect smile. And she was shorter up close than she appeared across the room as well, which also surprised him. He bet she wasn't more than five-foot-four inches tall and she had the most intense brown eyes that seemed to just look through him.

He couldn't believe he had gotten brash enough to invite her to have breakfast with him, and he swore he was shaking when she agreed.

Never, even back in high school, had he had a reaction like this with a woman. He had no idea what was happening.

Luckily the waiter taking their orders allowed him to bring back a part of his mind, at least enough to talk with her.

They made small talk about the beautiful hotel and how wonderful Boise was and how it was growing. Then she asked him if he would be staying for a time in the hotel.

"At least a month," he said. "I'm waiting here for a friend to return from Arizona."

She smiled at that.

"And you?" he asked.

"I also am waiting for a friend to return in a month or so," she said.

At that he smiled as well and they held each other's gaze for a long minute saying nothing before the waiter brought more of their breakfast meals.

Brice had no idea at all what was appropriate with a woman in this time period. So he flat decided to tell her that.

"I'm not experienced at all with being alone like this around such beautiful company," he said after they both started to eat. "So please do not hold any inappropriate comments against me."

She laughed and seemed to relax a little. "Thank heavens," she said. "I also have no experience at what my manners should be in this situation."

"So maybe we should hire the waiter to give us lessons?" he said.

Thankfully, she laughed. He loved her laugh, especially when it made it to her eyes. "I think we can just enjoy the company and we'll be fine."

"I like the sounds of that a great deal," he said, smiling at her.

She blushed.

He was starting to really love how easily she blushed.

So they continued to eat and make small talk and he slowly relaxed a little more.

And she seemed to relax a little as well.

As they both finished their coffee, he decided to be bold and ask if she would care to join him for lunch as well.

"I would love that," she said.

With that she picked up her journal and stood and he stood as well.

"I will look forward to lunch, Mr. Lincoln," she said.

"As will I," he said, bowing slightly and smiling. "And please call me Brice."

"Only if you call me Dixie," she said.

"It will be my honor," he said.

She laughed and turned and left the room and he sat back down, somehow managing to not spill the rest of his coffee on his journal.

He sat there for another half hour writing down his impressions of Dixie and wishing for the very first time for a computer to look her up and find out even more about her.

But it seemed that to learn about Dixie, he was going to have to do it the old-fashioned way. He was just going to have to talk with her.

And honestly, that sounded wonderful.

Chapter Twenty-four

August 22nd, 1901
Dixie's Timeline

SOMEHOW, DIXIE MANAGED to climb the six flights of stairs to her suite without stumbling. In fact, it felt more like she was floating she was so excited.

Brice Lincoln was more handsome up close than he had been across the room, if that was possible. And he seemed smart and interested in her.

She sat at the oak desk in her suite and wrote in her journal her impressions of him.

Every detail.

She could see his face clearly in her mind, again not something that usually happened with her.

After an hour, she went back to working on the math, double-checking to make sure that anything she did here would stay in this timeline. She filled two more pages of her journal with calculations before realizing that lunch was approaching quickly.

As was normal for her, she could lose vast amounts of time in math, lost in the calculations.

She used a wash cloth to freshen up, changed her dress into a lighter one more suited for the warming temperatures of the day, and then at her normal time, with her journal and pen in her hand, she started back down the stairs to have lunch.

She was mostly expecting that Brice Lincoln would not be there.

But she was so hoping he would be.

As she entered the dining room, Brice was sitting in his normal position writing in his journal.

He was slightly hunched over and seemed very intent on what he was doing. Maybe he was a novelist of some sort. She would have to ask him.

Bonnie had told her that it was normal for a woman of this time to keep a personal journal, so at least she had her cover story on what she was doing.

As she approached his table, she noticed that what he was working on was numbers.

Two steps away she froze.

Higher math.

He was working on higher math, just as she had been doing.

Math that did not exist in this time.

He looked up and slammed his journal closed, clearly stunned that she had gotten so close.

He scrambled to his feet, smiling at her and moving quickly around the table to hold the chair for her.

She barely made it to the chair and sat down.

"I hope you had a pleasant morning," he said, going back to his chair and moving his journal out of the way. "I'm so glad you could join me for lunch."

As he took his chair, she looked at him. Perfect teeth, just as she did. A journal just as she had. Working on higher math just as she was doing.

He was from a future, and more than likely another timeline.

Oh, shit, now what was she going to do?

He sat looking at her and as she didn't respond his smile slowly faded until it looked forced.

"I have a question for you," she said, her voice as controlled as she could make it.

"Anything," he said, now looking very worried.

"What is the name of the friend you are waiting for to return?"

Brice seemed stunned by that question and sat back. Then he said, "Duster Kendal."

"Oh, shit," she said, shaking her head and staring at the table. "This can't be happening."

"I'm sorry," Brice said, clearly surprised at her language. "I fear I am at a loss."

She took a deep breath and looked up into the worry covering his face.

"I'm waiting for Bonnie Kendal," she said. "I caught a glance at what you were working on."

For a moment Brice just looked puzzled, then slowly she could see a realization come over him.

With a quick glance around to make sure no one could overhear what she was about to say, she said, "I work for Bonnie and Duster Kendal in the year 2016."

She took her journal and opened it to some of the math calculations she had been doing this afternoon to figure out if she could stay with Brice in this time.

He glanced at her journal and his face went completely white.

Maybe even whiter than her normal skin color.

After a moment he swallowed hard and nodded. He then opened his journal and slid it toward her and there, in it, was almost the same calculations.

She could tell, at a glance, that he had been working to figure out a way to stay with her in this timeline.

"I also work for Bonnie and Duster Kendal in the year 2016," he said. "Only clearly in a very different timeline."

"Shit, shit, shit," she said softly.

It was all she could think to say.

And Brice said nothing.

Chapter Twenty-five

August 22nd, 1901
Brice's Timeline

ANOTHER TABLE of three men came in for lunch and sat close, so Brice and Dixie couldn't talk much at all.

For a few minutes, Brice was happy about that. It gave him some time to get his wits about him.

In another timeline, in an infinite number of timelines, actually, Bonnie and Duster had hired Dixie instead of him to help them with the math problems concerning the lodge.

So that meant she was as smart as he was about math.

Good looking and a math brain. How was that possible?

Somehow they were going to need to figure out together how this happened.

In all his work with Bonnie and Duster's math over the last year, he had never seen anything like this being possible.

Actually, at the moment, he wasn't even sure what "this" was. They were both from a future, but from futures in different timelines now together in just this timeline.

Across the table from him Dixie sat silently, clearly lost in her thoughts as well.

They both ate lightly, only picking at their food. Normally he enjoyed the grilled chicken and potatoes, but he only ate a little of each and sipped his iced tea.

Finally, as the lunch neared the end and it was clear that the three men close to them were not leaving anytime soon, Brice had to do something.

He took his journal and wrote in it "Lost River Suite. Sixth floor, south corner."

He slid it open so she could see his note.

She nodded and he took the journal back and closed it.

She took another bite, then took her journal and wrote it in and slid it so he could see.

"Avalanche Creek suite. Sixth floor, north corner. Join me after lunch when the hall is clear."

He nodded and smiled at her and for the first time during lunch she smiled back.

A few minutes later she stood and thanked Brice for a lovely lunch.

He stood and bowed to her as Duster had trained him to do.

She turned and left, moving toward the lobby and the staircase beyond.

He waited five minutes, sipping his tea, then stood and left, his journal in his hand.

He managed to walk up the six flights and since the wide, carpeted halls were empty in both directions, he knocked lightly on the suite with the brass tag Avalanche Creek on the door.

Dixie opened the door and smiled at him.

Damn he loved that smile of hers, and everything about her, even her short height.

"Mr. Lincoln," she said, nodding and indicating that he should enter.

"Ms. Smith," he said in return, smiling as he went past her. Her suite was almost identical to his, only with woman's clothes hanging in the wardrobe that he could see through the bedroom door.

She closed the door and he turned to face her.

"Holy crap," he said, "you have any idea what's going on?"

She smiled. "We'll figure it out. But first we need to get some basics out of the way."

He nodded as they stood about five feet apart, staring at each other.

"My real name is Dixie Smith," she said, "born in Phoenix, Arizona in July, 1988."

Brice nodded and followed her lead. "My real name is Brice Lincoln, born right here in Boise, Idaho in May of 1988."

"I have a doctorate in theoretical math from Princeton," she said.

"I have a doctorate in theoretical math from Harvard," he said.

"I was hired by Bonnie and Duster Kendal just over a year ago, moved to Boise to work for them, and this is my first long trip into the past."

Brice nodded. "Same exact thing. Did they show you the lodge and the remains of Roosevelt under the lake?"

"They did," Dixie said, smiling. "That damn road in there scared hell out of me."

"Yeah," Brice said, laughing, "and the one going up to the mine above Silver City was no joy ride."

She laughed with him on that and then they both stood there smiling at each other.

Damn he found her attractive.

Beyond attractive.

"Then there is one more thing we need to get out of the way," she said, "before we get down to the brand new math problems our presence here together has seemed to have uncovered."

"What's that?"

She walked forward and pulled his head down to her height and kissed him.

He was so shocked at the incredible feeling that it took him a moment to finally kiss her back.

And then, after a few minutes of kissing, he picked her up and carried her into her bedroom and quickly discovered how really impossible women's clothing of 1901 actually was to remove.

Chapter Twenty-six

August 22nd, 1901
Dixie's Timeline

AFTER A QUICK and intense session of making love (once they got her out of her clothes) they both lay on her feather bed, naked, panting in the warming afternoon heat.

His body was amazing, clearly a runner as she was, and clearly in shape. And as they made love, they fit together perfectly. Never, ever, had she felt anything like that before.

She hadn't been a prude, but sex and relationships hadn't really been much of her life before this.

Now she wanted to just roll back on top of him, even in the warmth, and make love to him again and again.

He was just staring at her body as well and she liked that. She hadn't had a man do that before, just lay naked beside her and stare at her.

"You know," he said, "you have one of the most perfect bodies I have ever seen."

"Seen a lot of them, have you?" she asked, laughing.

"A few in real life, more on beaches, and a bunch in magazines. You outclass them all."

She rolled over and kissed him, then said simply, "That was a sweet thing to say."

It was. Not only was he smart and amazingly good looking with a smile that would kill, but he was sweet. There had to be something wrong with him.

"It's the flat truth," he said. "And for the last few days I've been double-checking all the math that Bonnie and Duster did to make sure that if you were from this timeline I wouldn't cause problems doing exactly this."

She laughed. "I was doing the same thing. Seems we now need to take that math to the next level and see what this is going to do to our original timelines."

"Boy, do you have that one right," he said.

"Did you have a job offer before Bonnie and Duster hired you?" Dixie asked.

"I was looking at Cal Tech," he said. "And they seemed to be looking at me as well."

"So was I," she said, nodding. In fact, until Bonnie and Duster came swooping in with an insane offer of money to do research with them, she had almost said yes to the Cal Tech job.

"How much do you want to bet our alternate selves in our original timelines are teaching there?"

He shook his head. "No bet."

"How in the world did Duster and Bonnie not see each other before they left?"

"Duster left the day I first saw you in the restaurant," Brice said. "We had only been here two days and spent almost no time in the hotel."

Dixie nodded. "Bonnie left two days earlier and I spent two days in this room before getting enough courage to go downstairs to eat."

"Well, that explains some of it," Brice said. "But you don't think they did this on purpose, do you?"

"I don't see how they could," Dixie said. "But communication between timelines might be possible, I suppose."

"Now that's yet another math problem as well," Brice said.

Dixie knew that their entire situation was a giant mathematical puzzle. And with luck, together, they would figure it out.

He just kept staring at her white skin, her body, while running his fingers through her long hair. She loved that he was doing that. She didn't feel exposed at all, lying there completely naked in front of him. That was not something she had ever done with any other man in her life.

She was learning all sorts of new things about herself.

"Maybe together we can figure out why they could remember two timelines after the lodge," she said.

"Maybe," he said. "But there's one thing we have to do first."

"And what's that?" she asked, giving him a serious look, but hoping what he was going to suggest.

"This," he said.

He leaned in and kissed her breast, which sent shivers through her body. He then lifted her over and on top of him.

She giggled, feeling him getting quickly aroused under her.

Thirty minutes later they both decided they needed a cold bath.

Together.

And that, of course, led to more that needed to get out of the way before they could get to work.

Plus a lot of water on the floor.

Finally, by dinner, after a short nap, they were actually ready to get to work.

And both starving and facing the reality of the 1901 time period once again.

How could they eat together and talk freely?

Chapter Twenty-seven

August 22nd, 1901
Brice's Timeline

BRICE LOVED THAT they were both still naked and lying on the big feather bed as they talked about what to do next. Figuring out dinner turned out to be more difficult than they thought. They both wanted to eat together, but not down in the hot dining room. This time of the day it would be far, far too uncomfortable to eat there.

And more than likely it would be too crowded, so they wouldn't be able to talk freely either.

In fact, Brice had found it too hot to eat in any restaurant close by in the evening since the temperature was in the nineties each day at least.

"I have a standing dinner order," Dixie said, "to be brought to my room at 6 p.m. I'm sure you could have an order brought to your room as well, and then we just eat in here."

Brice climbed out of bed and got his pocket watch from his vest. It was five.

He turned back to her and flat couldn't speak. She was just laying there, her hair spread out on the pillow, her legs slightly open, her wonderful body comfortable being completely nude in front of him.

He stammered for a moment and then said, "If you don't cover up some, we're not going to make dinner at all."

She laughed and reached down and pulled a sheet up over herself.

"That better?"

"No, not hardly," he said. "But at least I can think a little."

She waved the sheet, flashing him, then laughed and pointed to him.

"That naked body of yours isn't helping the situation either."

"Sorry," he said and grabbed his cowboy hat and put it over his crotch. "That better?"

She laughed that wonderful laugh of hers and then said, "Dinner. That's the topic."

"Oh, yeah," he said, forcing his mind back on food instead of climbing back in with that wonderful woman naked in bed. "I'll get dressed and go down and order something to be brought to my room also at 6 p.m. that I can carry easily."

"Did you bring running shorts, or boxer shorts with you?" she asked.

"I did," he said. "I've been wearing them in the evening and to bed."

"Bring those with you as well when you come back with dinner," she said.

"It gets warm in here until the sun goes down and the evening breeze kicks up. We might as well be 2016 comfortable."

"I agree completely."

He managed to get dressed while she watched from the big bed, then he kissed her long and hard before finally pulling away and heading toward the door. He picked up his journal and pen and then with only one look back at the naked woman in the bed, he eased the door open to check if anyone was coming from either direction.

Both halls were empty, so he went out quickly and headed for the staircase. Ten minutes later he had his dinner ordered. It would be delivered at 6 p.m. in his room.

It felt very, very odd to be in the room alone, even though that was how he had spent most of the time since Duster had left. Suddenly Dixie was in his life and he wanted to be with her.

He forced himself to sit at his desk and start the process of figuring out the math behind how they could meet in a timeline.

He knew that in an almost infinite number of timelines he was doing the same thing right now.

There had to be something about the crystal cave that allowed this to happen, something about the physical nature of a timeline being expressed in a crystal that altered the math calculations.

But that didn't calculate out either.

Almost before he realized it there was a knock on his door and dinner had arrived.

He asked the waiter to just leave it on the tray. He might be eating with a friend and the waiter nodded and just left.

The steak smelled wonderful and the potato looked perfectly cooked. He had also ordered a full pitcher of iced tea with ice in the pitcher and a glass full of ice.

He put his journal and pen on the tray with his food, wrapped up a running shirt and running shorts and stuffed them inside his suit coat pocket and picked the tray up, balancing it carefully as he opened the door.

Again the wide, carpeted hallway was clear and he headed down the hall.

A moment later he was back in Dixie's room, unseen as far as he knew.

Her dinner had been delivered as well and was on the table in the round corner of her room. Since her room was on the north corner of the building, no sun was beating in as it did in his room. Her windows were open letting in a soft evening breeze that smelled of hot sagebrush.

Since her dinner had been delivered, she had changed into running shorts and a sports bra and had pulled her hair back and tied it away from her face.

He put his tray on the table and then turned and kissed her.

And she kissed him back and pressed into him.

When they finally broke apart, she looked him right in the eye. "You were only gone an hour and I missed you. How is that possible?"

"I don't know," he said after kissing her again. "But I felt the same way. So I'm not going to question it. I just want to enjoy every second of it."

"And that's a plan I really like," she said.

He went into the bedroom and took off his suit and vest and shirt and pants and put on his running shorts and tee shirt.

He went back into where she was already sitting at the table. She looked up and smiled as he walked barefoot toward her. "We've traveled back to 2016 and haven't left the room."

He laughed. "Sure looks that way."

Chapter Twenty-eight

September 25, 1901
Dixie's Timeline

FOR OVER AN entire, wonderful month, they continued the same routine they had set up the first day. Dixie flat loved every minute of it, every day of it.

They slept the nights together in her room, and she felt wonderful cuddling against him every night, her naked body against his.

Then at sunrise, Brice went back to his room and met her an hour later for breakfast in the dining room.

They went back to her room after breakfast and worked on timeline math until lunch. They seemed to just think the same with the math and he was the first person who could talk to her at the same level professionally.

And that was wonderful.

Then they had lunch together in the dining room, sometimes working, sometimes just making small talk if anyone sat too close to them.

Then they spent the time together for the rest of the afternoon working and ate dinner together as well in her room.

The days were wonderful and not once did she get tired of having him with her. They talked, worked, laughed, and made love.

They made a lot of love, actually. Neither of them seemed to be capable of keeping their hands off the other one. And Dixie didn't mind that in the slightest.

He had become a part of her, something she would have said impossible a month before.

And they had made progress on the math as well.

Both of them were convinced that the limited aspects of the physical nature of the crystal cave caused the ability to cross over timelines as had happened with the lodge, and that had happened to them.

Brice had assigned a random limited number of two hundred million to the crystals within a hundred paces of the table to plug into the equations they were coming up with.

It worked, which shocked Dixie.

By simply assigning a set number, all their math suddenly made sense.

They had their equation.

They had the answer. Granted, it was a very complex answer, taking almost two pages of each of their journals just to write out in small symbols.

And they would need to check it on a computer when they got back to 2016.

But they both knew it was right.

They were both almost giddy with excitement. The trip for both of them had been completely successful.

They had also figured out mathematically a way to use crystals not attached to the wall as a form of time travel machine outside of the crystal cave. Those crystals were detached from the wall and stacked when Duster's great-great-grandfather had broken through into the crystal room. Both Dixie and Brice remembered seeing the stack of crystals, each one representing a timeline, sitting near the door.

But now they had one major issue they flat couldn't figure out how to handle.

Bonnie and Duster would be returning.

Bonnie and Duster were married, but not to each other in this timeline at the moment.

Dixie's Bonnie was married to a Duster still doing dishes back in the cavern.

Brice's Duster was married to a Bonnie also doing dishes back in the cavern.

They needed to figure out a way to tell their bosses when they returned.

But mostly, she and Brice had started working on how to meet each other in their own timelines in 2016. They had decided that doing that could very well end up being the hardest thing they had to do when they returned.

Neither could even begin to guess what they would be doing after a year of teaching.

They both knew they were the same person in the other timeline, but they just both hoped their counterparts hadn't met someone else and gotten married.

If that turned out to be the case, they had worked out a few times to return to and meet and live lifetimes in the past.

But more than anything, they decided they both wanted to be a couple in 2016.

The only problem was convincing the other two parts of themselves in 2016 that was a good idea.

And both of them were sure that their counterparts were going to think the other person completely crazy. Just as they both had thought Bonnie and Duster crazy when they told them of the lodge.

It was just after eight in the evening, as they sat talking about how to make their future selves fall in love that a knock came at the door.

In over a full month, that had been the first time that had happened.

Brice grabbed his journal and dinner tray and moved quickly to the bedroom area.

"Who is it?" Dixie asked, moving toward the big door to the hallway. She could feel her stomach twisting. Had someone discovered them and were they going to be tossed out of the hotel?

Or something worse?

"It's Bonnie," the voice said from the other side of the door.

Dixie laughed and looked back at Brice who only shrugged and smiled.

It seemed it was time to face the boss, at least her boss.

Dixie moved over to the door and unlatched it, then looked out carefully at Bonnie, who smiled.

There was no one in the wide hallway behind Bonnie, so Dixie indicated Bonnie should come in.

Bonnie looked tired and dusty. She had on her riding clothes and clearly had just arrived, since her saddlebag was still in her hand.

Dixie quickly closed the door behind Bonnie and latched it, then hugged her boss.

"Great seeing you as well," Bonnie said, smiling. "How did it go? Are you all right?"

"I'm wonderful and we made progress on the lodge problem," Dixie said. "I think we have it solved."

"Wonderful!" Bonnie said, smiling. Then it clearly sunk in what Dixie had said.

"We?"

Dixie nodded. "I had a little help."

"In 1901 you had higher level math help?" Bonnie asked, a worried and puzzled look crossing her tired face.

"Did you know," Dixie said, smiling at her boss and friend, "that in other timelines in 2016, you didn't hire me. You hired a wonderful man by the name of Brice Lincoln."

"I know," Bonnie said, still frowning. "It was basically a coin flip between the two of you. How did you know that?"

Dixie could see the light starting to dawn on Bonnie.

"Nice meeting you, boss," Brice said, stepping out of the back room behind Bonnie. He was wearing only his running shorts and tee shirt and looked like he was completely from 2016. "I'm the guy that lost the coin flip in your timeline and seemed to have won it in others."

Bonnie spun around.

Then when she saw him she said simply, "Shit."

Dixie laughed. "That's exactly what I said when I realized who he was."

"I think I'm starting to get a complex," Brice said, smiling.

Chapter Twenty-nine

September 26, 1901
Brice's Timeline

THEY CONVINCED BONNIE to go get a bath and some sleep and they would talk about it at breakfast.

Dixie had said to her, "We worked out the reason mathematically this happened. We'll explain it all, honest."

"Is your Duster back yet?" Bonnie had asked Brice.

"Not yet," Brice said. "You get to be the first one to hear all this."

Bonnie had nodded and said she would meet them at breakfast.

After Bonnie left, Brice and Dixie sat in the living room area, her tucked against him, talking. He loved that she was sitting beside him like this, her legs curled up, the side of her face against his chest. He didn't want to lose this, and right now, for the first time, he was afraid he might.

Dixie was clearly thinking the same thing. "I don't want to lose you," she said, hugging him.

"We might be able to just talk Bonnie and Duster into staying for a lifetime," Brice said. "They've clearly done that a number of times."

"So you want to spend a lifetime with me?" Dixie asked.

"As many lifetimes as I can manage," Brice said, surprised that he felt that strongly. "Either in our timelines or back here the two of us."

"I agree completely," she said, again hugging him.

They spent the next hour setting exact times to return to the past and locations in the crystal room to hook to on the wall in order to increase the chances of hitting the same timeline again.

Brice knew their chances were very good to spend time together that way, lifetimes together.

But what he was worried about was Dixie convincing her future Brice to join her while he failed at convincing his future Dixie.

Dixie said she was worried about the same thing, only the other way around.

They finally decided if that happened, they would still return to a point in the past and meet to at least tell the other person what happened. But the thought of that made Brice really sad.

He was in love with a person in his own time that he hadn't met yet. The Dixie of his time might not love him. He knew that in an infinite number of universes, she wouldn't.

And in an infinite number of timelines she would.

Nothing was for sure when it came to relationships. And that scared him more than he wanted to think about.

They finally went to bed and made love passionately, as if it might be their last time.

And then the next morning, he went back to his own suite, changed clothes, and went down to the dining room first as he had done for a month.

A few minutes later Dixie joined him. And right behind her came Bonnie.

Brice had tipped the waiter to not seat anyone close to them so they could talk. So after they were all seated, Dixie asked Bonnie, "How was your trip to San Francisco?"

"It was wonderful and sad," Bonnie said, a haunted look in her eyes. "I didn't want to leave. I never do."

Brice glanced at Dixie who was frowning. "I assume that's not something you want to talk about just yet."

"Maybe never," Bonnie said as the waiter came up to take their order.

After he was out of earshot, Bonnie looked first at Dixie, then at Brice. "So tell me how this happened?"

Together they relayed the events of their first five days and how Dixie had seen Brice working on the math in his journal.

"And you've been a couple ever since I assume," Bonnie said.

"We have," Brice said, smiling.

"We were very careful," Dixie said.

Bonnie laughed. "I'm sure you were. But I'm sure all the hotel staff knew what was happening. You will discover that people are people no matter what time. And western people in this time were very forgiving of some things for a certain class of people."

Dixie blushed and Brice just laughed. He still loved how Dixie blushed at the drop of a hat. Actually, he loved just about everything about her.

"So after breakfast you want to show me the math on all this?" Bonnie asked, "Or wait until we get back?"

"I think showing it to you now, together, would be a good idea," Dixie said.

"And also showing it to Duster when he gets here," Brice said. "When we go back, we won't be together."

"I agree," Dixie said. "Since we worked this out together, better to present it together."

Bonnie nodded. Then after the waiter brought their coffee, she looked at both of them. "Have you thought what you are going to do when you get back?"

Dixie looked at Brice and he nodded and answered her question.

"We have," he said. "And we are hoping you will hire the loser of the coin flip in both timelines. So we can continue to work together."

"And if that person won't come on board?" Bonnie asked.

"Then we will meet here if you don't mind," Dixie said, "in the past, and be together as much as we can, as many years, as many lifetimes, as we can be."

At that Bonnie smiled and patted Brice's hand. "I think we can make the offer good enough that you'll come work for us and with Dixie."

"Thanks," Brice said. "But I have a hunch it might not take much more than a smile from Dixie."

Dixie blushed and Bonnie laughed.

Bonnie then looked at Dixie. "He's a romantic. Who knew?"

And at that Brice could feel himself blushing.

Chapter Thirty

October 4th, 1901
Dixie's Timeline

"FIGURES THAT DUSTER would push the limits of when he could return," Bonnie said at breakfast as the three of them sat at their normal table. For Dixie, the last week or so since Bonnie showed up had been wonderful.

The three of them ate meals together and then after breakfast they worked

on the math of the various issues facing them.

Then they had lunch together and worked through the afternoon as well.

For the first time, Dixie was seeing how amazing Bonnie's math mind really was. And during the week Bonnie had helped them fine-tune a number of theories.

Then Bonnie would leave them and let Dixie and Brice have their dinner together and the evening alone.

Dixie had loved those evenings as well as they talked about everything they could think to tell the other person about their lives to help that person when they went back to 2016.

But after a few days they had decided that the best way to get the other person on board was the Roosevelt Lodge, just as Bonnie and Duster had done.

They asked Bonnie and she agreed.

So by breakfast that morning they had their plan worked out.

"What do you mean push the limits?" Dixie had asked after the waiter left from delivering their coffee.

"It's going to snow in the mountains around Silver City in three days," Bonnie said. "Makes getting back in there tough after that."

"Not that tough," Duster said as he walked up toward them, smiling.

Dixie was surprised and pushed back slightly from the table.

Brice looked surprised as well.

Duster had on his normal suit and vest and the long oilcloth duster and cowboy hat. He looked freshly bathed and as if he had a night's sleep.

He leaned over and kissed Bonnie on the cheek and then sat down in the empty chair as the three of them stared at him.

"What? You weren't expecting me?" Duster said to Brice, who still looked stunned. "I got in late last night, didn't want to bother you."

Then he turned to Bonnie. "What made you decide to join the fun and who is this wonderful young woman who has joined us?"

Dixie reached out her hand and shook Duster's firm hand. "I'm Dixie Smith. Remember, I lost the coin flip and you hired Brice here."

Duster opened his mouth to say something, then closed it as a look of puzzlement came over his face.

Dixie knew that Duster suddenly not only remembered her, but realized that Bonnie, in just over two minutes, could not have brought Dixie to the past.

Bonnie laughed, but said nothing, just letting Duster figure it out for himself.

Duster waited as the waiter brought him a cup of coffee as well, then leaned forward. "I think a few words on what the hell is happening might be helpful."

Dixie and Brice both just eased back slightly from the table. Dixie figured it was time for the grown-ups to talk.

Now Bonnie really laughed. Then she smiled at Duster and said, "Thank you for the nice greeting kiss, but the woman you meant that for I understand is back doing dishes in the mine in your timeline. I promise to not tell my husband, who also claims he would do the dishes in my timeline while we were gone."

Duster looked at Dixie and she smiled. Then he looked at Brice who only shrugged.

Then Duster said simply, "Oh, shit."

"That's it," Brice said. "I now officially have a complex."

Dixie and Bonnie both laughed. Dixie so wanted to go kiss Brice, but remembering what year she was in, she just sat there and smiled at him.

"This is all a good thing," Bonnie said, smiling at Duster, who looked flat-out confused. "Not only together have they mathematically solved our lodge problem while we were off traveling this last month, but they also explained mathematically how all this could happen. The equation alone fills pages of their journals."

Duster just nodded.

"And they came up with a few other nifty things," Bonnie said, "we might want to play with when we go back and can crunch some numbers on a major computer or two."

Duster just shook his head and sat back, obviously trying to clear his head and think.

Dixie remembered that feeling after she had realized who Brice actually was.

Finally Duster looked at Brice. "I assume you two are a couple, right?"

He indicated Dixie with a nod.

Dixie smiled at the man she had fallen in love with over the last month as he smiled at her.

"We are," Brice said, turning to face Duster. "As much as two people can be in love who are not from the same timelines."

"They hope to solve that problem when we all return," Bonnie said.

Duster nodded and looked at Bonnie, then at Dixie. She could see a slight smile forming on his face.

Duster turned to Brice. "I take you into the past and leave you for a month and what happens? You change a few billion timelines."

"For the better I hope," Brice said, smiling back at his boss.

"Sure looks that way," Duster said, laughing.

Then he turned to Bonnie. "I suppose this means we're hiring another assistant in a massive number of timelines?"

Bonnie nodded. "Think of it more as us being mentors for a short time. I have a hunch these two together are going to leave us in the dust mathematically."

"That good, huh?" Duster said.

Bonnie nodded. "That good. Wait until you see the equations these two came up with here in 1901 in journals."

Dixie smiled and could feel herself blushing.

And across the table from her, Brice was smiling and blushing as well.

Now he and Dixie just had to figure out a way to make sure they were a couple in 2016.

And to do that, they had to meet again.

And fall in love again.

Twice.

Chapter Thirty-one

October 6th, 1901
Brice's Timeline

"EVERYONE READY?" Duster asked from beside the brown mare he was going to be riding. The sun hadn't come up yet and the morning was cool and damp. They were outside the stable behind the hotel and Dixie was already mounted. Brice mounted up and then turned to wait for Duster to pay the bill with the stable and tip the man who took care of the horses.

They had decided to not take much of the clothing they had bought, just a few of the suits and each woman had a few of the dresses, all packed in saddlebags they could carry.

Around Brice the trees along a few of the wide side streets were already turning fall colors or orange and gold and browns. He looked up at the four corner towers of the red brick and stone Idanha Hotel and knew, without a doubt, he was going to miss the place.

He had really fallen in love for the first time in this hotel. That made the hotel a very special place that would always remain special in his mind for as long as he lived.

When he got back to the present, he would have to go downtown and see how they did with the renovation.

"It's actually getting cold out here," Bonnie said.

"It is," Dixie said.

Brice didn't mind. After being so warm for the last two months, being able to bundle up and be slightly chilled felt almost good. And he knew he was going back into early July heat in 2016. So being chilled for a little bit felt right.

Duster mounted up and indicated they should start down the nearly empty street headed west.

Brice looked over at Dixie who was looking up at the hotel as he had done.

"We'll be back," he said.

"I know," she said, smiling at him. "I might be with a different Brice and you with a different Dixie, but we'll be back."

"It's still us," Brice said. "That's the key to remember. We are the same in every timeline."

She nodded and said nothing.

She looked as worried as he was feeling.

Taking a break every hour, they rode easily for the first day, not pushing.

Brice was surprised that the saddle and riding wasn't bothering him as much this time. He mentioned that to Bonnie on one break and Bonnie had said it was because they were riding flat and that Brice had had two days of riding on the way here to get the muscles toned some.

Mostly, when the road allowed, he rode beside Dixie, but they didn't talk much. They both just wanted to be close to each other as long as they could.

That night Duster pitched three tents, one for him, one for Bonnie, and one for Brice and Dixie.

They just slept together, not making love, but just holding each other.

And that was all Brice needed. It was going to have to last him, he knew, for some time to come.

Chapter Thirty-two

October 7th, 1901
Dixie's Timeline

THEY HAD REACHED Silver City just before dusk and checked into the Silver City Hotel, even though they had no plans on staying in the rooms.

Silver City was still a going concern and Dixie could hear the music echoing from the saloons. The hotel was a two-story wooden structure that looked worn and tired and dusty.

Compared to the wonderful suite in the Idanha Hotel in Boise, this room felt more like a closet. It had a small bed in a metal frame, a scarred-up dresser with a bowl and pitcher of water, and peeling wallpaper. It smelled like mold. Clearly a place that had seen much, much better days and Dixie was very glad she wasn't spending the night in the room.

They all had their saddlebags and the money and their clothes. They all had gone to their rooms to rest and wash down a little from the grime from the ride.

Duster sold the horses to the ranch just a mile below the town and mentioned he might be back at some point to buy them back, for a profit of course.

Dixie was surprised that the air in the high mountain mining town had a sharp, cold bite to it and smelled of wood campfires and fireplaces.

As the sun set, the looming peaks around the city seemed to close in.

Duster had warned her and Brice that they would be climbing after dark back up to the mine, to make sure they weren't followed. So they needed to dress warm.

In her room, Dixie washed her face and arms, then put on another layer of clothing over her riding clothes and took out a pair of riding gloves she had bought in Boise but never used.

Then she stretched out on the bed fully dressed, trying to let herself rest.

There was a very good chance in just a few hours she was never going to see the Brice she loved again.

And there was a good chance the Brice in her timeline would want nothing to do with her.

Even though she knew the math of all of this, her heart was confused beyond belief. She didn't want to lose Brice, but to really have a life with Brice, she had to take this chance.

She knew he was taking the same exact chance in his timeline. And she knew he was as scared as she was. He wasn't trying to hide it, which she admired.

Thirty minutes later when the knock came at the door, she took a deep breath, stood and grabbed her saddlebag. It was time.

It was Bonnie at the door. "Leave nothing."

Dixie nodded and looked back to make sure she hadn't left something. Then she pulled the door closed behind her and followed Bonnie down the narrow hallway toward the exit at the end of the building.

They went down a staircase on the end wall and to a back street behind the hotel, then turned to the north up a dark, rough dirt street between a number of buildings that looked like they were boarded up.

More than likely those buildings were owned by people who left for the winter.

They saw no one along the way at all.

Duster had been right in a comment about Silver City in 1901. This town really was dying. Especially right before the first snowfall of the winter. It had the feeling of a town ready to drop into hibernation.

At the edge of town they waited in dark shadows near one boarded-up building and a few minutes later Duster and Brice strode up the dark street toward them.

Both of them were wearing their long oilcloth coats and cowboy hats. To Dixie, Brice was the most handsome man she had ever seen.

"This way," Duster said as he got close to them, his voice hushed.

Dixie took Brice's hand and followed Duster up the street while Bonnie followed behind them.

When the trail got too narrow, Brice dropped back and Dixie moved up right behind Duster, following in his footsteps, watching her every step in the dark on the trail.

Just about one hour later, Dixie was winded, but standing beside Brice on the flat top of the mine tailings. She was both freezing and sweating from the climb at the same time.

Below them the few remaining lights of Silver City sparkled in the cold night air.

Duster and Bonnie both checked around the mine and inside the shack to make sure no one was close, then Duster used his key to open the big rock beside the mine entrance.

They all four crowded in and the rock slid closed and a moment later Dixie stepped into the mine as the lights came up.

Part of her had almost wanted to believe over the last two wonderful months that this place had all been a dream. But now it was very, very real again.

They all headed to the big room and right on through to the big crystal cavern.

Dixie had her saddlebag on her shoulder and almost dropped it at the fantastic sight of the crystal room.

"Do you ever get tired of seeing this place?" Brice asked Bonnie and Duster as he stopped beside Dixie.

"Never," Bonnie said.

"I'll never get tired of it," Dixie said.

She looked at the man she loved. "Do you have your journal?"

He quickly dug into his saddlebag and held it up for her to see.

"Do you?" he asked, stuffing his journal back into the saddlebag.

She pulled her journal out and held it up for him to see.

He nodded. "We'll make this work."

"I know," Dixie said.

Then she pulled his head down to her height and kissed him as hard as she could kiss him.

He kissed her back.

Finally they broke and she said, "I love you, Brice Lincoln. Make the me in your timeline love you as well."

"I love you as well," he said to her, smiling. "But I have a hunch that making you do anything you don't want to do might not be a good idea."

"Then make it my idea to love you," she said, laughing.

Damn she was going to miss this man. More than she wanted to think about.

With that they kissed once more and moved over to where Bonnie and Duster stood near the machine.

Brice put his hand on the machine and looked at Dixie.

Dixie put her hand on the machine beside his and looked into his eyes.

She loved this man more than she could imagine, yet she was leaving him.

She was leaving him for a chance to be with him again.

A moment later Bonnie and Duster touched the wooden box as well and then Duster unhooked the wire.

And Duster and Brice vanished.

She had been looking in Brice's wonderful green eyes and he had just disappeared, as if he had never been.

Dixie stepped back from the wooden box and watched as Bonnie carefully undid the wires and then carefully marked the crystal on the wall.

Dixie needed to know that crystal. She needed to make sure that one world, that one timeline inside that one crystal did not get lost because that might be the only one where she would know Brice was for certain.

It was in that timeline they had made plans to meet again if their plans in 2016 failed.

The Brice she loved wasn't in that crystal anymore either. But it was her gateway to him.

How could he be gone?

What had she done?

Bonnie finished marking the crystal and moved over toward Dixie.

"Are you all right?" Bonnie asked, her voice soft.

Dixie didn't dare speak. She just shook her head.

Bonnie put her arm around Dixie and turned her gently toward the door.

Dixie had promised herself she wouldn't cry.

She failed that promise.

Chapter Thirty-three

July 8th, 2016
Brice's Timeline

BRICE WATCHED CAREFULLY as Duster marked the crystal on the wall where he had spent those two wonderful months with Dixie. He needed that carefully marked and Duster did exactly that.

Duster then indicated that Brice should follow him out of the crystal room and back to the kitchen.

But instead Brice just stood there, remembering how he had been looking into the large brown eyes of Dixie and she had just vanished.

The woman he loved was living in one of the crystals around him, and he knew he was in one as well.

He knew the math of how they had met in that one timeline, and more than likely an almost infinite number of other timelines as well, but knowing she was in those crystals in that cave made him not want to leave it.

"She lives in this timeline as well," Duster said, coming back in to stand with Brice. "As well as all of those."

"I know," Brice said.

"Now," Duster said, "as time tends to do, we move forward and find her."

Brice nodded.

"But first," Duster said, "we have to try to explain all this to Bonnie."

"Yeah, that's going to be interesting," Brice said.

Duster just laughed at that.

They went out and dropped their saddlebags on the big empty table near the racks of clothing and Brice grabbed his journal and followed Duster toward the big kitchen area in the back of the cavern.

"Didn't quite get the dishes done," Bonnie said, smiling as they joined her, not sitting down.

Brice was having a very hard time realizing that for Bonnie, this Bonnie, only just over two minutes had gone by.

"You two want some dinner?" Bonnie asked.

Brice suddenly realized that he was hungry. They hadn't bothered to eat in Silver City while there.

"We would love some," Duster said. "That damn climb never seems to get any easier."

"So what did you think of your first extended time in the past," Bonnie asked Brice, moving toward the fridge.

"Interesting," Brice said.

Duster broke out laughing like Brice had told the world's funniest joke.

Bonnie frowned and looked puzzled.

"We're taking showers first," Duster said, managing to stop laughing, "and changing back into our modern clothes. Then we'll explain it all."

Brice nodded. "Very interesting. Very long story."

"You were only gone two months," Bonnie said, frowning. "Right?"

"Yup, just two months," Duster said, chuckling. "Just as we planned."

He walked over to Bonnie and kissed her and then said, "Showers, we need showers."

He turned and headed toward the bathrooms in the back of the big cavern. "You get the women's shower," Duster said to Brice, indicating that Brice should follow. "They use funny soap."

Twenty minutes later Brice felt almost human again. The first shower in over two months was something to treasure.

He got back into his tee shirt and jeans and running shoes and looked at himself in the mirror.

He now looked nothing like the man in the suit and vest and cowboy hat of 1901.

He went out and sat at the big kitchen table, putting his journal on the table in front of him. The place smelled wonderful of sizzling steaks on a grill.

Bonnie gave him a glass of iced tea and some apple slices to hold him until the steaks she was cooking finished up. Then she went back to mixing a salad.

A minute later Duster came out looking clean and refreshed as well.

She gave him a glass of iced tea as well and Brice slid the apple slices toward him.

"All right, you two," she said. "What exactly happened?"

Duster just shook his head and looked at the slice of apple he had taken.

"I met a woman on my fifth day in the hotel after Duster left," Brice said.

Bonnie smiled. "Wonderful. Was she beautiful?"

"Very beautiful," Brice said, smiling and nodding. "I was working on some math in my journal about what would happen if I spent time with her in the past for a few different timelines."

Bonnie nodded. "We did that math and you've reviewed it already."

"I know," Brice said. "But I wanted to make sure, so I was doing it again when she came up to the lunch table where I was working and saw my journal."

"Oh, oh," Bonnie said, smiling. "I bet that was hard to explain."

"Well, sort of," Brice said.

Duster snorted and started laughing.

"What the hell is so damn funny?" Bonnie asked, again looking puzzled.

"The woman knew what I was working on," Brice said. "She recognized it. Her name is Dixie Smith."

"How could a woman in 1901 recognize higher math?" Bonnie asked.

Then she stopped, frozen, the only sound in the cavern was the sizzling steaks.

"Dixie Smith?" Bonnie asked. "Short cute redhead?"

Duster laughed even harder.

Brice nodded. "She was there waiting for you to return, just as I was waiting for Duster to return."

"Oh, shit," Bonnie said, her face white.

"I get that a lot," Brice said.

Chapter Thirty-four

July 8th, 2016
Dixie's Timeline

BONNIE WALKED DIXIE back into the big cavern and they put their saddlebags on the empty table near the racks of clothing, then Bonnie walked her toward the kitchen.

Dixie carried her journal in her hand. There was no chance she was going to let it out of her sight at any point. She might even sleep with it under her pillow when she got home, just to have Brice close.

As they entered the kitchen area, Duster turned around and saw that Dixie was trying to not cry.

"She met someone," Bonnie said to Duster. "She'll be fine after a shower. But we need something to eat. Maybe a salad and some bread?"

Bonnie pointed Dixie toward the men's restroom and shower area and Dixie stumbled into it, mad at herself for crying. She wasn't the crying type, but seeing Brice just vanish into another timeline in front of her had been hard.

Really, really hard.

Impossibly hard.

Dixie had to admit, the shower did help a lot. This was the first shower in two months. She had enjoyed the baths, especially the ones with Brice, but she had missed a good hot shower.

After getting dressed again in her modern clothes and slipping on her tennis shoes, she went back out to the kitchen, her journal solidly in one hand.

Bonnie wasn't there yet and Duster asked her if she wanted some iced tea as Dixie sat down at the big kitchen table.

"I would love some," she said. "And don't worry, I'll be all right. I'll tell you all about it when Bonnie gets out."

Less than a minute later Bonnie joined them and touched Dixie's shoulder before going over and kissing Duster long and hard.

"What was that for?" he asked, smiling at her.

"Been wanting to do that for a few days now," she said, smiling and winking at Dixie.

Dixie laughed and that made her feel better as well.

"Need some help with a dinner for us hungry travelers?"

"Bread's warming in the over and I've tossed together a salad," Duster said. "Anything else?"

"That sounds wonderful," Bonnie said and kissed him again with some passion.

Duster looked puzzled. "Guess I'm going to have to fix salads more often."

Dixie laughed, as did Bonnie.

"So you want to tell him who you met?" Bonnie said.

Dixie nodded. "Two days after Bonnie left I got up enough courage to go down to the dining room in the hotel for lunch. This handsome man was sitting there by himself working in a journal."

"You didn't forget you were in 1901 and go introduce yourself or something?" Duster asked.

Dixie laughed and with each laugh she was feeling better and better. "No chance of that. I saw him every day for five days at both breakfast and lunch. We made eye contact and smiled at each other, but nothing else."

"Okay?" Duster asked, taking the wonderful-smelling bread from the stove.

"So the next morning at breakfast I decided to go introduce myself. He was a perfect gentleman and asked me to join him for breakfast and I did."

Dixie didn't want to tell Duster she had wanted a lot more at that point, but had acted the perfect woman for the time.

Duster brushed some butter on the top of the hot bread and put them in a basket and slid them onto the table, then went back for plates and napkins.

"But as I walked up to join him for lunch," Dixie said, "I saw what he was working on in his journal. It was the same math I had been working on in my journal."

Duster put plates in front of them. "Not possible."

Bonnie was now smiling, enjoying this moment a great deal clearly.

"I know that," Dixie said. "He had told me he planned on being in the hotel for at least a month waiting for a friend to come back. So after seeing the math, I asked him the name of his friend. He was waiting for you."

Duster just stood there, his mouth open. Finally he said, "Again, not possible."

"Very possible," Dixie said as Bonnie started to laugh. "His name is Brice Lincoln."

"The guy we almost hired instead of you?" Duster asked, looking panicked at Bonnie, who just nodded.

"So not only did I fall in love with a man in the past," Dixie said. "He's also from another timeline."

"Oh, shit," Duster said.

"That's exactly what I said when he told me he was waiting for you," Dixie said.

Laughing, Bonnie got up and patted Duster on the shoulder. "Sit down, I'll finish the salad. Wait until she shows you the really amazing equations the two of them worked out on our problem with the lodge, and on how it was mathematically possible for them to meet in the first place, and also a few other nifty things they came up with."

"The two of you worked together on the math?" Duster said, dropping into a chair at the table.

"We did," Dixie said. "For over a month."

"And together," Bonnie said, "they may be better than we are."

"We're pretty good," Dixie said, smiling at the clear memory of Brice's face. "And we're very much in love."

Damn she loved that man. But she was going to have to get him to love her all over again in his timeline.

The idea of that just scared hell out of her.

Just meeting him again scared her more than she wanted to admit.

How was she ever going to meet a man for the first time that she had already made love to every night for well over a month?

She doubted any dating manuals dealt with that problem.

Chapter Thirty-five

July 8th, 2016
Brice's Timeline

AFTER THE WONDERFUL steak dinner and telling Bonnie the full story, they headed out into the early evening air.

As they headed across the trail toward the Cadillac SUV from the mine, Brice realized that he had woken this same morning in the Monumental Summit Lodge. He had been gone for two months, fallen in love with a wonderful woman, and only part of one day had passed.

That was going to take him some time to really understand, even though he knew all the math of it.

They worked on their plan for hiring Dixie on the way back, and how they would even go about it. They all decided that the best thing to do, if possible, was to just hire her to work with Brice in Boise and not say a thing about the lodge or the mine.

Then, after a month, or two months, or a year if it took that long, they would decide if she was capable of handling the mine. Just because she had been able to do that in one timeline didn't mean she would be in this one.

All of this seemed so uncertain, Brice hated it.

So after he got home to the wonderful condo he was renting in Boise just after eleven in the evening, he logged on and looked up anything he could find about Professor Dixie Smith. And except for one faculty picture at Cal Tech, there was very little.

He just stared at the picture, missing her more than he could ever imagine missing someone.

It was Dixie in the picture, but not Dixie.

But yet it was the same Dixie. Only difference was he had worked for Bonnie and Duster for a year and she had taught for a year. She was Dixie.

Bonnie and Duster said that in their search for an assistant, they had private investigators look up everything they could about her and would send those files to him as soon as they got home.

Ten minutes after Brice started his search, he got the e-mail from Bonnie with the files.

Beside the files, the e-mail said, "Get some sleep. We'll pick you up at 5 a.m. We're headed for California."

Brice knew that there was little chance of sleep, but he was determined to try. He loaded the files Bonnie had sent onto his laptop. He would study them if he had time on the plane or in California. Then with his journal from 1901 tucked under his pillow, he laid down and tried to rest.

In that journal was a note from Dixie to herself in this timeline, written in her own handwriting. It said simply, "Yes, I know this all sounds crazy, but trust this man and Bonnie and Duster. And trust the math."

He must have dozed some because the alarm woke him at 4 a.m. He took a quick shower and was outside waiting when they pulled up.

"Breakfast is waiting on the plane," Bonnie said as Brice climbed into the back seat.

Fifteen minutes later, with almost no traffic on the wide Boise streets, they pulled up beside Bonnie and Duster's private Gulfstream Jet.

Fifteen minutes after that, they were in the air and headed for California.

Chapter Thirty-six

July 9th, 2016
Dixie's Timeline

AFTER BREAKFAST on the plane, both Bonnie and Duster stretched out to sleep, but Dixie decided to read over the files Bonnie had sent her last night about Brice.

From what she could tell, everything he had told her about himself over the last month or so was the total truth. Finally, she closed her laptop and put her seat back to think and rest.

Bonnie woke her as the plane was approaching the Bob Hope Airport in Burbank. It was the closest airport to Pasadena and CalTech.

Dixie had visited CalTech before accepting the job with Bonnie and Duster and had loved the campus. She hadn't really been that fond of the LA area, but when on the old, tree-covered campus with all the historic stone buildings, she had felt almost at home.

She just hoped Brice, after a year, didn't feel too much at home that he wouldn't want to leave.

A limousine was waiting for them when they got off the air-conditioned plane into the heat of the Southern California summer. The three of them didn't talk much on the short drive to the campus.

Dixie was starting to get so nervous, she could hardly walk or talk. She had decided that a casual look of jeans, an expensive blue blouse, and her red hair pulled back off her face was the best way to dress. But now she was questioning everything.

Bonnie had on her standard jeans and silk blouse with her brown hair pulled back off her face.

Duster dressed as Duster always dressed, in jeans, an expensive shirt, cowboy boots, a cowboy hat, and his long oilcloth coat. Even though it was already almost ninety degrees outside, the coat seemed to keep him cool.

On the drive to the campus, Duster did say something that surprised Dixie, but shouldn't have. "I've talked with the president of the board for CalTech," Duster said. "He's fine with us being here to talk with Brice about a job."

She knew how powerful and rich her two bosses were, but sometimes she just forgot that. Now they were putting all the energy and brains behind helping her be with Brice.

She knew they were also doing it for themselves, because she and Brice had proven that together they were better than being apart.

But Dixie felt like they were doing all this for just her. And she had no idea how she would ever thank them.

The limo left them off into the heat at the California Boulevard entrance and Bonnie pointed to the big, square, white-stone building on the right. "That's the Alfred Sloan Laboratory for Mathematics and Physics. Brice is teaching a small undergraduate class in there this hour and will be done in about twenty minutes."

Dixie knew the building well and had loved it on her tour here.

"So where shall we wait for him?" Dixie asked.

Duster laughed and strode toward the big building leaving the two women to follow.

"Duster isn't much for waiting," Bonnie said, smiling at Dixie and taking her arm.

Dixie was glad she did because she wasn't sure she would walk that well on her own. So much for being the strong, independent woman. There was no chance she could have come here on her own to meet Brice.

None.

The Sloan building had been built back before the Second World War and had high hallways with stone arches every twenty steps.

"Always loved this place," Bonnie said, smiling as they followed Duster into the air-conditioning.

"It has a very welcoming feel to it," Dixie nodded as their footsteps echoed on the tile floor. "Think we can convince Brice to leave it?"

Bonnie laughed. "We convinced you to not come here, didn't we?"

Dixie laughed. "That you did."

Ahead of them Duster found the right wooden door with a gold number eighteen on the outside and waited for them to join him before opening the door and letting them go in.

Bonnie went in first and looked around, then slid over to chairs against the back wall and sat down.

Dixie didn't dare look toward the front of the small, high-ceilinged classroom, so she just followed Bonnie. Duster came in last, letting the door close fairly loudly behind him.

The room was filled with long, scarred-up wooden tables and metal chairs.

Duster sat down beside Dixie and took off his hat.

At that moment Dixie looked up. About ten students were turned, looking at them, and Brice sat on the edge of an older table at the front of the room, looking very surprised.

Dixie just stared at him and he just stared at her.

Brice had on jeans, a blue tee shirt, and running shoes. His hair was still cut short and he was as handsome as she had ever seen him look.

Somehow Brice managed to look away from Dixie's gaze and at Bonnie and then at Duster.

His face went white as he recognized who they were. He quickly stood from where he had been sort of seated on the edge of the table and managed to get himself together a little.

Dixie was impressed. She hoped that when they came to see her she was able to react as well and not melt into a babbling mess.

"Everyone," Brice said. "I would like to introduce you to two very special guests who have just joined us. I have never had the pleasure of meeting them, but with us is Bonnie and Duster Kendal, two of the greatest math brains working on the planet."

Everyone who had been staring at them before now turned again with wide eyes.

"Thank you," Duster said, waving his cowboy hat. "Just carry on with what you were doing."

Brice actually laughed. "I think we're finished for the day. Dismissed."

Everyone stood, closing their laptops, and Duster and Bonnie and Dixie stood as well.

Not one of the students had the courage to introduce themselves as they left, and honestly Dixie didn't blame them. She was sure if a student was in this school, sitting in this kind of higher math class, they knew who Bonnie and Duster were.

Bonnie and Duster were legends, basically. It would be like having Einstein walk into the back of the classroom.

Finally, only Brice and Dixie and Bonnie and Duster were left in the room.

Duster walked toward the front of the room and extended his hand. "Great meeting you finally," Duster said. "I've heard a lot about you."

"It's an honor and a surprise," Brice said, shaking Duster's hand, then Bonnie's hand.

Dixie could tell he was barely holding it together and she didn't blame him in the slightest.

"And this is our colleague Dixie Smith," Bonnie said, introducing Dixie.

Dixie managed a smile at Brice and looked into his wonderful green eyes, the same green eyes she had seen vanish to another timeline yesterday in the crystal cavern.

He took her hand and she could feel the attraction and the electricity.

"Wonderful meeting you," Brice managed to say, not letting go of Dixie's hand.

She so wanted to just jump him and kiss him and never let him go, but she didn't dare. She didn't want to take any chance of scaring him away.

So she finally reluctantly let go of his hand.

"We're here for one reason," Duster said. "We need your help."

Brice opened his mouth and then shut it.

Dixie understood that reaction completely. When Duster had said that to her, she had done the same fish-out-of-water reaction.

"Sit for a minute and I'll tell you what we are offering," Duster said.

All four of them moved chairs out from behind the older wooden tables in the room and sat facing each other. Dixie sat next to Brice, but somehow managed to not reach over and try to hold his hand.

"I'm not sure how much you have followed our work," Bonnie said, "but we are working on the mathematical theory of alternate universes."

"Cutting edge," Brice said, nodding, keeping his focus on Bonnie and Duster.

"We will offer you thirty times what you make here as a salary plus housing and an office in Boise to come work with us," Duster said.

Again Brice opened his mouth and then closed it, clearly shocked.

"I have talked with the president of this fine institution of learning," Duster said, "and he is willing to release you from your contract and cover your classes while you work with us. And your job will remain here if you decide to return at any point. You can check with him on that."

"I don't know what to say," Brice managed to squeak out, then stopped and cleared his throat.

"I can tell you this," Dixie said. "It's a job that will challenge every mathematical skill you have and never once get boring."

Brice looked at her and she kept her gaze locked on his, doing her very best to will him to come join them.

Finally Brice looked back at Bonnie and Duster. "Can I have a little bit to think about it?"

"Of course," Duster said, standing and shaking Brice's hand.

Bonnie shook his hand and then Dixie did the same, again holding slightly too long onto the man she had spent almost two months with in another timeline.

But he didn't seem to mind.

"Here's my cell phone number," Duster said. "We'll be having lunch and will be glad to talk and answer any question you might have. But this evening our jet at the Burbank airport will be heading back to Boise. If you want to be on it, we'll have your apartment here packed and moved for you."

"In a hurry, huh?" Brice said.

Duster shrugged. "Time is an interesting thing. We are on the verge of making some fantastic breakthroughs mathematically, but could use your help to push the breakthroughs over the top."

Brice nodded. "You said thirty times my salary here?"

"I did," Duster said. "And a paid condo in Boise."

"And all four of us will be working together? Anyone else?"

"On the math, just the four of us," Duster said. "I don't trust anyone else, to be honest. But you can have staff if you want to help on mundane things."

"I'll call you shortly," Brice said after letting that sink in.

"Good," Duster said, turning and heading for the door.

Bonnie turned and followed her husband.

Dixie smiled once more at the man she loved. "It's more fun than you can ever imagine."

"I can imagine a great deal," Brice said.

Dixie smiled at him. "This job will beat even that. After all, look who you will be working for."

Brice glanced up at where Bonnie and Duster were just leaving and nodded.

"I think I need to wait for my alarm to wake me up," Brice said.

Dixie laughed. "I felt the same way a year ago when they offered me my job."

"Ever regret taking it?" Brice asked.

"Not for a second," Dixie said.

With that she turned and walked after Bonnie and Duster.

She knew Brice was staring at her as she left, but she didn't dare turn around.

No matter how much she wanted to.

Chapter Thirty-seven

July 9th, 2016
Brice's Timeline

FOR BRICE, the meeting with Dixie and Duster's job offer to her went about as good as could be hoped. He had been as scared and nervous as he ever got.

She had sure been shocked when two of the great math minds walked into her undergraduate class. He had no doubt that if they did the same thing to him in Dixie's timeline, he would be just as shocked.

Dixie seemed very interested in Duster's offer.

And Brice was very glad that clearly the attraction hadn't stopped at the other timeline. It was everything he could do to not just kiss her. But that would have been such a wrong move for the Dixie he knew. But even he could tell from her looks that she was just as attracted to him.

Brice knew that Dixie was forward in her emotional life, but she was forward in her own way and on her own time, and that was one of the things he loved about her.

As she had told him back in 1901, "Make me think it's my decision to want to be with you."

He had no doubt that right now she was on the phone with the president of the board of the university making sure that what Duster had told her was real.

"What's the president of the board going to say when she calls him?" Brice asked as they climbed back into the limo on California Boulevard. He felt very glad to be out of the July Southern California heat.

Duster laughed. "He's going to say what I told her, and he's going to encourage her to take the job, since working for us would be valuable if she decided to go back to the university at any point."

"How much did that cost us, dear?" Bonnie asked.

"Nothing extra, actually," Duster said. "We already endow two mathematics chairs here and fund a couple dozen mathematics scholarships. But I might have mentioned we were thinking of another donation to help with the updating of the Alfred Sloan building."

Bonnie laughed.

Brice just smiled and then said simply, "Thank you. To you both."

"We're doing this for us," Duster said, "not your sex life. What you two came up with in 1901 on pen and paper is simply stunning. We need you two working together as soon as possible."

"And what happens if she says no?" Brice said.

Both Bonnie and Duster laughed at that. "Did you say no? And clearly in another timeline, she didn't say no either."

"But a year has gone by and she might love teaching," Brice said, still beyond worried.

"You've never taught an undergraduate math class, have you?" Bonnie asked.

"You saved me from that," Brice said.

"Trust me," Duster said, "we're saving her as well."

"Which is why you burst in while she was teaching one of those undergrad classes, isn't it?"

Duster just smiled at Brice and Bonnie laughed.

"He's starting to catch onto us," Duster said.

"How fast they grow up," Bonnie said.

And with that all Brice could do was laugh as well.

Chapter Thirty-eight

July 9th, 2016
Dixie's Timeline

DIXIE WAS BOTH stunned and overjoyed when Brice called Duster and accepted the job two hours later. They had almost finished a wonderful fish lunch not far from the CalTech campus in a restaurant that looked like a cross between a bad Mexican restaurant and a shack on the beach.

Dixie had wondered about the place when the limo dropped them off there, but after the fantastic cod fish filet done perfectly with a light salsa, she needed to once again learn to trust Bonnie and Duster.

Dixie sat at the paper-covered table and listened to Duster's end of the conversation with Brice, smiling so hard that it hurt.

Bonnie was smiling as well.

"Pack a bag and meet us in an hour at the airport," Duster said. "Private terminal area seven."

Duster listened for a moment, then said, "Don't worry, I'll call the president and tell him you have joined us. He'll get your classes covered. And I'll send someone to pack your apartment and get it up to Boise tomorrow."

Again Duster listened, then said, "Glad to have you with us. See you in an hour at the airport."

With that Duster hung up and smiled at Dixie. "To say Brice is excited would be a giant understatement."

Dixie actually bounced in her chair, clapping her hands. "Thank you, thank you."

"Step one down," Duster said, smiling at her. "Now it's going to be up to you to ease him into the math and tell us when it's time to head to the Monumental Lodge."

Dixie nodded. "I'll go slow, I promise."

"That may be one of the hardest things you ever have to do," Bonnie said, patting Dixie's hand.

"You're telling me," Dixie said, laughing. "I wanted to jump Brice in front of the class when we walked in the door."

"Way, way too much information," Duster said, waving his hands as if trying to swat an annoying fly away.

Both Bonnie and Dixie laughed.

Dixie was far, far too excited to even try to finish the last of her wonderful fish lunch. Twenty minutes later they headed back out into the heat for the limo and the airport.

They were all three sitting in the plane when Brice walked out of the private terminal building and toward the plane. Dixie could feel her heart just about to beat out of her chest.

Brice looked as handsome as ever with his jeans and tee shirt and running shoes. He had a duffle bag slung over one shoulder and a laptop bag over the other.

Duster went out to meet him while Dixie and Bonnie stayed seated, sipping iced tea.

Duster brought Brice's bag up into the plane and handed it to a steward named Louis whom Dixie had found very nice. He was a cowboy-looking guy who often wore cowboy boots and a hat. Louis had two kids and a wife in Boise and all he did was stand by to help Bonnie and Duster with anything they needed.

But clearly he loved his job and Bonnie and Duster. Dixie had met him a few times when he had run errands at her office.

Duster introduced Brice to Louis and then said, "Grab a seat."

"Welcome aboard," Bonnie said.

"Yes, welcome," Dixie managed to say.

Brice took a seat facing Dixie and Bonnie and fumbled with his seat belt. He was directly facing Dixie. The four huge seats, one on each side of the aisle faced each other. So she was going to get to spend the entire flight facing the man she loved in another timeline.

Bonnie had been right, this was going to be the really hard part, not rushing anything.

"I know I'm going to wake up from this dream at any moment," Brice said, "and be really bummed this isn't real."

"It's real," Louis said, smiling. "But Bonnie and Duster tend to get that feeling from people they hire. So can I get you something to drink?"

"Iced tea would be wonderful," Brice said, laughing.

"We'll be headed for Idaho in about five minutes," Duster said, coming from the cockpit and sitting across the aisle, also facing Bonnie and Dixie.

"Never expected to be going back home this way," Brice said, indicating the wonderful large private jet around them. "This is fantastic."

"One of the perks with having more money than anyone can ever spend," Duster said.

"We try to spend it, don't we?" Bonnie asked.

Duster laughed and nodded as he took a sip from his iced tea.

Dixie managed to not say much as the plane taxied and then got into the air. Mostly she just listened to Bonnie and Duster talking with Brice about how much he liked teaching and what he had been working on.

At one point Brice said, "I didn't get a chance to do a lot of theoretical work this last year, with getting used to the teaching and all."

"What we are going to want you to do with us is all theoretical work," Duster said. "We'll give you a bunch of our work and we want you to spend day and night absorbing it. Dixie will help you get up to speed on anything you might need. She's completely familiar with our work and has advanced it some in the last year."

"Once Dixie thinks you are up to speed," Bonnie said, "we'll jump you into the deep end."

"And then all four of us go from there," Duster said.

Brice nodded and smiled at Dixie. "This is going to be fun."

"That it will," Dixie said, smiling back.

Both Bonnie and Duster laughed, so Dixie quickly asked a question she already knew of Brice and got him telling them about his work at Harvard.

Then he asked about her, and before she knew it, the plane was landing in Boise and Louis was taking Brice to a top hotel for the night.

And making arrangements with him to get his apartment packed and up here and his car driven up.

Dixie watched Brice go off with Louis and then turned to Bonnie and Duster. "Thank you both."

Bonnie smiled. "You are more than welcome. But just don't jump him before he gets settled."

"Again, too much information," Duster said, waving his hat at the two women and walking off toward the Cadillac in the parking area.

Dixie and Bonnie just laughed as they followed him.

Chapter Thirty-nine

September 4th, 2016
Brice's Timeline

BRICE WAS STUNNED how fast Dixie picked up on the work that Bonnie and Duster had done. She was the smartest person he had ever met and hungry to learn. She seemed to focus on the math day and night, asking Brice questions the next day in the office when there was something she seemed stuck on.

They had set her up an office in the same building as Brice, just down the hall from his, and hired a secretary to guard the reception area between them and make copies and run errands and a ton of other little stuff, including getting them lunch at times.

The two-story building actually was empty except for the two of them.

Bonnie and Duster owned it. It looked out over the Boise River from a small ledge just above the River Walk. The office was surrounded by cottonwood trees and even in the heat of the summer, the grass area around the office seemed to stay cool. In the evenings they often sat on the patio looking at the river and talking math.

Dixie had made her office as comfortable as his, with a couch, a huge desk, two large computers, and more whiteboards than anything else on the walls.

Somehow, even with the attraction, they had managed to not even kiss in almost two months. Brice wasn't sure if that was good or bad, but he was willing to be very patient. And as the summer wore on and Dixie got more and more familiar with the mathematics of what Bonnie and Duster had done, they became closer and closer as friends.

They shared the math, which was what they had shared when they met the first time in the other timeline. Now they were building that same connection in this timeline.

Over lunches and a few dinners, he had learned that she hadn't dated anyone at CalTech. And he had not managed to slip and say anything about her he couldn't have known from a simple hiring search.

Even though they were not a couple, he had enjoyed the two months more than he wanted to admit. And he had kept Bonnie and Duster completely up to speed, finally suggesting it was time for them to head to the lodge in the mountains.

That next morning they had picked up Dixie at six in the morning while it was still dark and headed out of town, going north into the Central Idaho Mountains.

He and Dixie were in the back seat and Duster and Bonnie were in the front with Duster driving as normal.

Both Brice and Dixie napped for the first hour of the drive and Brice managed to wake up some with coffee at a wonderful little café in Cascade, Idaho.

Then four hours later they were in the huge Monumental Summit Lodge. It was as stunning as Brice remembered it from a few months earlier.

They all checked into their rooms and met for dinner in the huge, high-ceilinged dining room.

"So this is the deep end?" Dixie had asked over dinner. "This place is something to behold. And in stunning condition considering how bad the weather must be up here in the winter."

"We help with the upkeep some," Bonnie said, smiling. "We know the owners."

"Do you own this place as well?" Dixie asked.

Brice had never thought to ask them that.

"Nope," Duster said. "But we have a special connection to it."

"We'll tell you tomorrow," Duster said.

Brice looked at them. "How about we tell her at breakfast tomorrow right here," he said.

"Don't want to head down that road again into the valley?" Duster asked, laughing.

"Since Dixie is from Phoenix and not really familiar with this area, I think right here is fine."

Bonnie nodded and Duster shrugged.

"This is all sounding so suspicious," Dixie said.

"Trust me," Brice said, "I just saved you a terrifying drive down a cliff face."

"Oh, thank you," she said, looking puzzled.

"Just remember the math you've been going over," Brice said, "and it will all make sense tomorrow."

Both Bonnie and Duster nodded and then Bonnie changed the subject, talking about the lodge and some other projects for the rest of dinner.

After dinner Brice suggested that he and Dixie go out on to the deck to sit and have a dinner drink.

"Remember, breakfast at six," Duster said as Brice and Dixie walked toward the deck to watch the colors of the sunset color the mountains below the lodge.

They sat in two chairs, both facing the Monumental Valley and sipping on their dinner wine. The summer air had an evening bite to it and smelled of warm pine needles. Brice flat loved being in the mountains like this, and if he had his way over the next few years, he would spend more and more time in them, maybe in the past for a lot of it.

"Down there is the lake covering the old ghost town that you talked about?" Dixie asked.

"It is," Brice said. "Worth seeing, but other things are more important tomorrow."

"What does this have to do with this lodge and the math I've been going over?" Dixie asked, turning to face him, a worried look in her eyes.

"A lot," Brice said. "And it's not bad stuff, I promise. But I want Bonnie and Duster to explain it to you as they explained it to me about two months ago."

"So you've sat here before?" Dixie asked.

"I have," Brice said. "But alone, not with such wonderful company."

"Thank you," she said. "And thank you for all the help the last two months."

"It honestly has been my pleasure," he said. "And we're just getting started."

"It feels that way to me as well," Dixie said. "In more ways than just the job and the math."

He looked into her wonderful brown eyes and he knew, he could see, she was starting to care for him. And more than anything else he wanted to just reach over and kiss her.

But he didn't.

After a moment she looked at him and sighed and then stood. "Is there a reason you won't kiss me? I know you want to and I want you to, you have to know that. Is there some dumb job reason or something?"

He laughed. "No job reason," he said.

He stood and moved over and bent down and kissed her.

And that felt better than he had remembered. It was wonderful as the cool night mountain air swirled over them.

She put her arms around him and held him against her.

Finally they came up for air.

"Now that was better than I had imagined," she said.

He almost said *And better than I remembered* but stopped himself just in time.

"That was wonderful," he said.

And he kissed her again.

Then when they came up for air the second time, she took him by the hand and pulled him toward the staircase up to their rooms.

"Where are we headed?" he asked, laughing.

"To do something I wanted to do the first time I saw you walk into my classroom."

"Lead on, professor," he said, laughing.

Chapter Forty

September 5th, 2016
Dixie's Timeline

DIXIE AWOKE IN the wonderful feather bed and rolled over and kissed Brice softly on the lips. The man was more handsome than any man she had ever met and she had wanted to kiss him for the last two months, but had managed to just keep her hands to herself and let him work.

But now, up here at the big lodge, while sitting on the big deck, he had finally asked her why she hadn't kissed him, if it was a job rule that he didn't know about with Bonnie and Duster.

She had laughed and kissed him and they had ended up making wonderful love in the big featherbed in her room.

But now they needed to head to breakfast, to shock Brice with the reality of the math, and then take him to the crystal cavern.

"That's nice," he said as she kissed him softly to wake him up just as she used to do months earlier in Boise. He had liked it then as well.

After one long kiss, she pushed back a little and said, "Time for breakfast, professor. But even with what Bonnie and Duster tell you this morning, this right here is real."

She kissed him again before he could ask a question, then she headed for her shower, very aware that he was watching her walk naked away in front of him.

"See you downstairs," she said, turning and giving him a big smile, then moving on into the bathroom.

She half expected him to join her in the shower, but he didn't. And she beat him to the breakfast table in the big dining room by only a minute.

Bonnie and Duster were already there, sipping orange juice.

Dixie smiled at Bonnie and winked and Bonnie damn near fell out of her chair laughing.

"Is this something I need to know about?" Duster asked.

Bonnie kissed her husband on the cheek and said simply, "No, dear."

Bonnie took a deep breath and tried to focus on eating her wonderful breakfast of ham and eggs and homemade bread. They were almost done when finally Brice pushed his mostly empty plate away. "All right, the suspense is killing me. What's up?"

Dixie couldn't eat another bite. Somehow, in Brice's timeline Bonnie and Duster had talked him into this. But the idea of losing him now scared her more than she wanted to think about.

"You like this lodge?" Duster asked, taking one last bite of his ham before also pushing his plate forward.

"I love it," Brice said, nodding. "I wouldn't mind going down to see the old town under the water, but I know work comes first, if staying in this wonderful old lodge can be called work."

"We built it," Duster said.

Brice frowned.

"It can't be possible," Bonnie said. "We know, but we actually built this, paid to have it designed and furnished in 1903 in another timeline."

"Okay," Brice said. "So what's the joke?"

"Math is never a joke," Duster said. "You've been going over all the math since we hired you. You know mathematically that other timelines are probable."

"Knowing mathematically and going to the alternate timelines are two very different things," Brice said, clearly getting angry.

Dixie forced herself to remain silent, but her stomach was twisting up with worry.

"Very, very true," Bonnie said. "But didn't your work on math clearly show you the possibility of time having a physical nexus in each universe that in a form connects time and energy and matter together."

"It did," Brice said. Then he looked at Duster and Bonnie and then at Dixie, who just sat staring into his wonderful, and clearly panicked, eyes.

After a moment he asked softly, "Are you telling me you found the nexus between timelines?"

"We'd like to show it to you," Duster said, "if you are up for an adventure today."

Brice turned and looked at Dixie. "And you believe all this?"

"I've stood in the nexus," Dixie said. "It is a crystal cave that is more stunning than anything that can be described in beauty. And more infinite than any of our calculations can imagine."

"And you went to another timeline?" Brice asked.

"Twice so far," she said, nodding. "One short, one for a few months."

She did not tell him that she had met him on that trip. Duster and Bonnie had figured that telling him about their history would be up to her, and better done on a trip into the past. She had agreed.

"You know this is impossible to believe," Brice said, pushing back slightly from the table.

"For the moment," Duster said, "trust the math, trust the three of us, and let us show you the cave. It will make a lot more sense when you see it, both mentally and mathematically."

Brice took a deep breath, then looked at Dixie.

"Trust us," Dixie said, using her most convincing look. She didn't want to beg Brice, but if she had to, she would. She was that much in love with him.

"All right," Brice said, after a moment. "Show me this physical proof of the math. Where is it?"

"A drive from here," Duster said, smiling and standing. "Get your stuff and I'll check us out."

Bonnie stood and smiled at Brice. "Remember who we are and remember the math. And if nothing else, trust Dixie."

With that she moved to follow Duster.

Dixie reached over and pulled Brice to his feet. Then she kissed him.

He seemed very confused, which she had no doubt she would be in his spot.

"You think this is real? This nexus?" Brice asked as they turned and headed toward the huge log staircase up to their rooms.

"I don't think it's real," Dixie said. "I know it is and more than anything else in the world, I want you to see it."

He looked down at her for a moment and she smiled up into his wonderful concerned gaze.

"Either I've gone nuts or all of you have," Brice said as they started up the stairs.

"Well, nuts or not," Dixie said. "I really enjoyed last night."

"So did I. Very much so."

"Good," she said. "So let's go see a cave and then get back to more of last night as soon as possible. Keep your priorities straight there, mister."

"You said that, didn't you?" he asked, laughing as she opened her room door and went to get her suitcase.

"And I meant it," she said, smiling back at him. "Now go get your stuff."

When he laughed and moved off, she sighed with relief and packed her bag quickly.

Chapter Forty-one

September 5th, 2016
Brice's Timeline

BRICE COULD TELL that Dixie was getting more and more nervous as Duster bounced the big Cadillac SUV up the steep grade toward the mine. She was holding on with one hand on a handle above the door and another gripping the back of Bonnie's seat in front of her.

This was Brice's second ride up this rut-fest of a cattle trail that Duster seemed to think was a road. And he didn't much like it any better this time.

But the last trip up here, in just a few short hours in this timeline, he had taken two trips to other timelines and spent almost two months with the Dixie from another timeline in a wonderful suite in Boise.

More than anything on the planet, he wanted to get back there with her now. But not the Dixie of that other timeline, but this Dixie sitting beside him right now. Except for the year of experience teaching at CalTech, she was the same Dixie he had fallen in love with.

He and Bonnie and Duster had planned that if Dixie decided to take a chance and go with them to the mine, they would follow the same routine they had done with him.

Bonnie would first take her out into the snowstorm in October 1878, then the four of them would go back to August 1901 and head to Boise.

Finally Duster pulled the Cadillac up into a stand of trees and got out.

Brice let out the breath he had been holding out of fear and relaxed.

"That was fun," Dixie said. "If you like climbing inside the agitation cycle of a wash machine."

Bonnie laughed as she also opened her door and climbed out.

The smell of hot pine needles and sagebrush washed through the car before Brice could get his door open. The smell relaxed him even more.

"I don't have sunscreen on," Dixie said as the heat hit her.

The sun was almost directly overhead and hot, even though it was September.

"Not going to be out in the sun long enough to worry about," Bonnie said.

They left all their stuff in the car and followed Duster along a trail leading toward a big mine. On the drive here, Dixie had asked all sorts of questions, including the history of the mine and how this was found in the first place.

And she had asked how Duster and Bonnie had built a lodge in their own timeline.

"We did it, but the we that did it were from another timeline," Bonnie had said. "Which is why we hired Brice in the first place, to help us figure out why that had happened and why we could remember both timelines."

"Did you solve that?" Dixie had asked, looking over at Brice.

"I did with help," Brice had said. "I'll show you that math after we get back to Boise."

He had decided that since they had both worked on that math solving that problem, he would wait until she understood everything before showing it to her.

They made it across the narrow trail over the old ruins of Silver City a thousand feet below them.

Brice stayed close to Dixie as Duster opened the big rock and they crowded into the entrance and then into the mine tunnel.

"Oh, shit, this is real," Dixie said.

"More than you can ever imagine," Brice said.

He took her hand and helped to get her through the protective holograms and then into the big storage cavern.

Then without slowing, they went on through the first cavern and into the big cavern of crystals.

To Brice, it was more beautiful than he had remembered it two months before. He got about five steps inside and just stopped, staring at the slightly rose-colored crystals shining from the walls with an energy all their own.

Small crystals, large crystals, in clusters and alone.

Billions of crystals that he could see in just a quick glance and the cavern went on into the mountain into the distance as far as he could see. He doubted he would ever get used to this place.

Dixie did the same thing he had done when he had first come into the cavern. She made it about five steps and then just sat down on the hard dirt floor.

Bonnie came over after a moment and helped her up.

Dixie had a haunted look in her eyes.

"It's real," Dixie said softly.

"It is," Bonnie said.

"This is a physical representation of all of time," Dixie whispered.

"Not all of it," Duster said. "Just our area of it, and that goes off into infinity and other dimensions in that direction."

Duster pointed down into the mountain and the caverns that could be seen going into the distance like looking at facing mirrors.

"Come on," Bonnie said, "the two of us need to take a little trip."

"We'll get the hot chocolate going," Duster said, smiling as he finished hooking up the machine to a random crystal on the wall and then set the date on the machine.

Brice went over and made sure the crystal on the wall where he had first met Dixie was clearly marked. It still was. And Duster was not using it.

"What are we doing?" Dixie asked.

"There's just something I want to show you," Bonnie said.

She had Dixie put her hand on the wood surface of the machine on the big wooden table and then nodded to Duster.

Duster connected the wires and the two women just vanished.

"Wow, that's something to see from this side," Brice said, shocked.

Duster laughed. "That it is. Come on. Two minutes and fifteen seconds is a damn short time to make hot chocolate."

Brice stared at where Bonnie and Dixie had vanished, then followed Duster back toward the kitchen in the big cavern.

Chapter Forty-two

September 5th, 2016
Dixie's Timeline

WITH DIXIE'S HELP, Bonnie almost had the hot chocolate done when

Brice and Duster appeared from the crystal cavern. They both looked cold and Brice was actually shivering. He moved like his mind was not attached to his body. He managed to get to the table and sit down.

Dixie didn't know what to say. She remembered very clearly that first short trip out onto the main tailings in that 1878 snowstorm and how cold and shocked she had been when she came back.

Finally Brice looked at her. "It is real. But it can't be."

"My feelings exactly," Dixie said as Bonnie put a mug of hot chocolate in front of Brice and another in front of Duster. To Dixie it smelled wonderful and she remembered how that smell had helped calm her after that first jump to another timeline.

"The math tells you this is possible, doesn't it?" Bonnie asked Brice.

Brice nodded as he sipped the hot chocolate.

"So trust the math," Bonnie said, tossing a bag of small marshmallows on the table, then sliding a cup of hot chocolate in front of Dixie and then sitting down with a cup herself.

Even though it had to be over eighty outside right now, Dixie was glad for the hot chocolate. Just the memory of that intense cold on that mine tailings in the winter of 1878 chilled her.

For the next half hour they talked and finished their drinks, letting Brice get used to the idea that beyond that wall was a cavern filled with billions of alternate timelines represented by glowing crystals.

And that he could travel to any of them he wanted and stay as long as he liked.

Then Duster pushed his mug away from him and stood. "Let's take a trip to a warmer time, stay a month or two, let you experience the past to get used to all this."

Brice started to open his mouth, then shut it.

Dixie laughed. She had a hunch she knew what he was thinking.

"We'll only be gone for two minutes and fifteen seconds from here," she said, touching Brice's hand. "No matter what happens back in the other timeline."

Brice nodded.

Dixie knew he understood the math of it all. But knowing the math and combining that math with a reality that seemed impossible were two very different things.

"I'll head back a couple months early, get us some horses and supplies," Duster said. "You guys get ready. Let's go for August 13, 1901. Morning if you can."

Bonnie nodded.

Dixie was about to object. That had been the date she and Bonnie had gone back to when she met Brice. But that was in another timeline and if the four of them showed up that day, a new timeline would split off, one where she and Bonnie had not gone back.

And where Brice and Duster had not gone back two days later.

They would form a new timeline and that seemed perfect to Dixie.

Chapter Forty-three

August 13th, 1901
Brice's Timeline

THEY HAD ALL gotten what supplies and money they would need ready and gone back to the crystal room. Duster again hooked up the wires to a random crystal that was not marked as having been used before, then set the date on the big wooden box, hooked the wire and vanished.

To Brice, he doubted he would ever get used to someone just not existing in front of him. No sound, no phasing out, just one minute there, next gone.

"Okay," Bonnie said, making sure that Dixie was right beside her as she reset the timer on the box for two months after Duster had left.

Brice made sure he was on the other side of Dixie to help her. She was looking scared to death, but managing to hold on for the moment.

"When I say now, we all touch the box at the same time," Bonnie said.

Dixie nodded and Brice could see she was ready.

Dixie hovered her hand over the box and Bonnie said now.

All three of them touched the box at the same time.

It felt like nothing happened.

Bonnie stepped back from the box and said to Dixie and Brice. "Let's go see if that husband of mine got into trouble the last two months."

"And if he did, or he's not out there," Dixie asked as they got to the cavern door.

"We pull the wires and yank him back to 2016 and find out what happened," Bonnie said. "It's happened more than once."

"I'd love to hear some of those stories," Brice said.

Bonnie laughed. "Have Dawn and Madison tell you the story of their first trip back."

"Dawn and Madison?" Brice asked. He hadn't remembered meeting anyone by that name over the last year.

"Dawn Edwards and Madison Rogers," Bonnie said as they got to the big supply cavern.

"The two famous historians?" Dixie asked. "They go back in time?"

"They do," Duster said, coming toward them from the kitchen area. He was dressed in his oilcloth long coat, jeans, cowboy boots, a plaid shirt, and a cowboy hat. He looked like he had just come in from outside since his face was slightly flushed and he had a glass of water in one hand.

"In fact," Bonnie said, "Dawn and Madison helped build the lodge and have lived in the lodge and raised their family there many, many different times."

"Yeah, there's an advanced math problem we haven't got a handle on," Duster said. "Why is it that in every timeline their kids are different?"

Brice just shook his head.

"You mean beyond normal variations of sperm and egg?" Dixie asked.

"You are the same in all timelines," Bonnie said. Their kids should always be the same in each timeline as well, but their kids are not, they vary. Beyond Duster and I at the moment."

"We're hoping you two can help on that one as well," Duster said.

Dixie looked at Brice, clearly shocked and struggling.

"Trust the math," Brice said to her. "You know the math, believe it, so trust it."

Dixie nodded and took a deep breath.

Duster kissed Bonnie.

Brice just shook his head. To Duster, two months had passed. To Bonnie, only a few seconds.

"You get into trouble?" Bonnie asked as they turned and headed for the clothing area of the big cavern.

"No more than normal," Duster said, laughing. He looked back at Brice and Dixie. "She always asks me that as if I'm going to tell her."

Brice laughed, but Dixie just looked even more shocked.

Duster had gotten them supplies and four good horses and within an hour of arrival, the four of them were leading their horses on the trail across the hillside toward where the Cadillac was parked in 2016. Now, in 1901, it was a barren hillside, long ago logged off and pock-marked by fresh mine tailings dripping down the steep slope toward the dying town of Silver City below.

They rode an hour and walked an hour in the growing heat of the August day. Brice was thankful for that, since it had been a few months since his last time on a horse and he hadn't gotten that used to it them.

And the heat was brutal in the afternoon, more than likely climbing into the high nineties with no humidity at all. Dry as a bone.

They drank a lot and Dixie kept a wide, floppy hat on and her exposed skin slathered in suntan lotion. Being red-haired with fair skin made this weather downright dangerous to her.

As far as riding, clearly Dixie was having the same issues with soreness he had had to start. She said she hadn't managed to go riding, something she loved, since she took the teaching job at CalTech, so she was well out of practice.

"You can ride all you want, now," Bonnie said, smiling. "Call it part of the job description."

Dixie smiled, for pretty much the first time in the entire day.

Brice knew she was having troubles and just stayed close to her and tried to help where he could without being in the way.

They camped the first night near the Snake River among some cottonwood trees. Duster showed them both how to take care of the horses and Brice was glad for the refresher.

They pitched three tents in a small clearing right over the river so they could get the fresh breeze from the water. One tent for him, one for Dixie, one for Bonnie and Duster.

Brice felt slightly disappointed he would not be sleeping with Dixie on this first night in the past, but she looked wiped out and he felt the same way. After a great dinner of steaks and small potatoes that Duster cooked over the open fire, they all went to their tents after washing everything up and hanging the food in a tree and taking care of the horses.

Next thing Brice knew was the smell of bacon and eggs and talking around the campfire. He managed to change shirts and slip on his oilcloth coat that looked very similar to Duster's coat before climbing out of the tent. The morning air near the river had a chill to it that Brice knew he would miss in a few hours.

Bonnie and Duster were talking and laughing around the campfire. You could never tell that they were two of the most famous and brilliant mathematicians of all time. They looked very much like they fit perfectly in 1901.

And clearly both were very comfortable here.

There was no way Brice could tell they both had lived for over a thousand years in different timelines. Clearly being able to switch timelines and live entire lifetimes while only being gone for a few minutes in their own world allowed a person to live a very, very long time.

In fact, Brice doubted there would be an upper limit on it. He'd have to crunch the numbers when they got back to Boise. But right now he had something far, far more important to worry about.

He was worried, very worried, about Dixie getting settled and understanding what was happening.

If he remembered his first trip back here right, he had peppered Duster with questions all the second day. Brice still had a bunch, but he had a hunch Dixie would have even more.

Brice had splashed water on his face and managed to comb his hair before Dixie poked her head out of her tent.

"That smells wonderful," she said, standing and stretching.

"Almost ready," Duster said.

All Brice could do was stare at her and think how fantastically beautiful she was. Even in the morning climbing out of a tent after a long day of riding.

He really was in love with Dixie, especially this Dixie of this timeline. Of that there was no doubt.

Chapter Forty-four

August 15th, 1901
Dixie's Timeline

DIXIE WAS SURPRISED how much she could ride instead of walk the second day. She had expected to be saddle sore, but it wasn't that bad and the tight muscles in her legs relaxed as she got more relaxed. Clearly the riding she had done the first time back here had helped her get ready for this second trip. Brice seemed to be doing all right, but

she could tell he would be very sore by the time they got to Boise.

From the river to the ferry and then into Caldwell, Brice peppered Bonnie and Duster with questions. Many of them were questions Dixie had wanted to ask Bonnie, but just never got around to it.

They were great questions. Brice was clearly settling in and understanding far faster than she had her first trip back here.

Last night she had so wanted to go crawl in his tent and sleep with him, but they were both so tired, it had worked out better that the two of them just slept.

The hotel in Caldwell was as bad as she remembered it and she decided that instead of taking a chance with the bed, she would sleep in her own bedding on the floor. Better to do that than catch lice.

She found out the next morning over breakfast in a small dining hall that all of them had done the same thing.

That afternoon they rode up to the Idanha Hotel in downtown Boise and left their horses in the stables behind it.

The day was getting hot, but not as hot as Dixie knew it would get in a few more days. She needed a cool bath more than anything to get off the grime and dust that she felt like coated everything.

"Wait until you see this place," Dixie said, smiling at Brice.

"They remodeled and restored this in our time," Brice said, staring up at the towers on the four corners of the building and the stone and brick. "But I never took the time to go look at it."

"It's amazing how history can just sit right in front of us all the time and we never see it," Duster said.

"I love this place," Bonnie said. "But you two ought to see the fantastic hotels in San Francisco. Pure class and luxury."

Duster laughed. "And not my style at all."

"Yes, dear, I know," Bonnie said, shaking her head.

Dixie was just as shocked the second time at the spectacular beauty of the hotel as they entered.

The huge front lobby seemed larger than she remembered, with the oak trim on everything, the stone floors with scattered carpets and furniture, and light stone columns.

The towering windows let in the bright summer sun making the insides feel as bright as being outside.

The open doors and windows were managing to keep a slight breeze blowing through the big rooms, keeping it moderately cool for the moment.

Duster had them wait in the middle of the big lobby and went and got their keys.

Brice just stared at the ornate room and plush furnishings. "This is amazing, simply amazing."

"It is a wonderful place," Dixie said.

"I made reservations a month ago," Duster said as he came back over to them after just a few minutes.

He handed Brice a key. "Sixth floor in the Lost River suite on the south corner."

He handed a key to Bonnie. "Our regular suite, the Dutch Flat suite on the east side."

Then he handed a key to Dixie and smiled. "I have you back in the Avalanche Creek suite. I hope that's all right?"

"It's perfect," Dixie said, taking the key and staring at it.

She had made it back here, back to 1901 and the Idanha Hotel. And she was standing with the love of her life, someone she wasn't certain she would ever be with here again.

If it was possible, she loved this Brice more than she had loved the first one she met here.

Now she just had to figure out a way to tell this Brice what happened to her the first time she had come here.

She had no idea what he might say.

Chapter Forty-five

August 16th, 1901
Brice's Timeline

BRICE HAD SMILED and nodded his thanks when Duster put Dixie back in the Avalanche Creek suite. She didn't know it, but she would love that suite. And at some point he would tell her how she had been there before.

Another alternate timeline her. And what had happened. But telling her scared him to death. He felt like this news might be the news that drove her away from him.

That first night they had a comfortable dinner down the street in one of Duster's favorite steak houses. Both women dressed in fancy dresses and both wore wide-brimmed hats to keep the sun from their skin. Dixie had her striking red hair pulled up and tucked around under her hat.

Brice and Duster wore suits with vests and cowboy hats.

Dixie looked flat stunning as far as Brice was concerned, even dressed as she was for this time.

After dinner they retired back to the hotel.

They all planned on meeting at six in the morning for breakfast, just as the hotel dining room opened.

Bonnie and Duster walked up the flights of wide stone stairs slowly in the heat ahead of Brice and Dixie, said goodnight at the top, then turned toward the east.

The wide, carpeted high-ceilinged hallway at the top of the stairs went in two directions. Oak wood trim and lined wallpaper covered the walls between stone pillars with lamp sconces every ten feet giving the hallway a clean, almost bright light.

Dixie and Brice turned in the other direction from Bonnie and Duster.

Dixie had gushed about how much she loved her suite at dinner and thanked Bonnie and Duster at least twice for bringing her to the past and hiring her in the first place.

"Thank Brice," Duster had said at one point during dinner between bites of steak and the best tasting butter bread Brice remembered ever tasting. "He was the one who suggested we get you on board for some of the coming math problems we're all going to be trying to solve."

Dixie had just nodded to that, but he could tell that the brilliant mind of hers hadn't missed that comment in the slightest. Up until that comment, hiring her had all been Bonnie and Duster.

As they walked in the direction of Dixie's corner suite, she looked up at him and smiled from under her wide-brimmed hat. "I know this might be improper for a woman of my status in this time, but would you like to come in."

Brice bowed slightly to her. "I would love to."

When they got to the big oak door with the bronze plaque that read Avalanche Creek, she stopped and pulled out her key.

"Any idea where that is at, or if it even exists?" She pointed at the sign.

"Actually," Brice said, "I do. It's a small creek in the Monumental Creek drainage about three miles below where the town was buried under water."

She smiled at him and nodded and he had a hunch he had just slipped as Duster had slipped. He would have had no reason to look it up.

They looked both ways down the hallway to make sure no one was watching, then she opened the door and they both went inside and she closed and bolted the door behind them.

She had left two windows open, one in the bathroom and one in the corner of the living room in the round tower area of the room and a slight breeze had kept the room fairly cool. One thing he had always loved about Boise was that even on hot days, the evenings and nights cooled off. It made the hot days bearable.

The suite was as he remembered it. All the wonderful afternoons and evenings they had spent at the table in the big round stone turret with its tall windows and perfect light. The two of them had solved Bonnie and Duster's math problem, and even more together.

Brice just stood gazing at the room, letting the memories wash over him.

After a moment he realized Dixie was staring at him and he smiled. "Great room."

"A wonderful place," Dixie said. Then she took off her wide-brimmed hat and flipped it on the couch, walked over to him, and pulled his head down to kiss him.

He melted into her, holding her, kissing her, wanting the moment to never stop.

And clearly she didn't want it to end either, but finally she held him at arm's length, looking up into his face. "I'm going to go down to the front desk and have the housekeeping staff bring up some hot water to take the chill off that ice water from the tap."

He nodded to that, but the kiss had pretty much taken his breath away and caused him to sweat even more than he had been before.

"Then," Dixie said, "I'm going to take a lukewarm bath to get a few layers of trail grime off."

"Good idea," Brice managed to say.

"You want to join me after the house-keeping folks leave?"

All Brice could do was stand there, his mouth open and his head nodding.

She laughed and pulled him down and kissed him again.

"Now get to your room, give the staff a good thirty minutes, change into your breakfast clothes, and bring a change of modern night clothes back. I assume you brought some."

"Running shorts and a couple of tee shirts," he said, nodding.

"Good," she said.

She kissed him again and then the two of them went back out into the hall and she went to the staircase to go down to the front desk while he headed for his suite.

Thirty minutes exactly, he went back to her suite and knocked lightly.

He heard a "Yes," from the other side.

"It's Brice," he said.

He heard the latch unbolt and the door swung slightly open and he stepped inside.

Dixie pushed the door closed and then turned to him, completely naked and smiling.

Again all he could do was stare at the most beautiful woman he had ever known.

In any timeline.

Chapter Forty-six

August 16th, 1901
Dixie's Timeline

THEY MADE LOVE before they got to the big tub. She had surprised Brice by being naked when he came back and he had just stood there staring at her, which she flat had loved.

When they finally got to the big tub in the bathroom, the water was cool, but not ice cold, perfect for the warm evening.

She had brought soap from the future and they used it to scrub each other down, washing off layers and layers of dirt and more suntan lotion from her than she wanted to think about.

But somehow, after being outside for more than three days, she hadn't really gotten any damage at all from sun. Most of that was because of the wide-brimmed hat, long sleeve blouses, and the lotion.

The bath felt wonderful and the big, soft towels even better.

As they were drying each other off with big fluffy white towels, Brice asked the question she had been worried about.

"What did Duster mean it was your idea to hire me?"

She turned and reached up and kissed him. Then she said, "Put on your running shorts and tee shirt and let's have a talk."

"That serious, huh?" he asked, looking into her eyes with those wonderful green eyes of his.

She nodded. "As serious as Bonnie and Duster telling you about the lodge and the crystal cave."

"Oh," was all he said.

He moved into the other room near the bed and quickly slipped on a tee shirt and running shorts while she did the same. It felt weird to be dressing in 2016 clothing in 1901, but alone like this, there was no reason not to.

"The table in the turret," she said.

He took one chair, then she took another facing him.

He looked worried and as she sat down he said simply, "Just blurt it out. Better to start that way."

She nodded. She had gone over and over this moment in her mind since Bonnie and Duster had managed to get him to go to work with her. Now was the time, the final step.

"In another timeline," she said, "you and I sat at this very table, dressed as we are right now, for almost two months every afternoon and evening, working on math in notebooks, trying to solve a math problem Bonnie and Duster had hired us to solve."

He opened his mouth, then shut it and sat back. "Of all the things I was worried about you saying, that wasn't it."

"What were you worried about?" she asked.

He brushed that question away with a wave of his hand. "Me just being worried you don't like me or couldn't be with me for some strange reason."

"Actually," she said, "that's exactly my worry with all this."

"So how did it happen?" Brice asked. "I assume the me you are talking about was from another timeline?"

Dixie nodded. "Bonnie and Duster, when looking for mathematical help on the problem they faced with the lodge happening, they boiled down the candidates to you and me. They called it a coin flip."

"In your timeline you won the flip and in other timelines I won the flip,"

Brice said. "Standard timeline branching decision."

"Exactly," Dixie said, relieved that he was understanding that much.

"So how could it happen that we met here?"

"Bonnie brought me back to this hotel and left me after a few days," Dixie said. "In the other timeline, Duster brought you back and left you here after a few days. They didn't see each other until they returned."

"So the Bonnie from our timeline met a Duster from another timeline?" Brice asked.

"That's right," Dixie said. "First time in the thousands of years they have come back here that had happened."

"Because of the closeness of the timelines you won the flip and I won the flip," Brice said, nodding, clearly lost in thought.

"Exactly," Dixie said. "And because your counterpart and I solved so many problems together, it was clear to Bonnie and Duster that we should work together."

"More than that I assume," Brice said, staring at her.

She nodded and took a deep breath. "I fell in love with you during those two months, and I am even more in love with the you sitting here now."

"You mean the counterpart me?" Brice asked.

"No, you," Dixie said, her voice as firm as she could make it and looking him directly in the eyes. "Except for your year of teaching, you are exactly the man I fell in love with. I fell in love with you at first here in this hotel. I just hadn't met you, the professor yet. And then I fell in love all over again with you, the professor you, while we worked together the last two months."

Brice opened his mouth again and then closed it, just staring at her.

She sat there letting that brilliant mind of his grapple with what she had told him.

Finally he said, "Did the counterpart me decide to meet you in his timeline?"

"He did," she said. "But you know the math of alternate timelines as well as I do. There were three major turning points in getting to right here."

Brice nodded. "I would either leave teaching or not leave teaching."

Dixie nodded. "Different timelines split off for each."

"I would walk away from the job when Bonnie and Duster told me about the lodge," Brice said.

Again Dixie only nodded. She knew that in a large number of timelines, she was sure Brice had both stayed teaching and walked away.

"And the third turning point is this moment right now," he said. "How will I react?"

She nodded. "And I'm scared to death. I want to be with you for a very long time, work with you, make love to you, laugh and talk with you and explore the boundaries of math and history together."

She just sat there after that, her heart racing as she stared into his green eyes.

He didn't seem to be even reacting. She had no idea what or how he was feeling. In the two months back here and in the two months after Bonnie and Duster had hired him, she had never seen him angry. Focused, yes, snippy with stupidity, yes, but never angry.

She didn't want to see him angry now. She didn't know what she would do if he turned his back on her.

Outside the sun was just setting, the sounds of music drifted through the air from a few nearby saloons. A wagon rattled past on the street below. All sounds she had grown to love with Brice facing her across this very table.

A Brice from a different timeline.

But still the same Brice.

They sat there for what seemed like an eternity. She wanted to give him time to think, so she somehow managed to say nothing.

Finally, he shook his head and sighed and sat forward. He looked at her as intensely as he could. Was he going to tell her to go to hell?

Was he going to be angry with her for tricking him to this point?

She wouldn't blame him for yelling at her.

"In your list of things that you wanted to do with me, you forgot taking baths together," he said. "Toss that in and you just might sway me to stay with you and do all those other wonderful things you mentioned as well."

She stared at him for a moment, blinking.

He wasn't upset.

Finally he smiled and she flat wasn't sure what to do next. She damned near fainted off the chair because she had been holding her breath.

She stood and moved over to him and sat on his lap and kissed him harder than she had ever kissed anyone before.

And he kissed her back.

Chapter Forty-seven

August 16th, 1901
Brice's Timeline

THE NEXT MORNING to get to breakfast, Brice and Dixie had done what they had done for almost two months in another timeline. They had waited for the coast to be clear and then left her room together to go to breakfast. But instead of him going back to his room for a few minutes to stagger their arrival, this time they walked down the stone staircase together.

Dixie looked ravishing in her blue summer dress and tall boots. She carried her large matching hat and had her red hair loose and pulled together with a decorative comb. He wore jeans, a vest and suit coat, and carried his cowboy hat.

He couldn't believe she hadn't been angry with him. In fact, after he told her, she had kissed him long and hard and then asked a ton of questions about her counterpart and how she handled being alone here in the past in the west.

Then they had made love in the big feather bed and drifted off to sleep in each other's arms.

For Brice, it had been wonderful. Two months of constant worry that he could get to that very moment with the Dixie of his own timeline, and he finally had.

The woman he loved was once again at his side and knew everything.

The dining room was like returning to an old home. The high ceilings and tall windows let in the morning light and a cool morning breeze. Each table was covered in a white cloth and each table had a flower in the center.

Dixie was shocked at how stunning the large dining room was and how wonderful the large stone and brick fireplace against one wall was.

"Where did I sit before we met?" she whispered as they entered.

Brice pointed to a table across the room. "And I sat where Bonnie and Duster are. We did a lot of nodding to each other for a few days at breakfast and lunch."

She laughed. "I'll bet. I'm a lady, you know."

"I'm not ever forgetting," Brice said.

"So," Duster asked, standing as Brice held the chair for Dixie and then went and sat down. "You on board now completely?"

"I am," Dixie said. "Brice told me all about my counterpart and how she handled being alone here and how we met. I hope she is having as much luck with the Brice of her timeline."

"An infinite number of her did, and infinite numbers of her didn't," Duster said.

"I feel bad for my counterparts that did not," Dixie said.

"As you know from the math," Bonnie said, smiling. "Timeline splits often come back together. I have a hunch that Duster and Brice and I can be very persuasive."

"Very," Dixie said, and laughed.

Brice loved that laugh, and those large brown eyes and everything about Dixie.

"Did you have any doubts when Brice told you?" Bonnie asked.

Brice had been worried about that question as well, but hadn't asked.

"Honestly," Dixie said, "I'm thinking the three major turning points to get me to this point are not really turning points. And I might be able to prove that mathematically given time, some computers, and help from Brice."

Brice just stared at her, as did Bonnie and Duster. The waitress interrupted them at that moment and took their breakfast orders. Brice almost said he would have his "regular" of ham and eggs and the wonderful butter bread and then realized he actually had never been to this restaurant in this timeline before.

As the waitress walked away, Duster asked Dixie, "Care to explain?"

"Looking back at the three turning points of hiring me, the lodge conversation, and Brice telling me about how we met," Dixie said, "I had no doubts at any of the points that would have been large enough to make me change my decision. I can't imagine making any other decision."

"So it would have to be a very different you who would make negative decisions along the way," Bonnie said.

Dixie nodded. "Very, very different than the Dixie that Brice met here in that other timeline and that you two hired."

"Well ain't that interesting?" Duster sat back shaking his head.

"The turning points would have then come earlier in your life," Bonnie said, clearly thinking and almost talking to herself. "Decisions on careers, studying math, accidently getting pregnant and so on."

"Yes," Dixie said. "Those turning point events all through my life caused me to be a person you almost hired or did hire. From there I don't think, knowing you three, that anything but this outcome was possible."

Brice had been stunned and had just sat listening because he had been just as worried about all the Brice counterparts in other timelines not wanting Dixie. So what Dixie was saying, that might not have ever been a timeline turning point.

Then he realized what Dixie had said about the math proving it and he jumped to the work he and Dixie had done in the other timeline and then eased it forward.

"We can show the equations on that, actually," Brice said. "It is a branch off the calculations that Dixie and I did on proving why you could remember the lodge being and not being in the same timeline."

"We figured that out mathematically?" Dixie asked.

Duster laughed and Bonnie just smiled.

"We did," Brice said. "And you were about to get to it in your review but I wanted you to know it was your math you were studying, so the lodge and coming here was the only way."

"So you two want to stay here and figure out this new problem for a month or so," Duster asked.

Brice looked at Dixie and she smiled. "I would love that."

"So would I," Brice said.

Bonnie nodded. "Looks like we're going shopping after breakfast. Can't have a lady staying at a fancy hotel wearing the same clothes every day, now can we?"

"And what will you two do?" Dixie asked. "Will you stay as well?"

Duster looked at Bonnie. "You want to stay or you want to do some traveling?"

"This hotel is wonderful," Bonnie said. "And Boise is very pretty this time of the year and into the early fall. I think I'll stay this time around."

"As will I," Duster said, breaking into a huge smile. "There's a great poker game in the basement of this hotel."

"The big tub in our room doesn't add into that equation?" Bonnie asked.

"Not unless you are in it," Duster said, smiling at Bonnie.

"Hush," Bonnie said, smiling. "The children are listening."

Brice was pretty sure his face was slightly red remembering what he and Dixie had done in that big tub in her room last night. And Dixie was flat out blushing.

"Promise me one thing?" Bonnie asked.

Duster nodded.

"We all meet for lunch every day and talk math," she said. "I'd like to be a part of where this math is going instead of just tracking it from behind."

"As would I," Duster said, smiling. "I'll make sure we have a corner table every lunch and no one is sat near us."

"We can sure talk about it more than just lunch," Brice said.

"We just might," Bonnie said, smiling.

"That we might," Duster said. "Damn, this is going to be fun."

And with that Brice couldn't agree more.

Chapter Forty-eight

October 7th, 1901
Dixie's Timeline

DIXIE ARRIVED by herself in the crystal cavern, stepped back from the wooden table and looked around at the incredible beauty of the massive room. This was the first time she had been alone in the room and it felt intimidating.

She now understood the math of this place, but actually standing here, looking at billions of alternate timelines, just awed her.

She turned toward the big steel door leading back into the supply cavern. It was locked, so she had beat the first Brice here for their arranged meeting.

She was mathematically certain he would be coming, but she and her Brice might be wrong with the math.

It was always possible. And that twisted at her stomach.

She and the Brice she had met while alone in Boise had agreed to meet just four hours after they left if they could. They were to tell the other one if they had had success in meeting the counterparts. But as it turned out, that had not been a mathematical issue.

As Duster had said, knowing the math of a situation in hindsight was a completely different thing than going through the situation first. Boy had he been right about that.

It was about eleven in the evening outside the mine, and more than likely snowing slightly. But she had no intention of going out there.

She just would wait here for the timeline Brice she had met first and tell him she was fine, that the Brice of her timeline was now with her. And that she loved him.

She had no doubt from the math she and her Brice had done over the last month in Boise that this first Brice had the same result with his Dixie.

The two timelines were just far, far too similar, more than likely only divided by a decision for a person to turn one way on the way to work or turn another, or something even far smaller that would have consequences down the road.

Either of them saying no to any of the major turning points was not likely, considering who they were in each timeline. And the math that she and her Brice had done in the 1901 Boise with Bonnie and Duster had backed that up.

Now her Brice stood with Bonnie and Duster in the crystal room in 2016, waiting the two minutes and fifteen seconds for her to return from this last meeting before they headed back to the modern Boise.

She had lived over a month since that breakfast in the Monumental Lodge telling Brice about this place. But in reality, her timeline reality, that had only been six hours before.

She moved over and opened the steel door that led into the storage cavern. Lights came up as she did, but again the place seemed empty. She went to a timer that Duster had hidden in one wall and checked the exact time and date.

She had arrived at 15 minutes before eleven in the evening on the correct date. One hour and fifteen minutes from now and she would unplug the machine and go back and know the original Brice wasn't coming.

But she knew he would.

She knew Brice.

She turned around and went back into the cavern, closing the steel door and locking it again. As she finished that and turned toward the wooden table and wooden box on top of it, Brice appeared, his hand on the wooden box.

He turned and saw her and smiled. "Waiting long?"

"Just a few minutes," she said, her heart racing.

"Duster and Bonnie have that timer pretty fine-tuned," Brice said, walking over to her across the dirt floor, but not hugging her or kissing her.

Now, for the first time, she understood how Bonnie and Duster felt when they met their counterparts. It just seemed wrong.

Her Brice, the man she now loved, was waiting for her to return.

"You and your Dixie do the math to prove there was no question this would happen?" she asked.

"Wonderful month in 1901 Boise in the Avalanche Creek suite," he said, nodding. "I love that place and that room."

"Same here," she said, smiling. "With Bonnie and Duster staying around the entire time and helping."

"That was wonderful," Brice said, nodding. "Are they all waiting for you in 2016 for you to return?"

"They are," Dixie said. "Yours?"

"They are," Brice said. "My counterpart will be worried."

"So will mine," Dixie said. "But they will only be waiting for just over two minutes. We have as long as we want."

Brice nodded. "We could take that extra time, but wouldn't you rather spend that time with your Brice?"

Dixie laughed. "I would."

Brice smiled. "So we kept our date and we're both fine. Let's go start our futures. This is just saying goodbye to a past."

"A great past that led to our futures," Dixie said, smiling at him. "You know, it's really hard to be sad knowing you are standing here waiting for me in 2016."

He nodded to that, and they turned back toward the wooden table with the machine.

"Who is going to pull the wire to send us into our futures?" Brice asked as they got close to the table.

"We both are," she said. "At the same time. That only seems appropriate, don't you think?"

"Perfect," he said.

They both got into position with a glove on one hand and the other hand on the wooden top of the machine.

"Dixie," Brice said, turning to look at her. "I love you in all timelines."

"Brice," she said, staring into his wonderful green eyes. "I love you in all timelines as well."

He smiled and she smiled back.

Then they both pulled the wires off the machine, sending them both back to their own timelines.

And their own futures with each other.

The First Four Seeders Universe Novels
Available at your favorite booksellers.

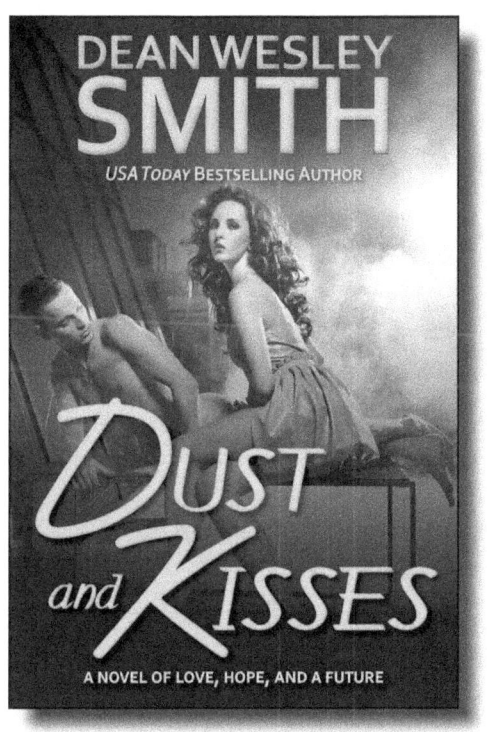

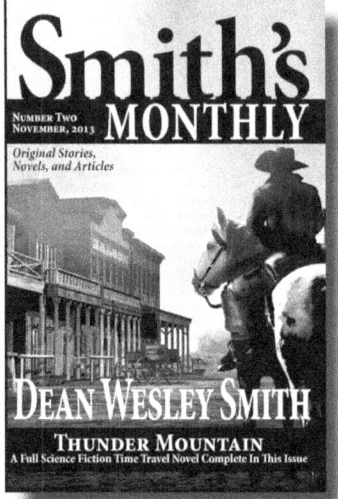

#1... October 2013   *#2... November 2013*   *#3... December 2013*

#4... January 2014   *#5... February 2014*   *#6... March 2014*

The First Full Year of Smith's Monthly!!!

Subscribe Now and start with any issue.
All are also available from all your favorite booksellers
in trade paper and electronic editions.

#7... April 2014

#8... May 2014

#9... June 2014

#10... July 2014

#11... August 2014

#12...September 2014

Don't Miss an Issue!

Subscribe

Electronic Subscription:
6 Issues... $29.99
12 Issues... $49.99

Paper Subscription:
6 Issues... $59.99
12 Issues... $99.99

And Continuing into Year #2. Don't Miss an Issue!

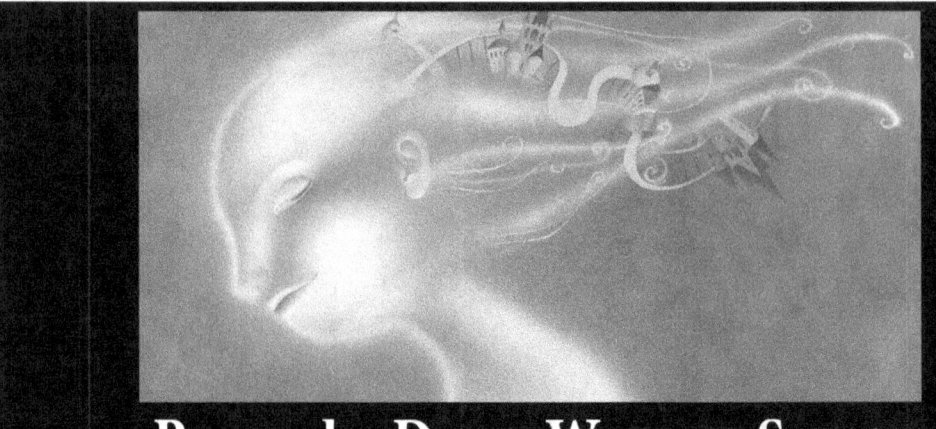

Poems by Dean Wesley Smith

Sotera

She's beautiful
lying there peacefully beside me,
sleeping.

Visions of future lovers
parade through her dreams
like a long line of dominoes
all standing on end.

She's running atop them, jumping
one to another
staying just barely ahead of their fall.

I'm the third. I have five dots.

I wonder what will happen
when she reaches the end.
Maybe I'm the end, I thought,
falling.

She's beautiful
lying there peacefully beside me,
sleeping.

(First published in Prize Poets '76 in 1976)

www.ingramcontent.com/pod-product-compliance
Lightning Source LLC
Chambersburg PA
CBHW081150170626
46813CB00009B/3141